FRANKLIN PARK PUBLIC LIBRARY

W9-AXM-122

FRANKLIN PARK PUBLIC LIBRARY
FRANKLIN PARK, ILL.

Each borrower is held responsible for all library material drawn on his card and for fines accruing on the same. No material will be issued until such fine has been paid.

All injuries to library material beyond reasonable wear and all losses shall be made good to the satisfaction of the Librarian.

Replacement costs will be billed after 42 days overdue.

THE **HARDY BOYS**

UNDERCOVER BROTHERS™

THE HARDY BOYS GRAPHIC NOVELS AVAILABLE FROM PAPERCUTZ

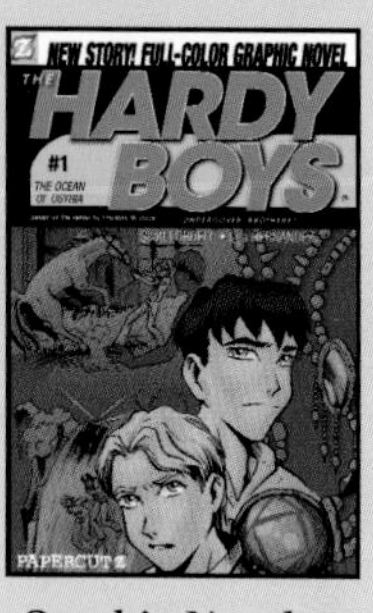
NEW STORY! FULL-COLOR GRAPHIC NOVEL
THE HARDY BOYS
#1
PAPERCUTZ

Graphic Novel #1
"The Ocean of Osyria"

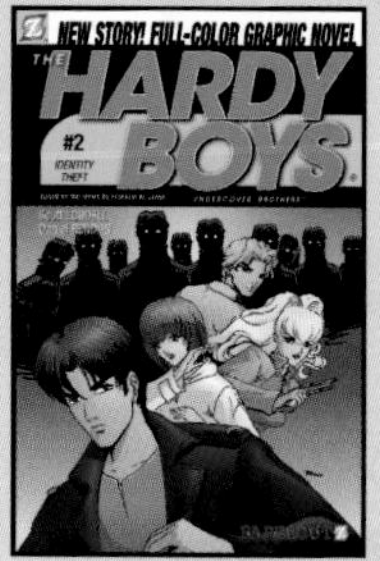
NEW STORY! FULL-COLOR GRAPHIC NOVEL
THE HARDY BOYS
#2
PAPERCUTZ

Graphic Novel #2
"Identity Theft"

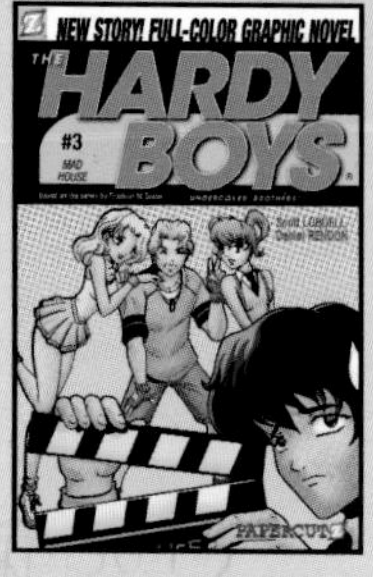
NEW STORY! FULL-COLOR GRAPHIC NOVEL
THE HARDY BOYS
#3
PAPERCUTZ

Graphic Novel #3
"Mad House"

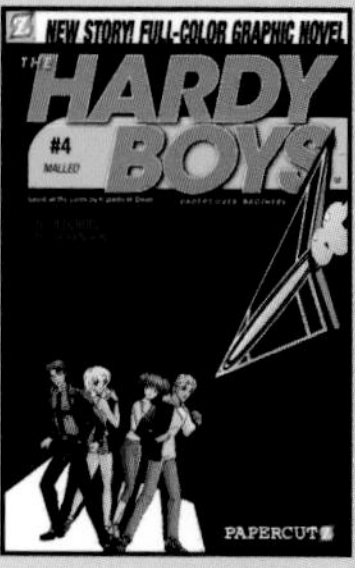
NEW STORY! FULL-COLOR GRAPHIC NOVEL
THE HARDY BOYS
#4
PAPERCUTZ

Graphic Novel #4
"Malled"

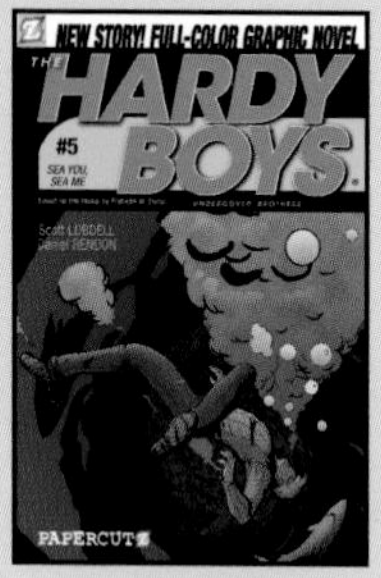
NEW STORY! FULL-COLOR GRAPHIC NOVEL
THE HARDY BOYS
#5
PAPERCUTZ

Graphic Novel #5
"Sea You, Sea Me!"

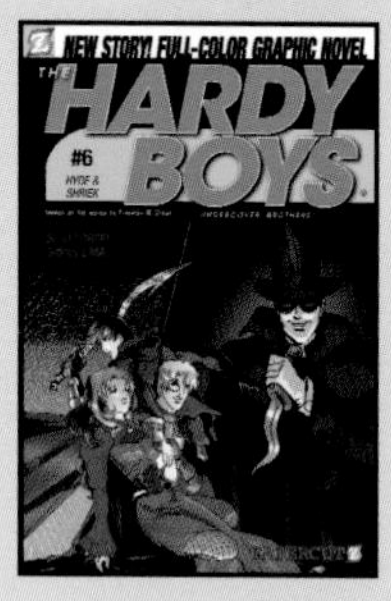
NEW STORY! FULL-COLOR GRAPHIC NOVEL
THE HARDY BOYS
#6
PAPERCUTZ

Graphic Novel #6
"Hyde & Shriek"

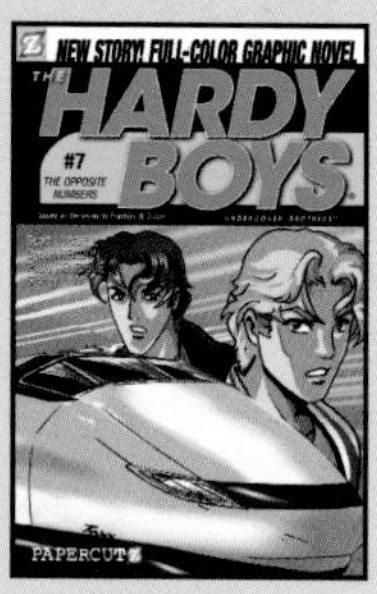
NEW STORY! FULL-COLOR GRAPHIC NOVEL
THE HARDY BOYS
#7
PAPERCUTZ

Graphic Novel #7
"The Opposite
Numbers..."

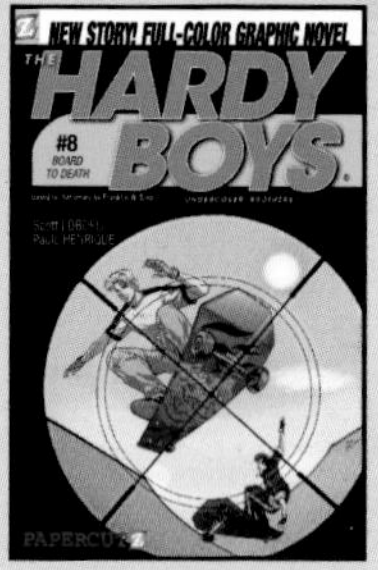
NEW STORY! FULL-COLOR GRAPHIC NOVEL
THE HARDY BOYS
#8
PAPERCUTZ

Graphic Novel #8
"Board To Death"

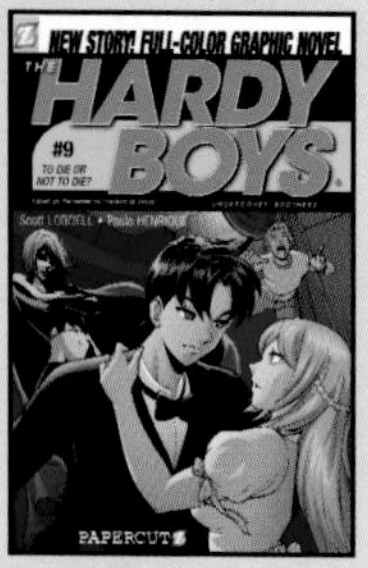
NEW STORY! FULL-COLOR GRAPHIC NOVEL
THE HARDY BOYS
#9
PAPERCUTZ

Graphic Novel #9
"To Die Or
Not To Die?"

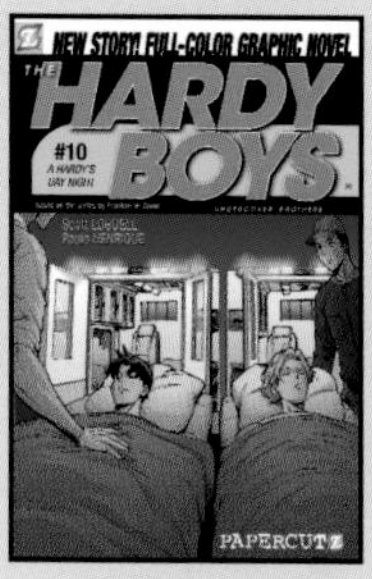
NEW STORY! FULL-COLOR GRAPHIC NOVEL
THE HARDY BOYS
#10
PAPERCUTZ

Graphic Novel #10
"A Hardy
Day's Night"

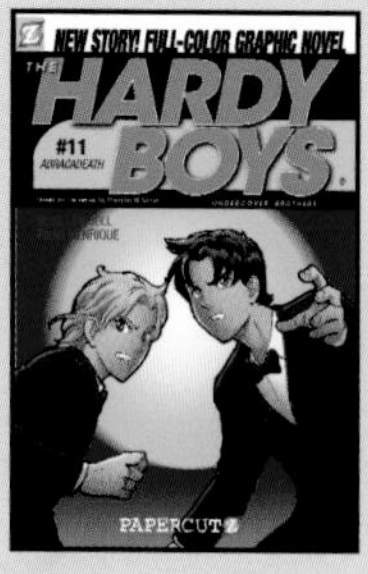
NEW STORY! FULL-COLOR GRAPHIC NOVEL
THE HARDY BOYS
#11
PAPERCUTZ

Graphic Novel #11
"Abracadeath"

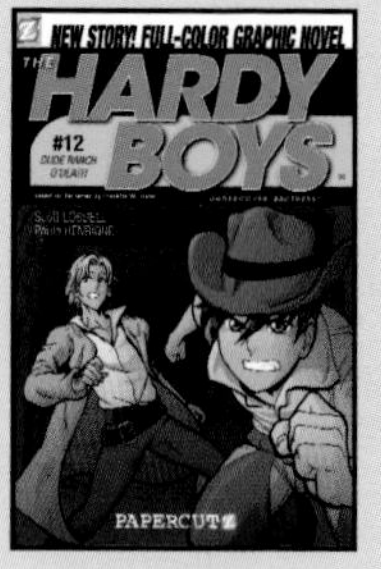
NEW STORY! FULL-COLOR GRAPHIC NOVEL
THE HARDY BOYS
#12
PAPERCUTZ

Graphic Novel #12
"Dude Ranch
O' Death"

www.papercutz.com

THE HARDY BOYS

UNDERCOVER BROTHERS™

#3

Mad House

SCOTT LOBDELL • Writer

DANIEL RENDON • Artist

Based on the series by
FRANKLIN W. DIXON

FRANKLIN PARK LIBRARY
FRANKLIN PARK, IL

PAPERCUT**Z**™

New York

J-GN
HARDY BOYS
369-9272

Mad House
SCOTT LOBDELL – Writer
DANIEL RENDON — Artist
BRYAN SENKA – Letterer
LAURIE E. SMITH — Colorist
JIM SALICRUP — Editor-in-Chief

ISBN 10: 1-59707-010-6 paperback edition
ISBN 13: 978-1-59707-010-2 paperback edition
ISBN 10: 1-59707-011-4 hardcover edition
ISBN 13: 978-1-59707-011-9 hardcover edition

Copyright © 2005 by Simon & Schuster, Inc. Published by
arrangement with Aladdin Paperbacks, an imprint of
Simon & Schuster Children's Publishing Division.

The Hardy Boys is a trademark of Simon
& Schuster, Inc. All rights reserved.
Printed in China.
Distributed by Macmillan

10   9   8   7   6   5   4

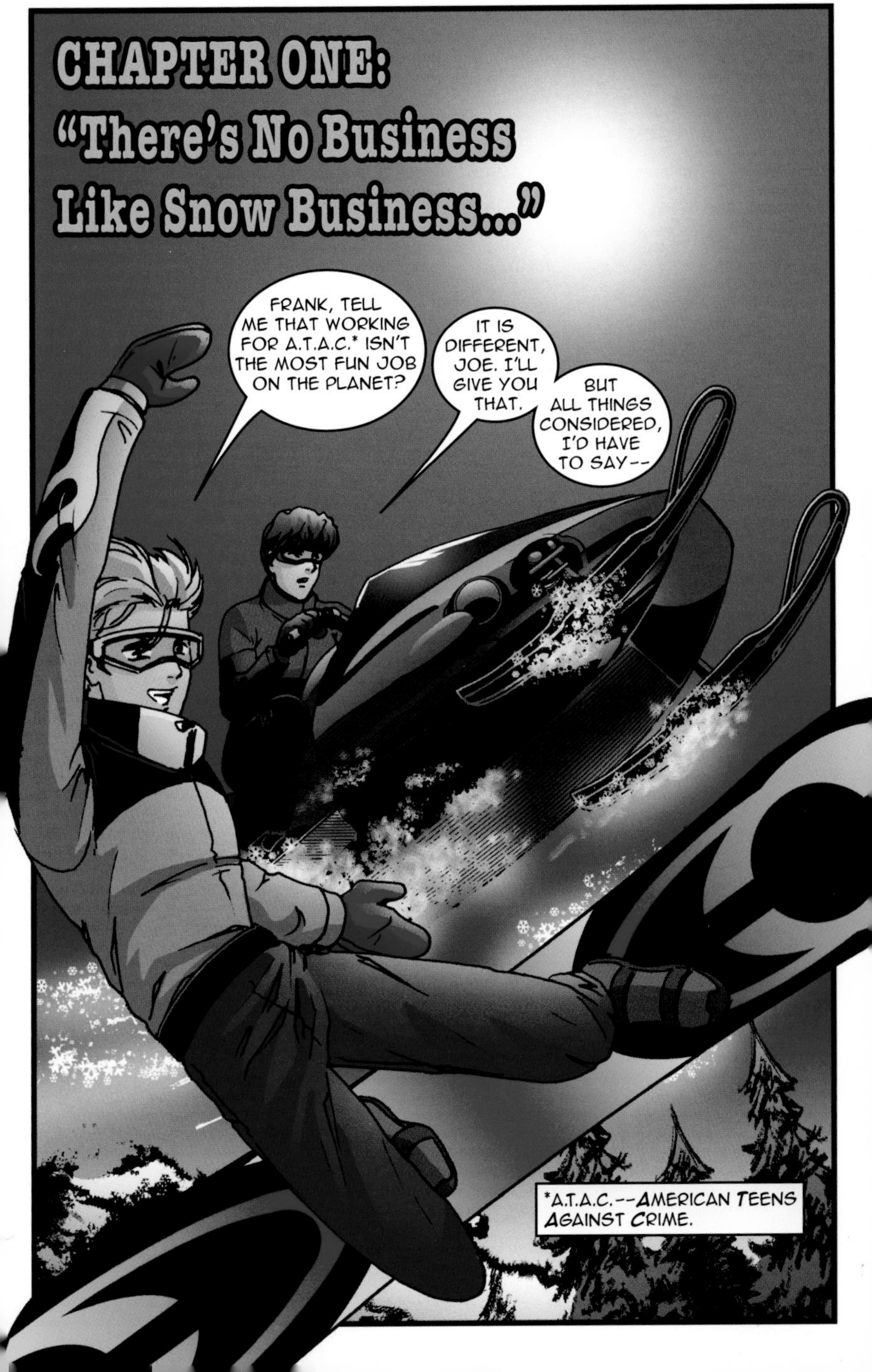
CHAPTER ONE:
"There's No Business Like Snow Business..."
FRANK, TELL ME THAT WORKING FOR A.T.A.C.* ISN'T THE MOST FUN JOB ON THE PLANET?
IT IS DIFFERENT, JOE. I'LL GIVE YOU THAT.
BUT ALL THINGS CONSIDERED, I'D HAVE TO SAY--
*A.T.A.C.--AMERICAN TEENS AGAINST CRIME.

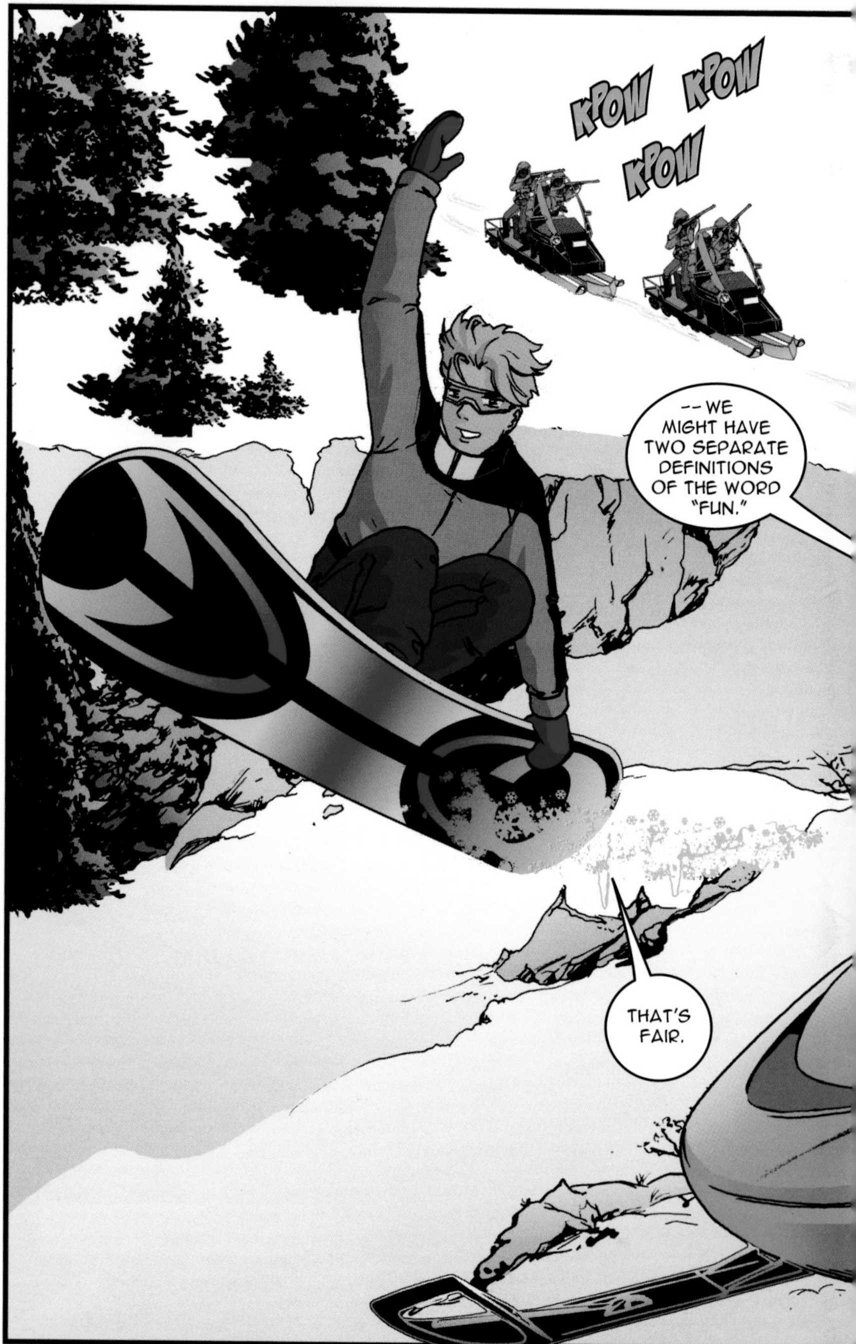
KPOW KPOW
KPOW
--WE MIGHT HAVE TWO SEPARATE DEFINITIONS OF THE WORD "FUN."
THAT'S FAIR.

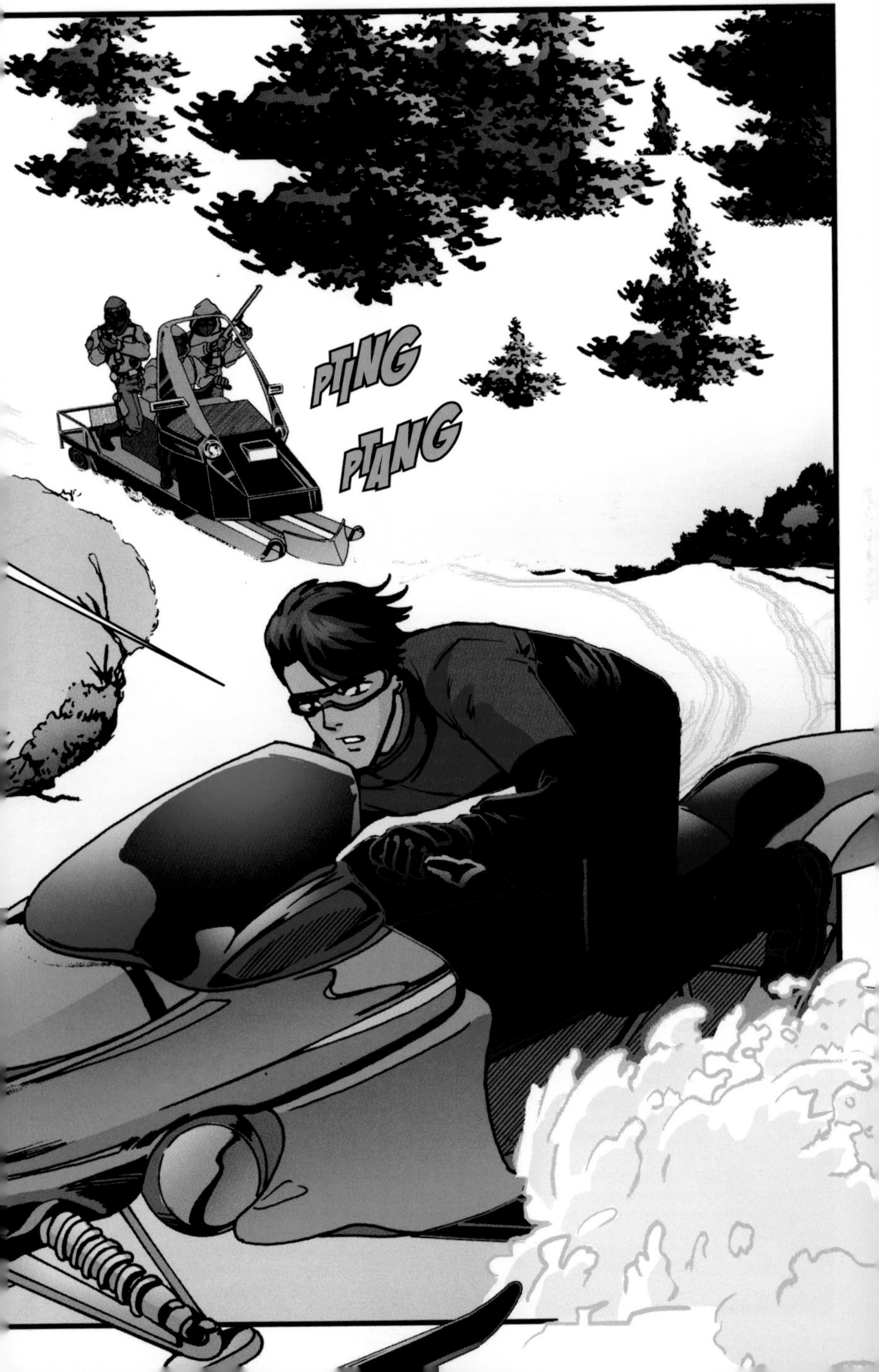
PTING
PTANG

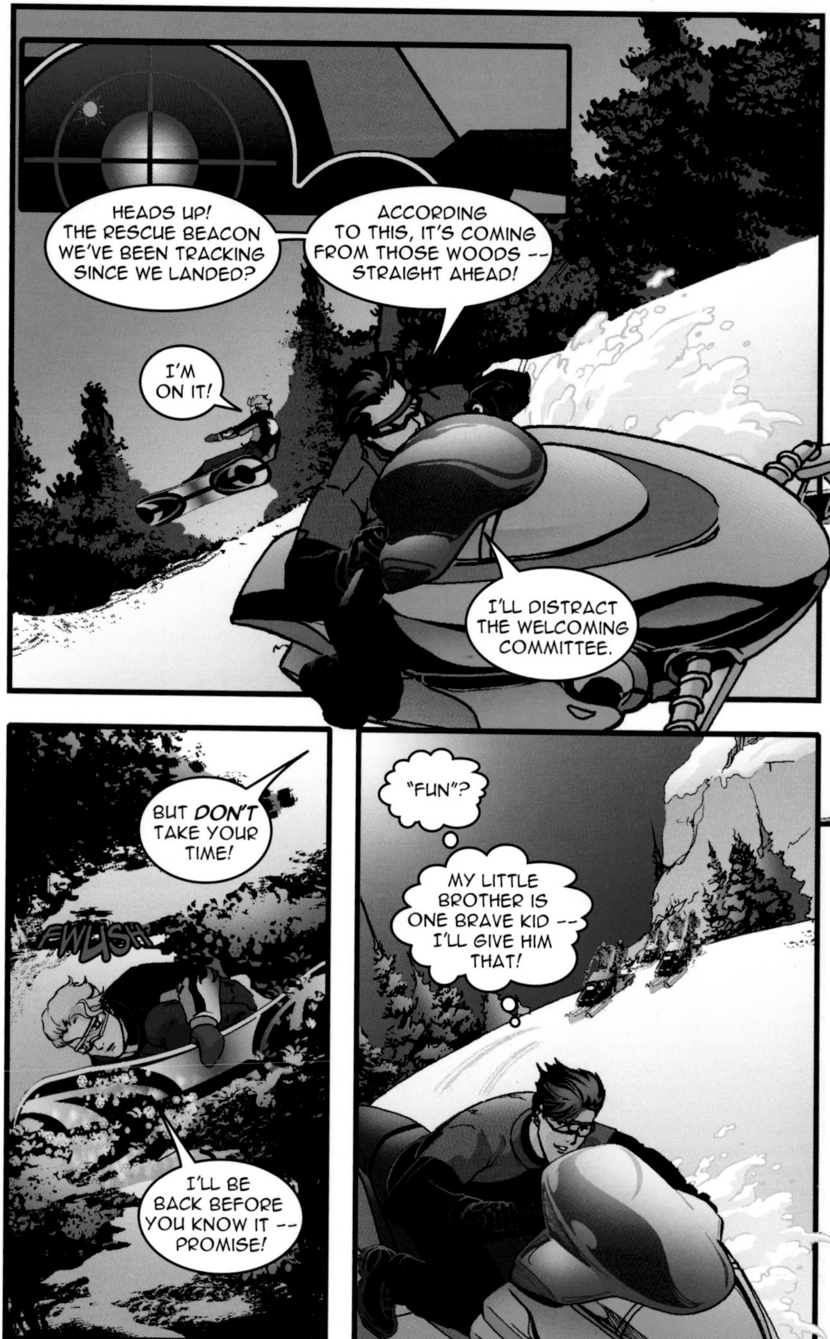
HEADS UP! THE RESCUE BEACON WE'VE BEEN TRACKING SINCE WE LANDED?
ACCORDING TO THIS, IT'S COMING FROM THOSE WOODS -- STRAIGHT AHEAD!
I'M ON IT!
I'LL DISTRACT THE WELCOMING COMMITTEE.
BUT DON'T TAKE YOUR TIME!
FWUSH
I'LL BE BACK BEFORE YOU KNOW IT -- PROMISE!
"FUN"?
MY LITTLE BROTHER IS ONE BRAVE KID -- I'LL GIVE HIM THAT!

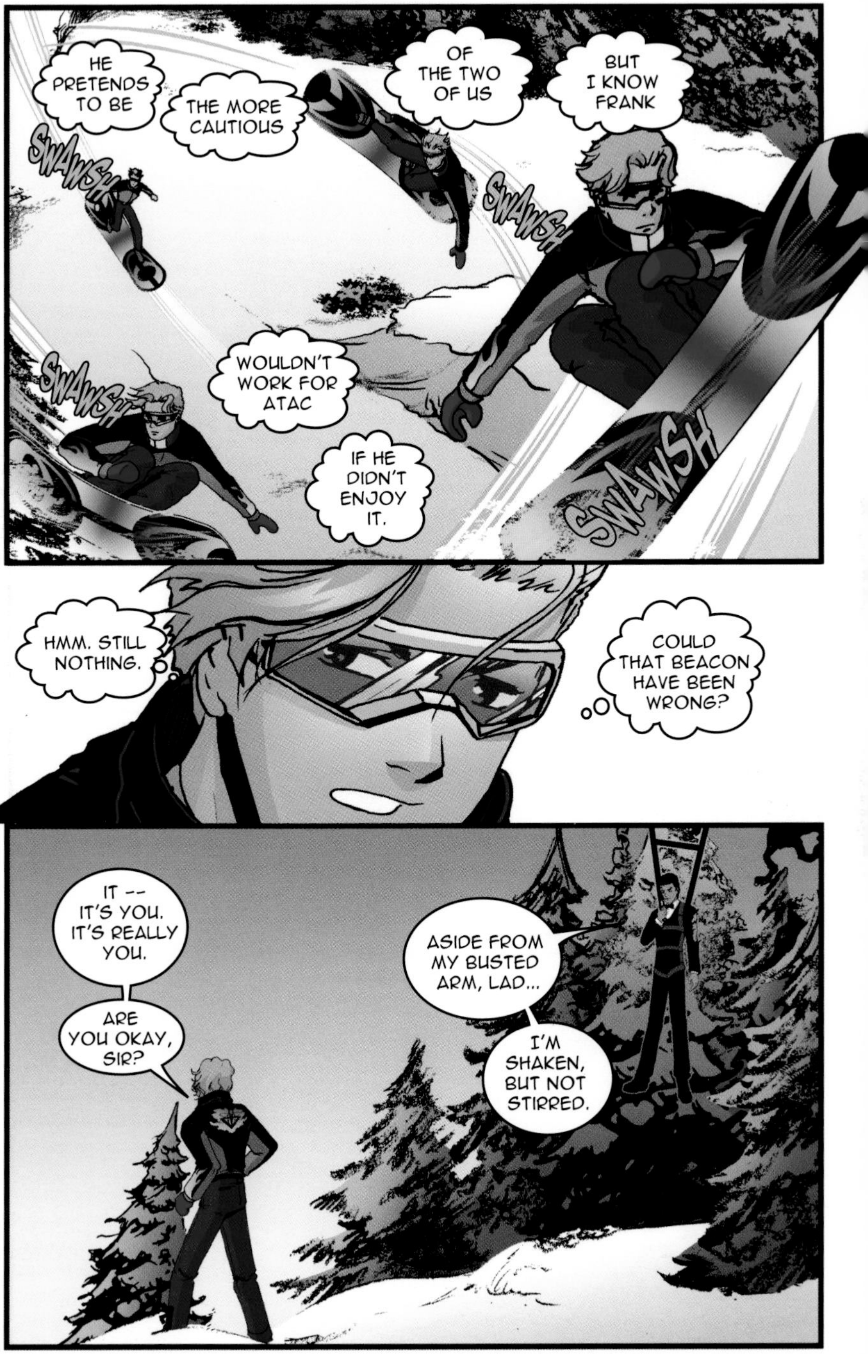
HE PRETENDS TO BE
THE MORE CAUTIOUS
OF THE TWO OF US
BUT I KNOW FRANK
SWAWSH
SWAWSH
SWAWSH
WOULDN'T WORK FOR ATAC
IF HE DIDN'T ENJOY IT.
SWAWSH
HMM. STILL NOTHING.
COULD THAT BEACON HAVE BEEN WRONG?
IT -- IT'S YOU. IT'S REALLY YOU.
ARE YOU OKAY, SIR?
ASIDE FROM MY BUSTED ARM, LAD...
I'M SHAKEN, BUT NOT STIRRED.

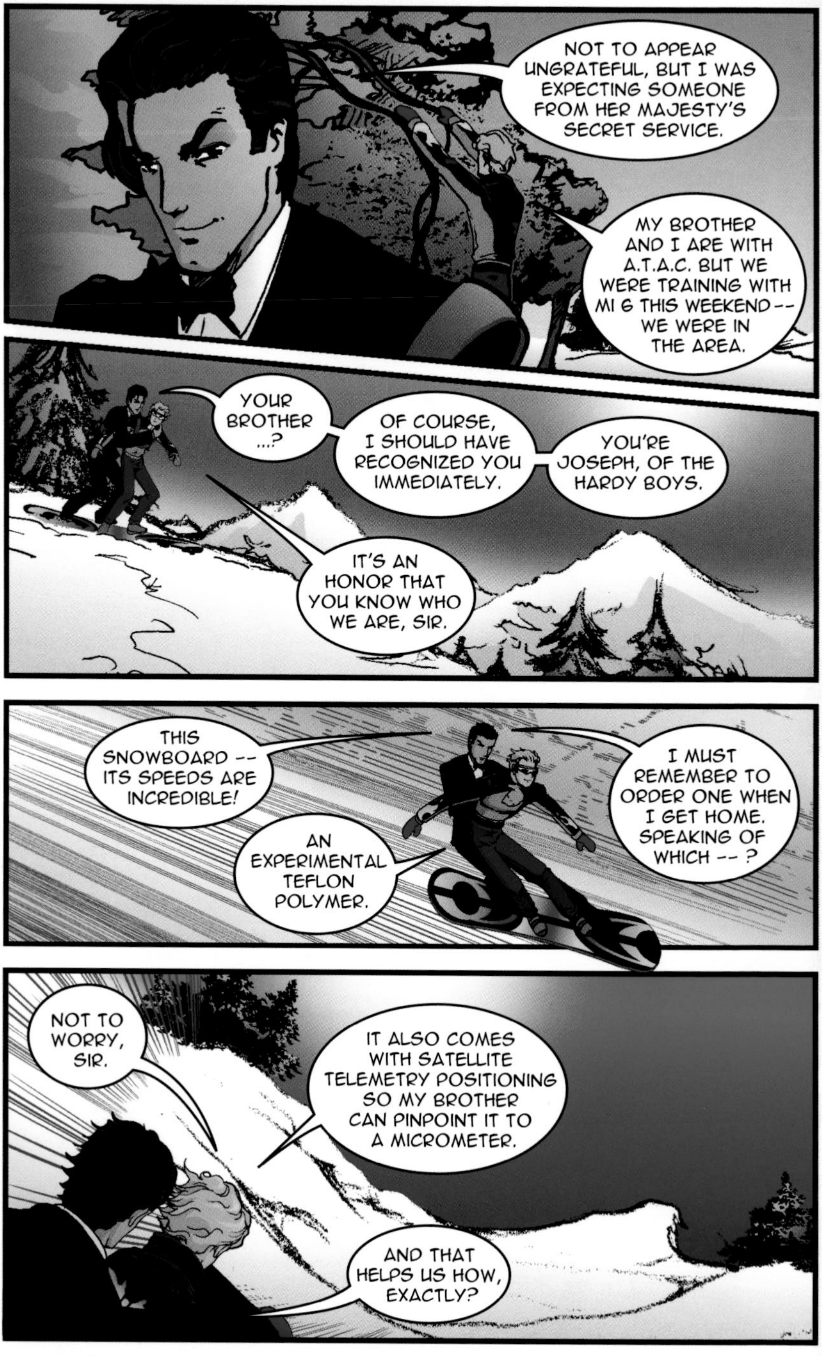

NOT TO APPEAR UNGRATEFUL, BUT I WAS EXPECTING SOMEONE FROM HER MAJESTY'S SECRET SERVICE.
MY BROTHER AND I ARE WITH A.T.A.C. BUT WE WERE TRAINING WITH MI 6 THIS WEEKEND-- WE WERE IN THE AREA.
YOUR BROTHER ...?
OF COURSE, I SHOULD HAVE RECOGNIZED YOU IMMEDIATELY.
YOU'RE JOSEPH, OF THE HARDY BOYS.
IT'S AN HONOR THAT YOU KNOW WHO WE ARE, SIR.
THIS SNOWBOARD -- ITS SPEEDS ARE INCREDIBLE!
AN EXPERIMENTAL TEFLON POLYMER.
I MUST REMEMBER TO ORDER ONE WHEN I GET HOME. SPEAKING OF WHICH -- ?
NOT TO WORRY, SIR.
IT ALSO COMES WITH SATELLITE TELEMETRY POSITIONING SO MY BROTHER CAN PINPOINT IT TO A MICROMETER.
AND THAT HELPS US HOW, EXACTLY?

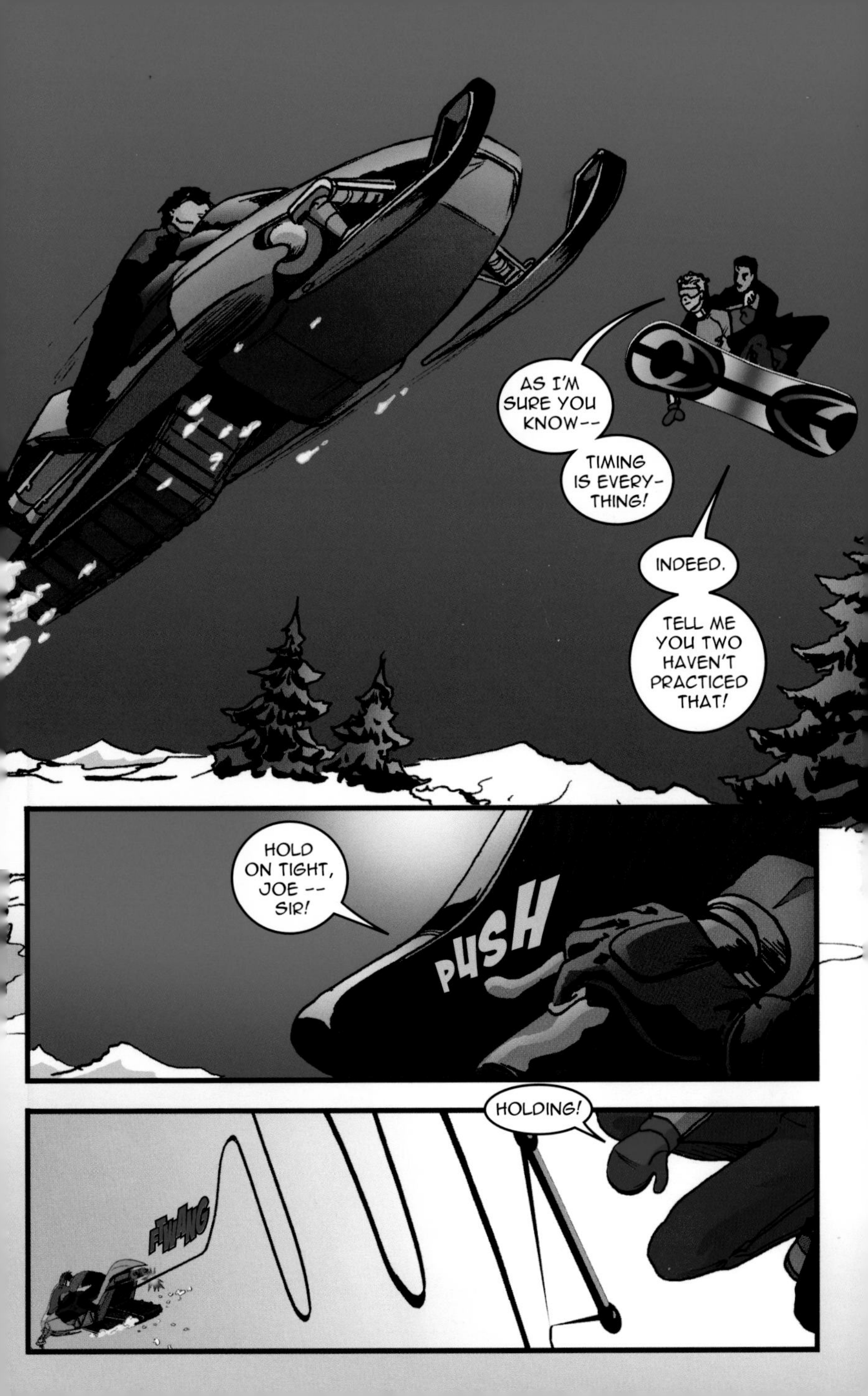
AS I'M SURE YOU KNOW--
TIMING IS EVERY-THING!
INDEED.
TELL ME YOU TWO HAVEN'T PRACTICED THAT!
HOLD ON TIGHT, JOE -- SIR!
PUSH
HOLDING!
FTWANG

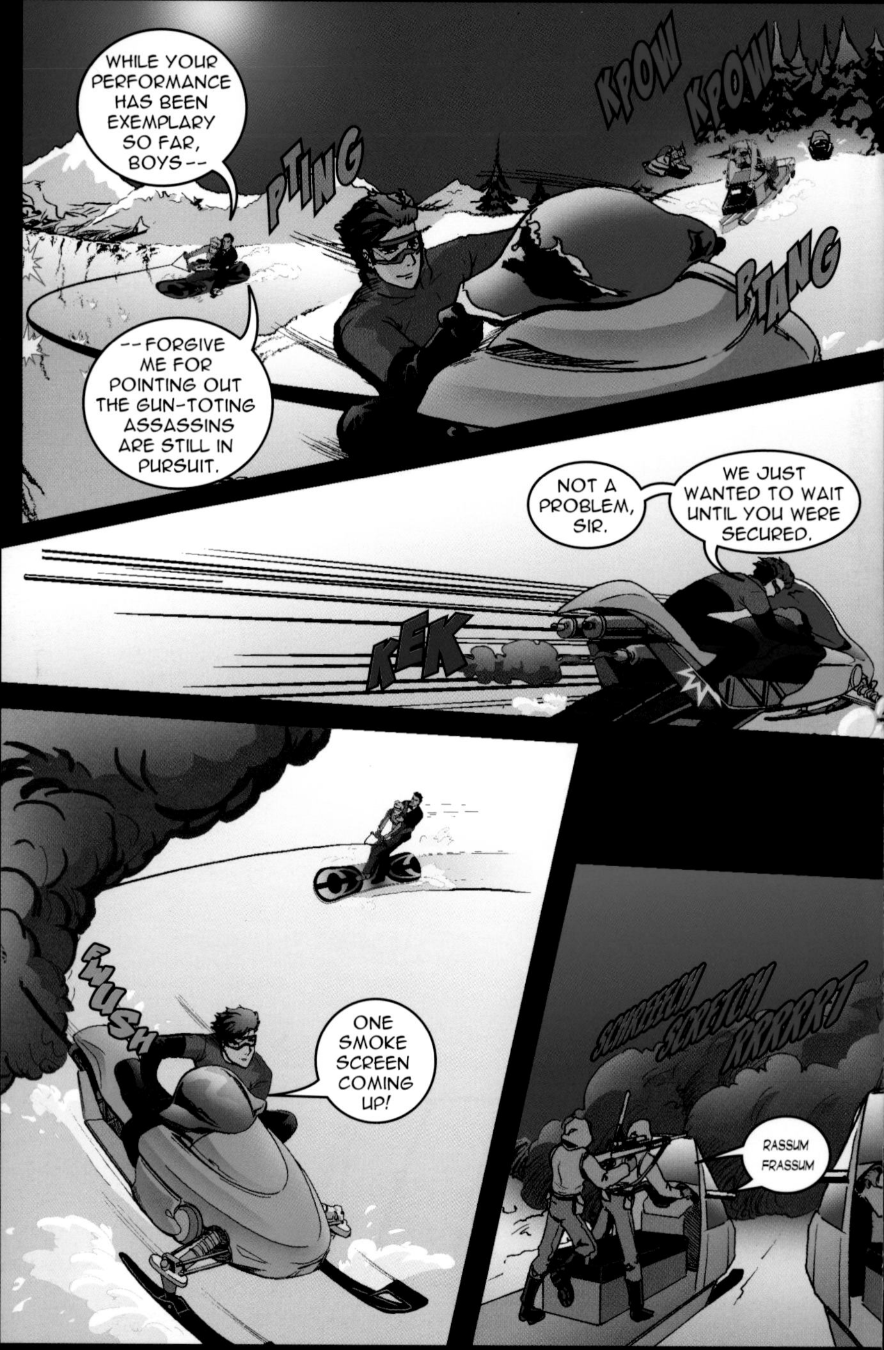
WHILE YOUR PERFORMANCE HAS BEEN EXEMPLARY SO FAR, BOYS--
PTING
KPOW
KPOW
PTANG
--FORGIVE ME FOR POINTING OUT THE GUN-TOTING ASSASSINS ARE STILL IN PURSUIT.
NOT A PROBLEM, SIR.
WE JUST WANTED TO WAIT UNTIL YOU WERE SECURED.
KEK
FWUSH
ONE SMOKE SCREEN COMING UP!
RASSUM FRASSUM

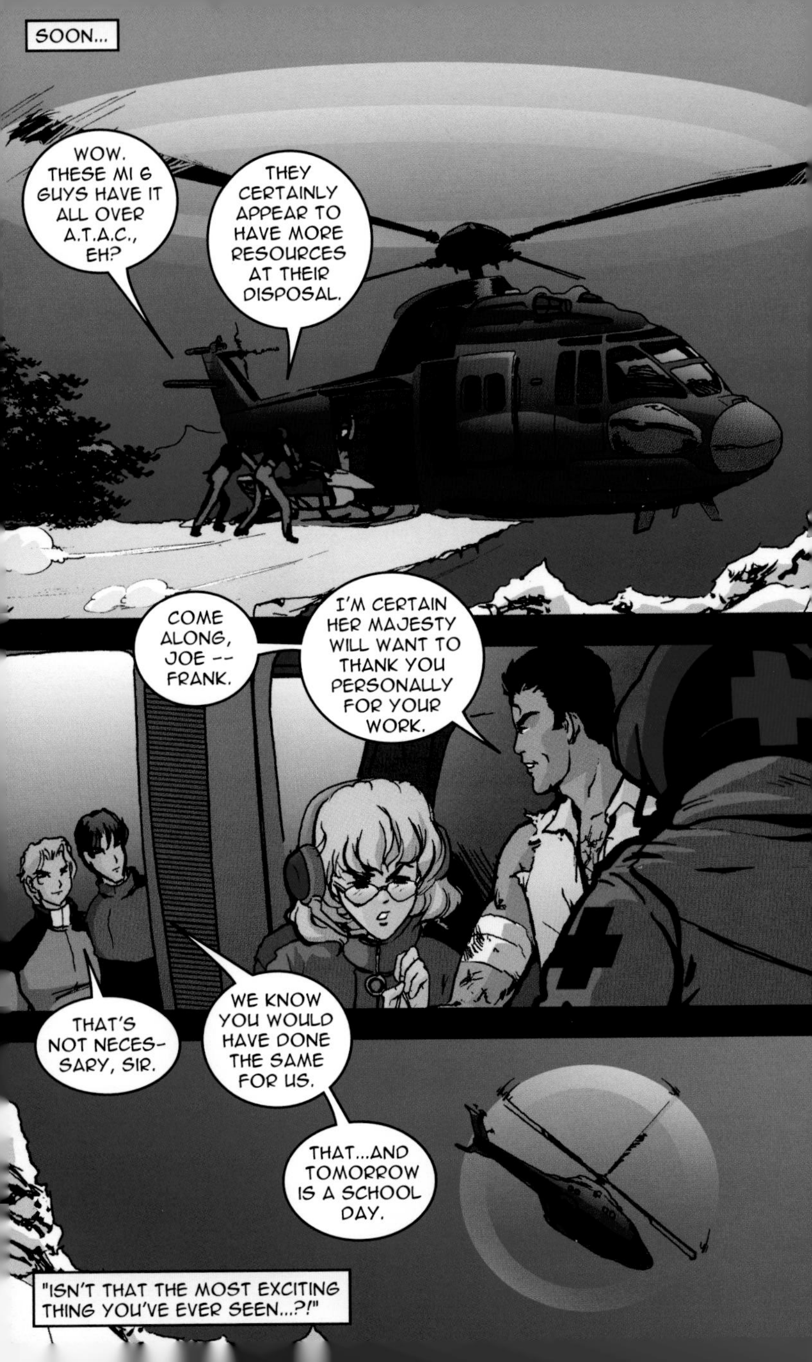
SOON...
WOW. THESE MI 6 GUYS HAVE IT ALL OVER A.T.A.C., EH?
THEY CERTAINLY APPEAR TO HAVE MORE RESOURCES AT THEIR DISPOSAL.
COME ALONG, JOE -- FRANK.
I'M CERTAIN HER MAJESTY WILL WANT TO THANK YOU PERSONALLY FOR YOUR WORK.
THAT'S NOT NECES-SARY, SIR.
WE KNOW YOU WOULD HAVE DONE THE SAME FOR US.
THAT...AND TOMORROW IS A SCHOOL DAY.
"ISN'T THAT THE MOST EXCITING THING YOU'VE EVER SEEN...?!"

CHAPTER TWO: "Thanks, But No..."

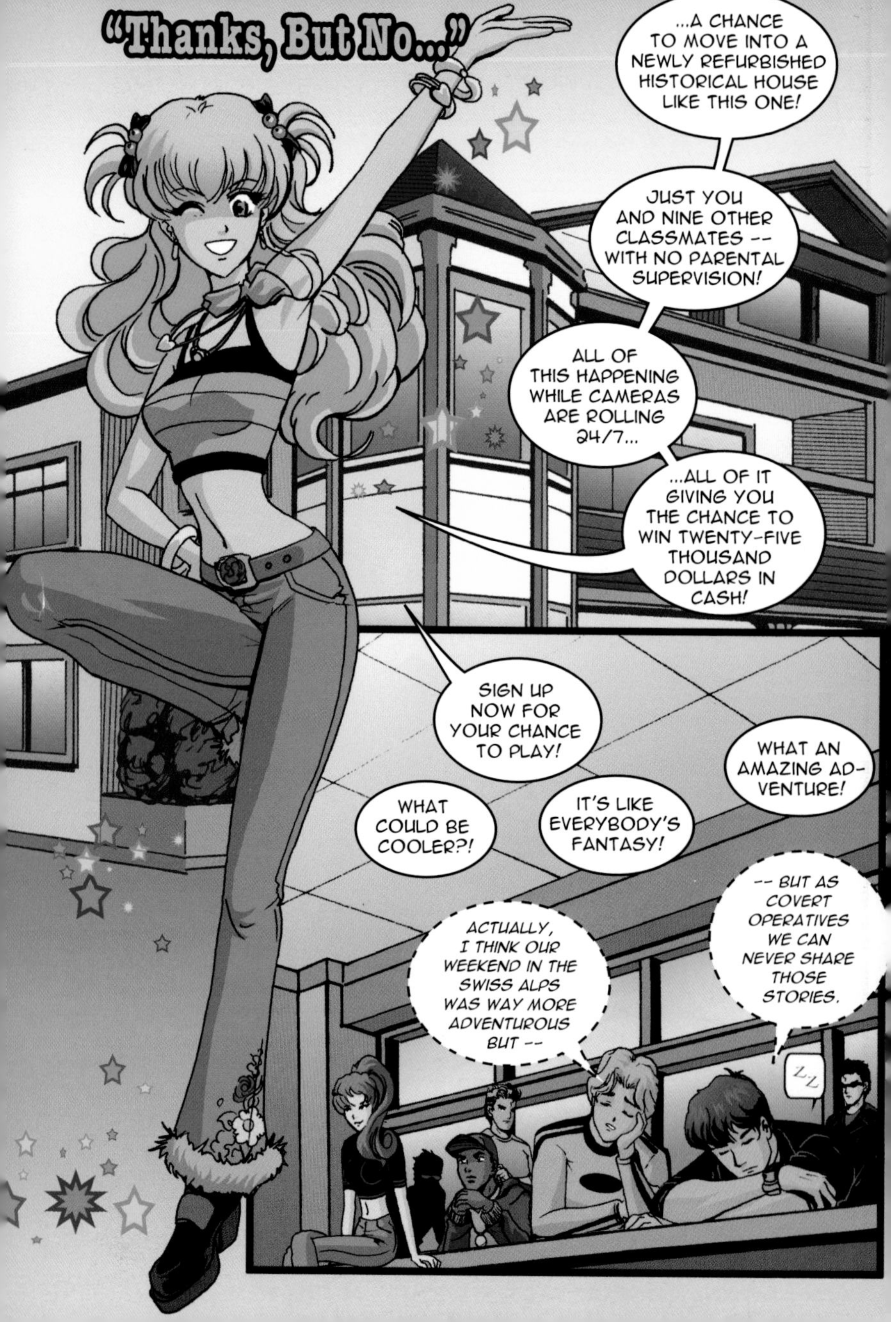
...A CHANCE TO MOVE INTO A NEWLY REFURBISHED HISTORICAL HOUSE LIKE THIS ONE!
JUST YOU AND NINE OTHER CLASSMATES -- WITH NO PARENTAL SUPERVISION!
ALL OF THIS HAPPENING WHILE CAMERAS ARE ROLLING 24/7...
...ALL OF IT GIVING YOU THE CHANCE TO WIN TWENTY-FIVE THOUSAND DOLLARS IN CASH!
SIGN UP NOW FOR YOUR CHANCE TO PLAY!
WHAT AN AMAZING AD-VENTURE!
IT'S LIKE EVERYBODY'S FANTASY!
WHAT COULD BE COOLER?!
ACTUALLY, I THINK OUR WEEKEND IN THE SWISS ALPS WAS WAY MORE ADVENTUROUS BUT --
-- BUT AS COVERT OPERATIVES WE CAN NEVER SHARE THOSE STORIES.
Z Z

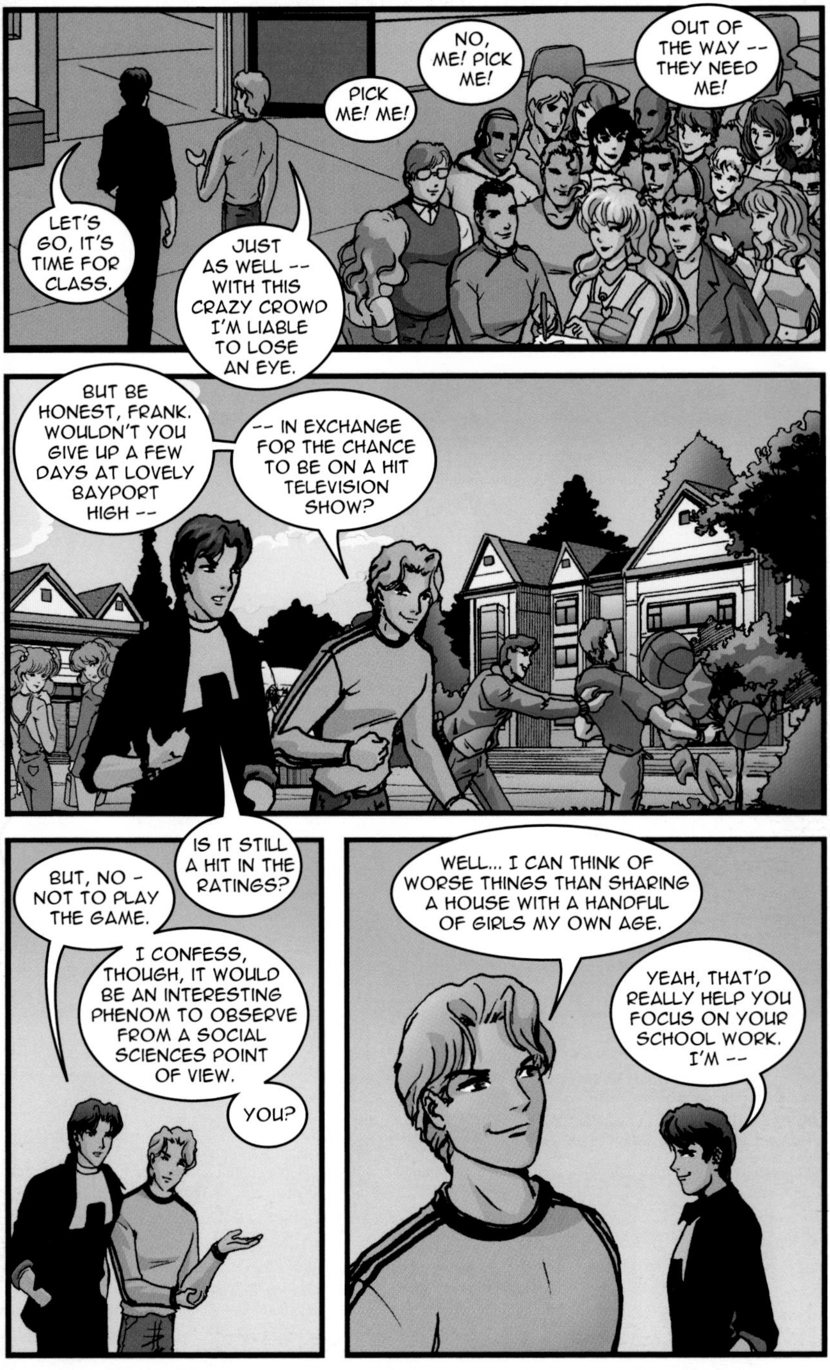
PICK ME! ME!
NO, ME! PICK ME!
OUT OF THE WAY -- THEY NEED ME!
LET'S GO, IT'S TIME FOR CLASS.
JUST AS WELL -- WITH THIS CRAZY CROWD I'M LIABLE TO LOSE AN EYE.
BUT BE HONEST, FRANK. WOULDN'T YOU GIVE UP A FEW DAYS AT LOVELY BAYPORT HIGH --
-- IN EXCHANGE FOR THE CHANCE TO BE ON A HIT TELEVISION SHOW?
IS IT STILL A HIT IN THE RATINGS?
BUT, NO - NOT TO PLAY THE GAME.
I CONFESS, THOUGH, IT WOULD BE AN INTERESTING PHENOM TO OBSERVE FROM A SOCIAL SCIENCES POINT OF VIEW.
YOU?
WELL... I CAN THINK OF WORSE THINGS THAN SHARING A HOUSE WITH A HANDFUL OF GIRLS MY OWN AGE.
YEAH, THAT'D REALLY HELP YOU FOCUS ON YOUR SCHOOL WORK. I'M --

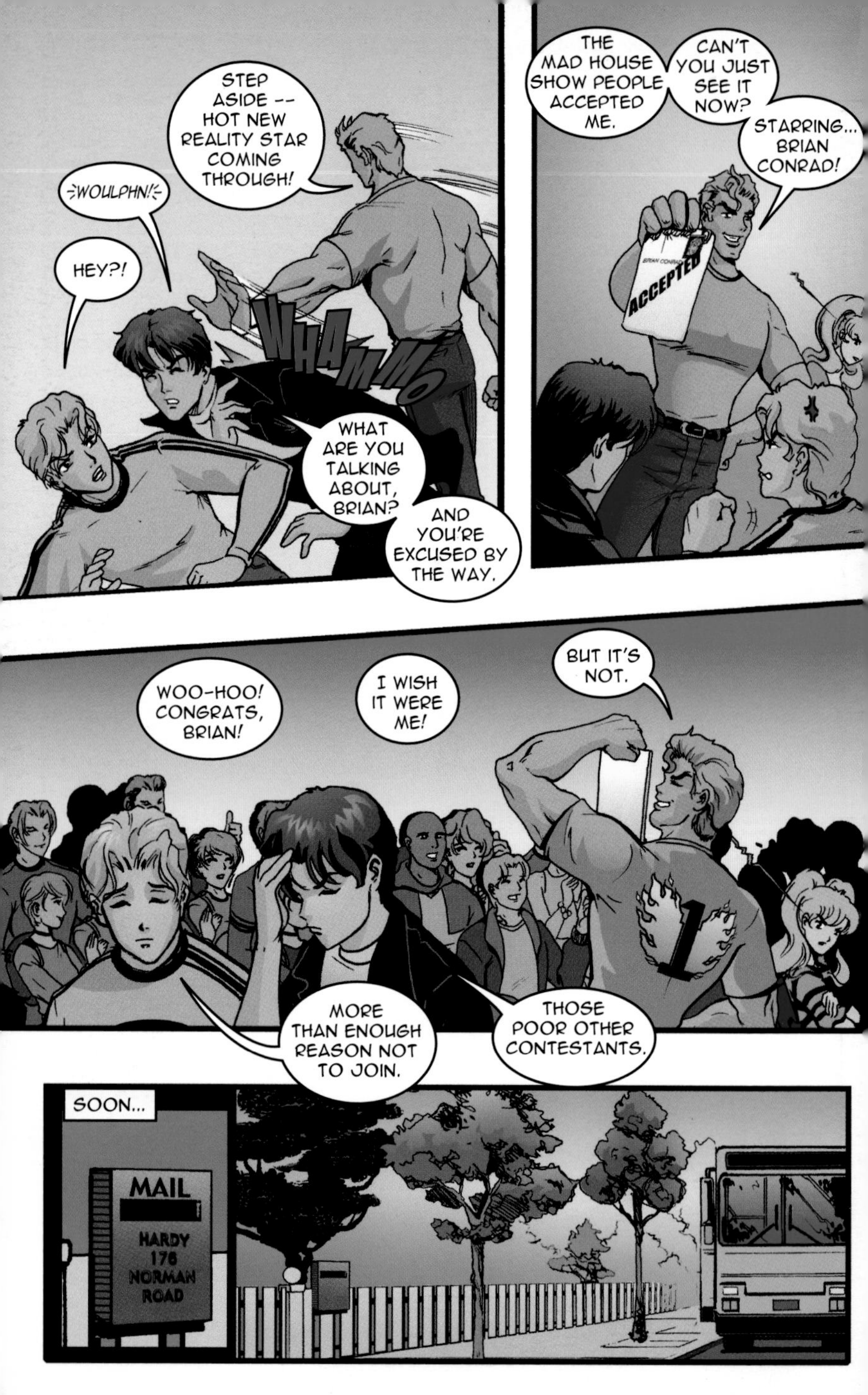
STEP ASIDE -- HOT NEW REALITY STAR COMING THROUGH!
WOULPHN!
HEY?!
WHAMMO
WHAT ARE YOU TALKING ABOUT, BRIAN?
AND YOU'RE EXCUSED BY THE WAY.
THE MAD HOUSE SHOW PEOPLE ACCEPTED ME.
CAN'T YOU JUST SEE IT NOW?
STARRING... BRIAN CONRAD!
BRIAN CONRAD
ACCEPTED
WOO-HOO! CONGRATS, BRIAN!
I WISH IT WERE ME!
BUT IT'S NOT.
MORE THAN ENOUGH REASON NOT TO JOIN.
THOSE POOR OTHER CONTESTANTS.
SOON...
MAIL
HARDY
176
NORMAN
ROAD

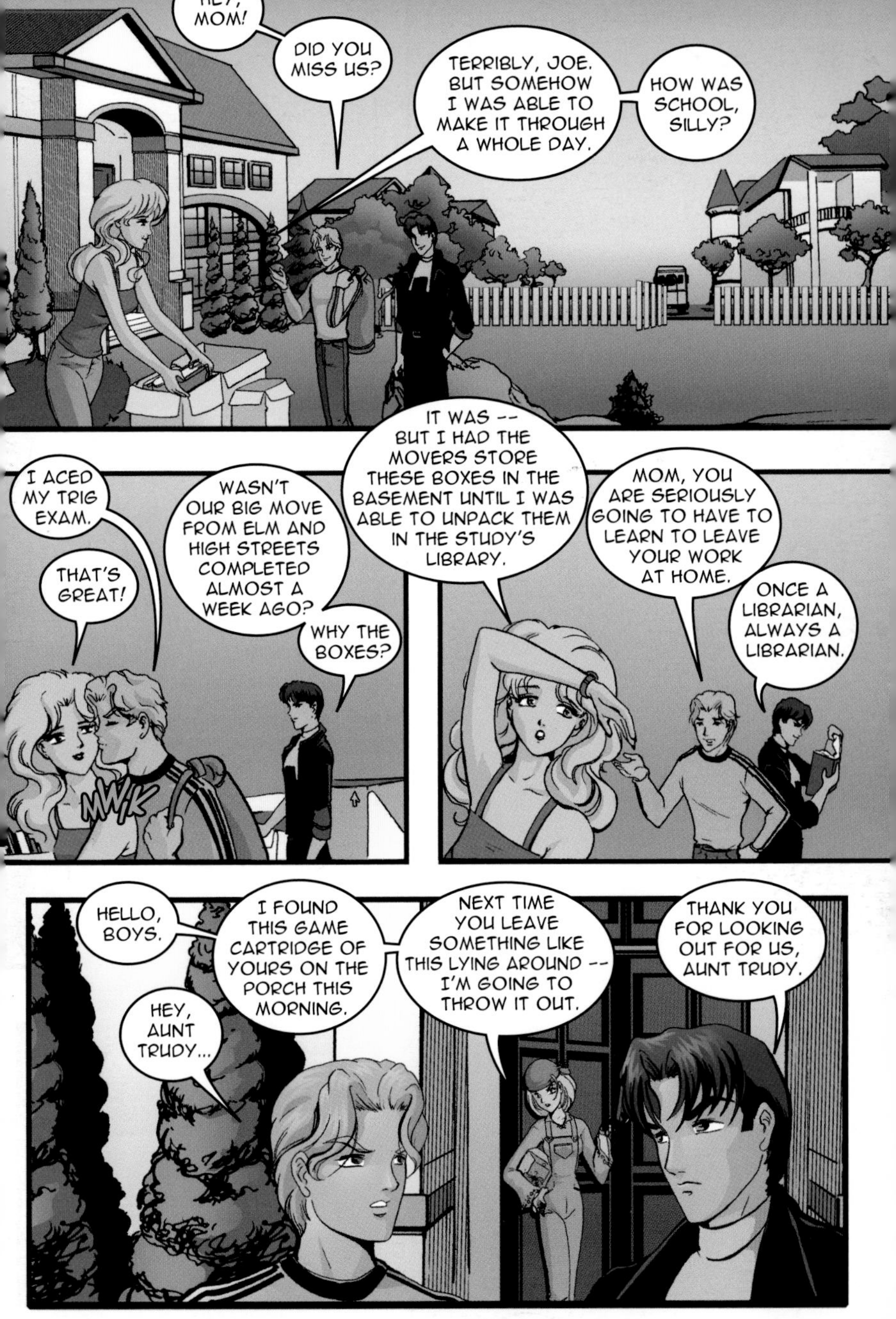
HEY, MOM!
DID YOU MISS US?
TERRIBLY, JOE. BUT SOMEHOW I WAS ABLE TO MAKE IT THROUGH A WHOLE DAY.
HOW WAS SCHOOL, SILLY?
I ACED MY TRIG EXAM.
THAT'S GREAT!
MWK
WASN'T OUR BIG MOVE FROM ELM AND HIGH STREETS COMPLETED ALMOST A WEEK AGO?
WHY THE BOXES?
IT WAS -- BUT I HAD THE MOVERS STORE THESE BOXES IN THE BASEMENT UNTIL I WAS ABLE TO UNPACK THEM IN THE STUDY'S LIBRARY.
MOM, YOU ARE SERIOUSLY GOING TO HAVE TO LEARN TO LEAVE YOUR WORK AT HOME.
ONCE A LIBRARIAN, ALWAYS A LIBRARIAN.
HELLO, BOYS.
HEY, AUNT TRUDY...
I FOUND THIS GAME CARTRIDGE OF YOURS ON THE PORCH THIS MORNING.
NEXT TIME YOU LEAVE SOMETHING LIKE THIS LYING AROUND -- I'M GOING TO THROW IT OUT.
THANK YOU FOR LOOKING OUT FOR US, AUNT TRUDY.

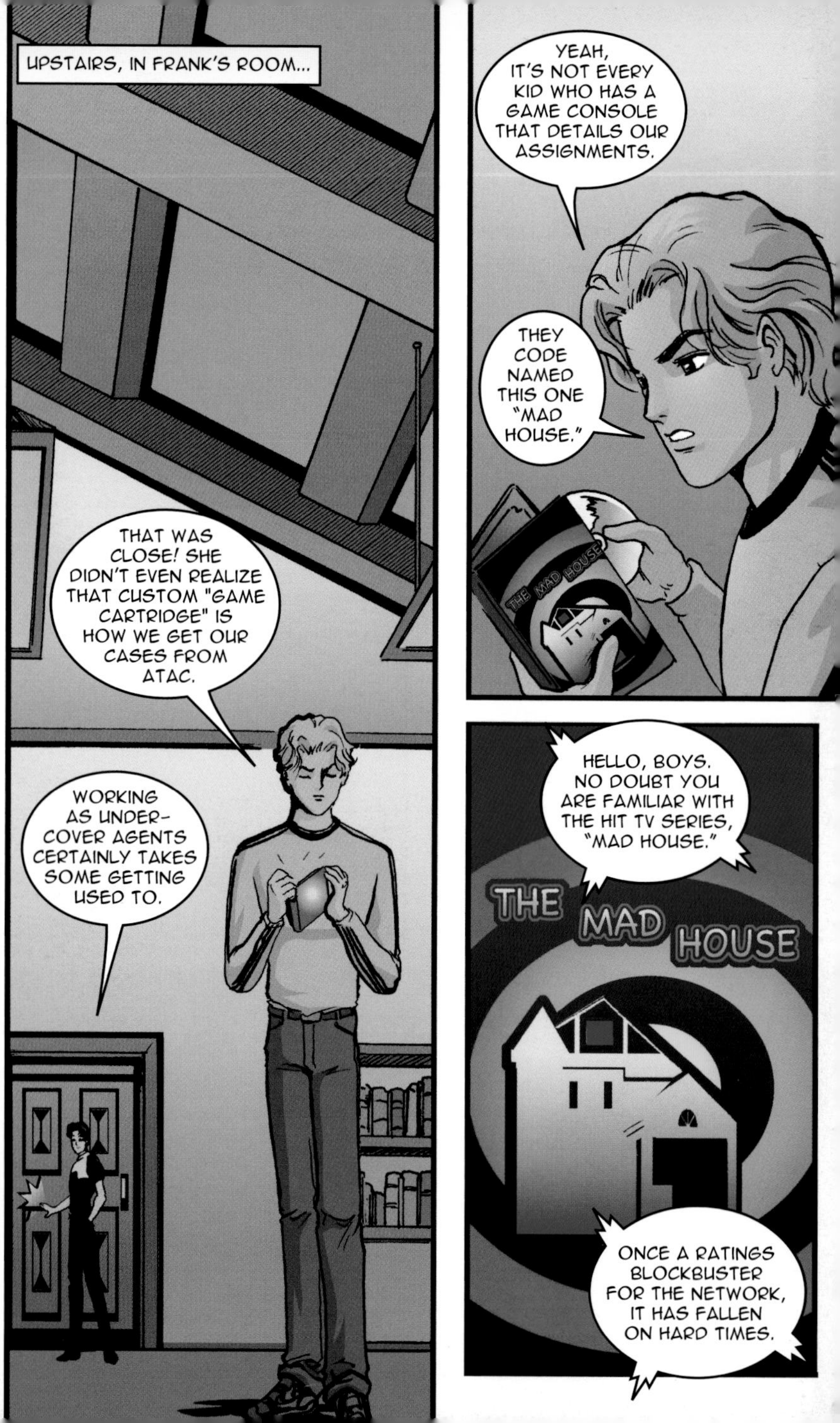
UPSTAIRS, IN FRANK'S ROOM...
THAT WAS CLOSE! SHE DIDN'T EVEN REALIZE THAT CUSTOM "GAME CARTRIDGE" IS HOW WE GET OUR CASES FROM ATAC.
WORKING AS UNDER-COVER AGENTS CERTAINLY TAKES SOME GETTING USED TO.
YEAH, IT'S NOT EVERY KID WHO HAS A GAME CONSOLE THAT DETAILS OUR ASSIGNMENTS.
THEY CODE NAMED THIS ONE "MAD HOUSE."
THE MAD HOUSE
HELLO, BOYS. NO DOUBT YOU ARE FAMILIAR WITH THE HIT TV SERIES, "MAD HOUSE."
THE MAD HOUSE
ONCE A RATINGS BLOCKBUSTER FOR THE NETWORK, IT HAS FALLEN ON HARD TIMES.

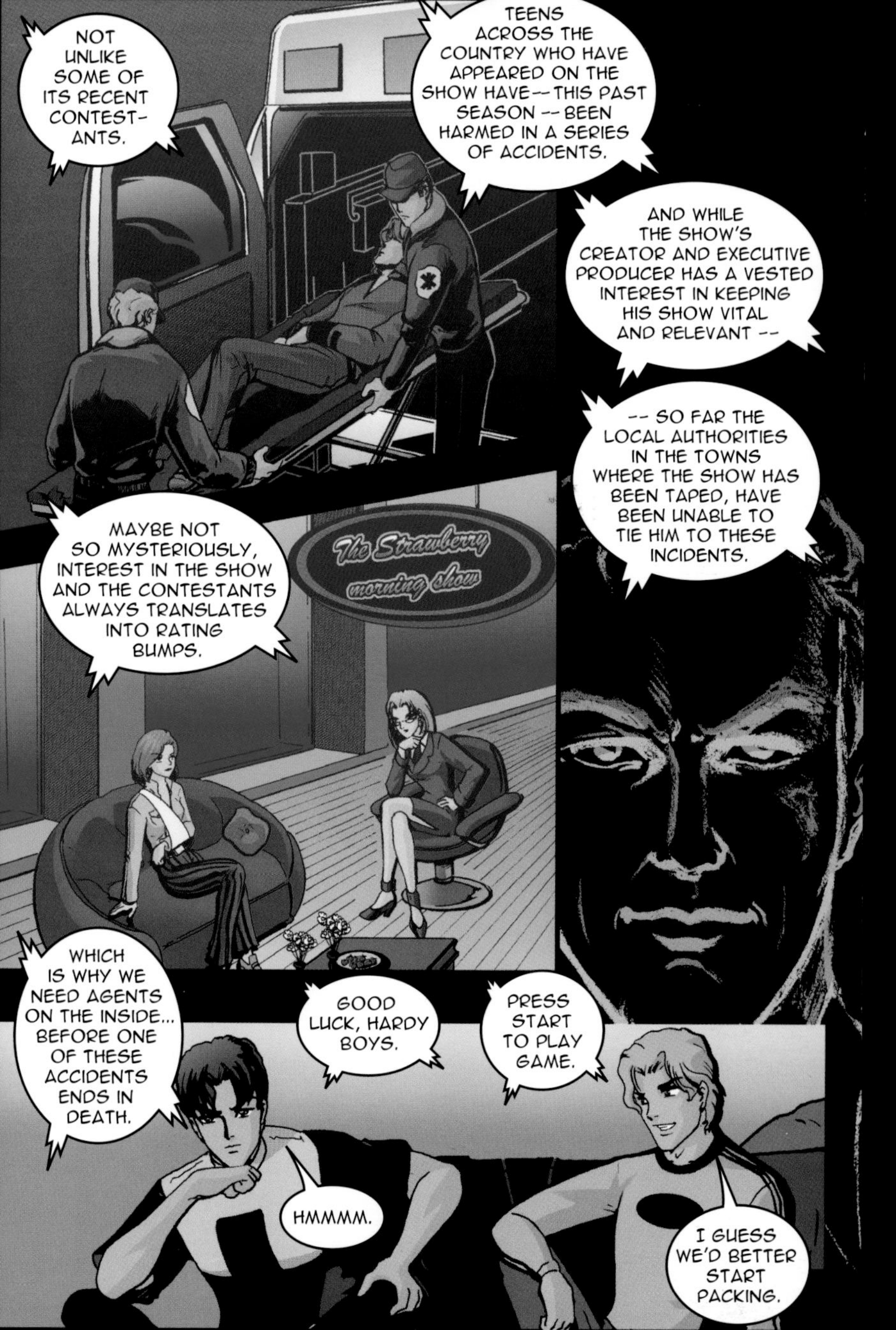
NOT UNLIKE SOME OF ITS RECENT CONTEST-ANTS.
TEENS ACROSS THE COUNTRY WHO HAVE APPEARED ON THE SHOW HAVE-- THIS PAST SEASON -- BEEN HARMED IN A SERIES OF ACCIDENTS.
AND WHILE THE SHOW'S CREATOR AND EXECUTIVE PRODUCER HAS A VESTED INTEREST IN KEEPING HIS SHOW VITAL AND RELEVANT --
-- SO FAR THE LOCAL AUTHORITIES IN THE TOWNS WHERE THE SHOW HAS BEEN TAPED, HAVE BEEN UNABLE TO TIE HIM TO THESE INCIDENTS.
MAYBE NOT SO MYSTERIOUSLY, INTEREST IN THE SHOW AND THE CONTESTANTS ALWAYS TRANSLATES INTO RATING BUMPS.
The Strawberry morning show
WHICH IS WHY WE NEED AGENTS ON THE INSIDE... BEFORE ONE OF THESE ACCIDENTS ENDS IN DEATH.
GOOD LUCK, HARDY BOYS.
PRESS START TO PLAY GAME.
HMMMM.
I GUESS WE'D BETTER START PACKING.

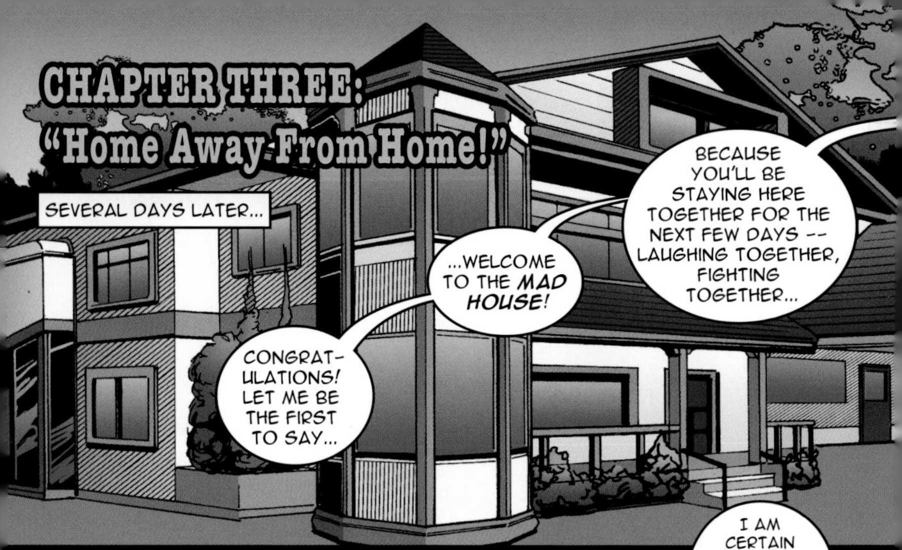
CHAPTER THREE:
"Home Away From Home!"
SEVERAL DAYS LATER...
CONGRATULATIONS! LET ME BE THE FIRST TO SAY...
...WELCOME TO THE *MAD HOUSE*!
BECAUSE YOU'LL BE STAYING HERE TOGETHER FOR THE NEXT FEW DAYS -- LAUGHING TOGETHER, FIGHTING TOGETHER...

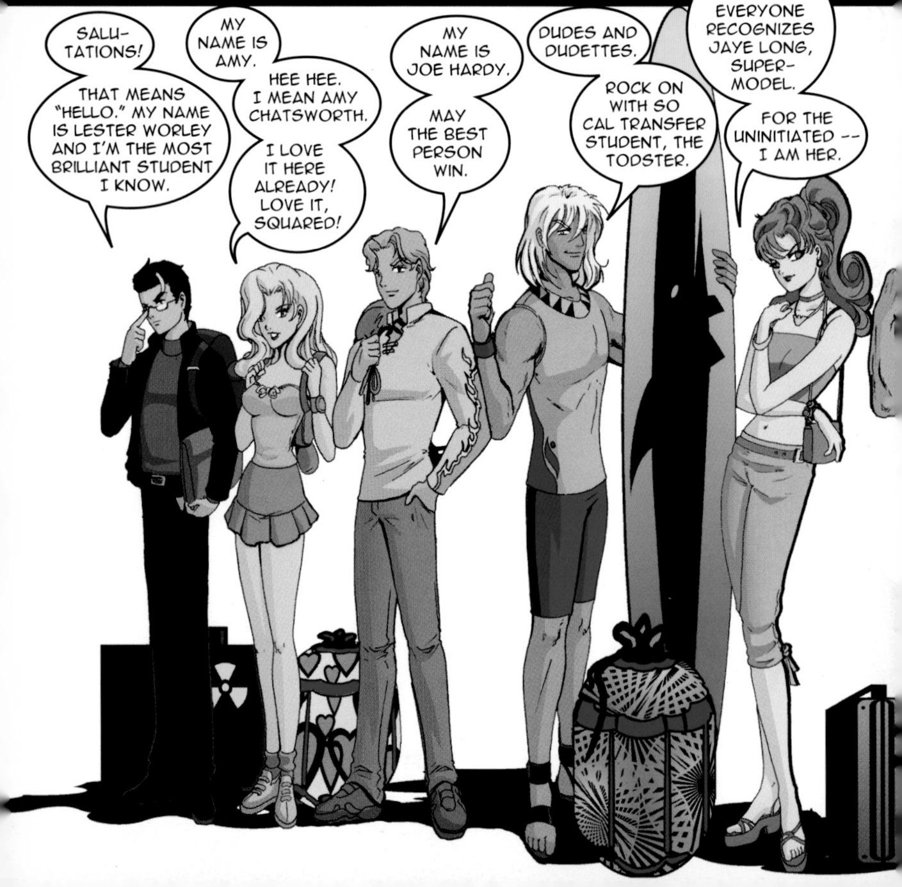
SALUTATIONS!
THAT MEANS "HELLO." MY NAME IS LESTER WORLEY AND I'M THE MOST BRILLIANT STUDENT I KNOW.
MY NAME IS AMY.
HEE HEE. I MEAN AMY CHATSWORTH.
I LOVE IT HERE ALREADY! LOVE IT, SQUARED!
MY NAME IS JOE HARDY.
MAY THE BEST PERSON WIN.
DUDES AND DUDETTES.
ROCK ON WITH SO CAL TRANSFER STUDENT, THE TODSTER.
I AM CERTAIN EVERYONE RECOGNIZES JAYE LONG, SUPER-MODEL.
FOR THE UNINITIATED -- I AM HER.

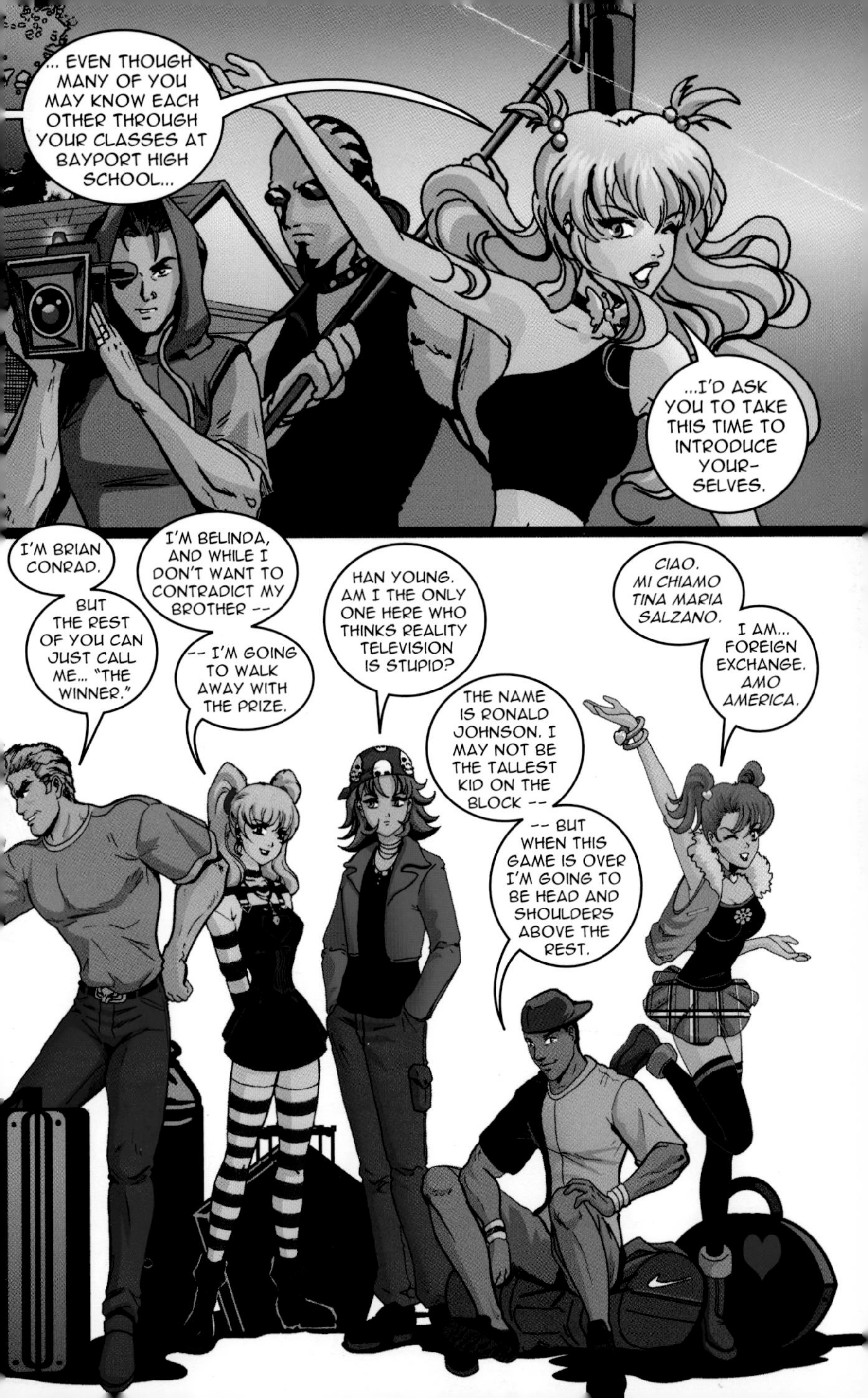
... EVEN THOUGH MANY OF YOU MAY KNOW EACH OTHER THROUGH YOUR CLASSES AT BAYPORT HIGH SCHOOL...
...I'D ASK YOU TO TAKE THIS TIME TO INTRODUCE YOUR-SELVES.
I'M BRIAN CONRAD.
BUT THE REST OF YOU CAN JUST CALL ME... "THE WINNER."
I'M BELINDA, AND WHILE I DON'T WANT TO CONTRADICT MY BROTHER --
-- I'M GOING TO WALK AWAY WITH THE PRIZE.
HAN YOUNG. AM I THE ONLY ONE HERE WHO THINKS REALITY TELEVISION IS STUPID?
THE NAME IS RONALD JOHNSON. I MAY NOT BE THE TALLEST KID ON THE BLOCK --
-- BUT WHEN THIS GAME IS OVER I'M GOING TO BE HEAD AND SHOULDERS ABOVE THE REST.
CIAO. MI CHIAMO TINA MARIA SALZANO.
I AM... FOREIGN EXCHANGE. AMO AMERICA.

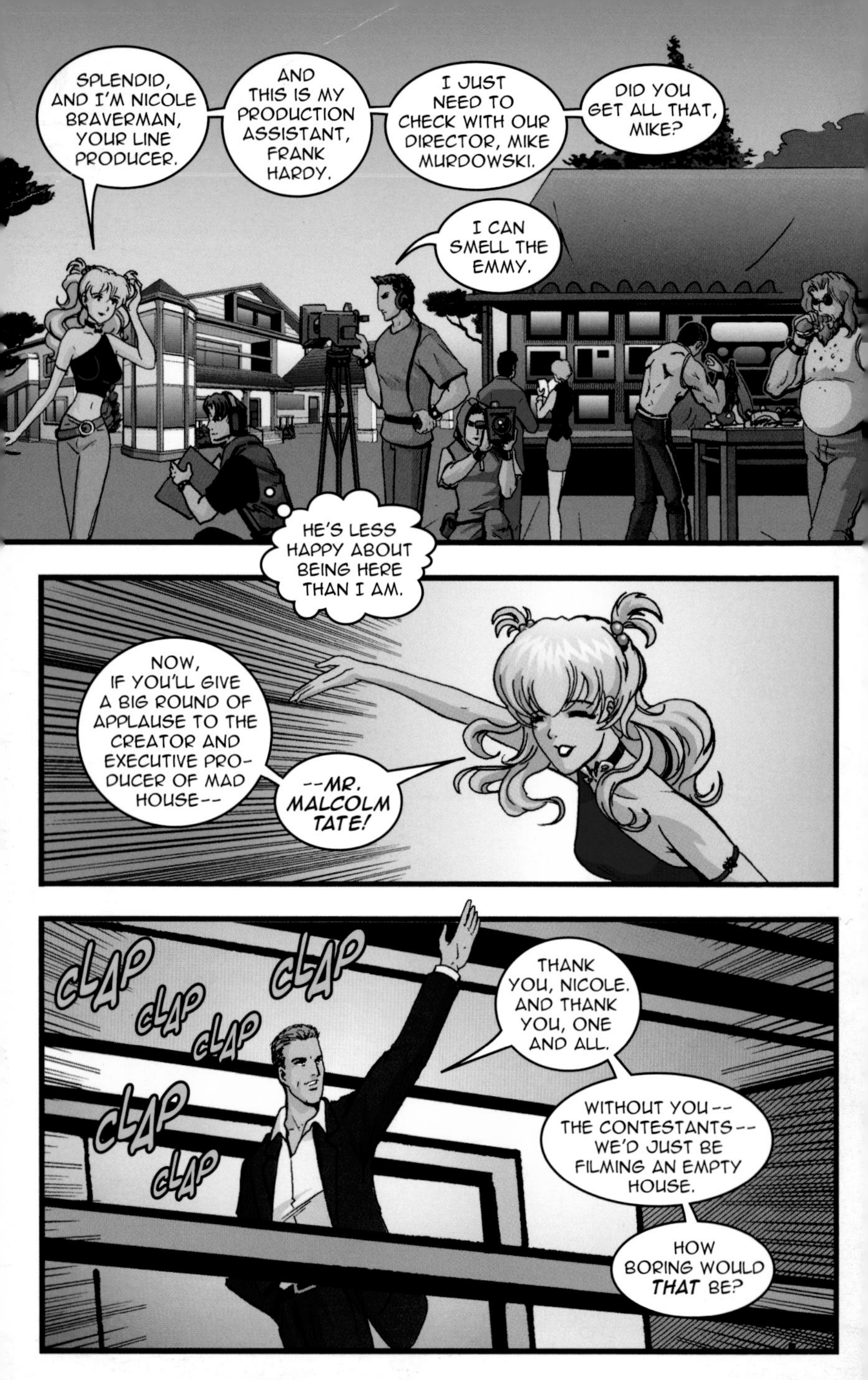
SPLENDID, AND I'M NICOLE BRAVERMAN, YOUR LINE PRODUCER.
AND THIS IS MY PRODUCTION ASSISTANT, FRANK HARDY.
I JUST NEED TO CHECK WITH OUR DIRECTOR, MIKE MURDOWSKI.
DID YOU GET ALL THAT, MIKE?
I CAN SMELL THE EMMY.
HE'S LESS HAPPY ABOUT BEING HERE THAN I AM.
NOW, IF YOU'LL GIVE A BIG ROUND OF APPLAUSE TO THE CREATOR AND EXECUTIVE PRO-DUCER OF MAD HOUSE--
--MR. MALCOLM TATE!
CLAP CLAP CLAP CLAP CLAP CLAP
THANK YOU, NICOLE. AND THANK YOU, ONE AND ALL.
WITHOUT YOU-- THE CONTESTANTS-- WE'D JUST BE FILMING AN EMPTY HOUSE.
HOW BORING WOULD THAT BE?

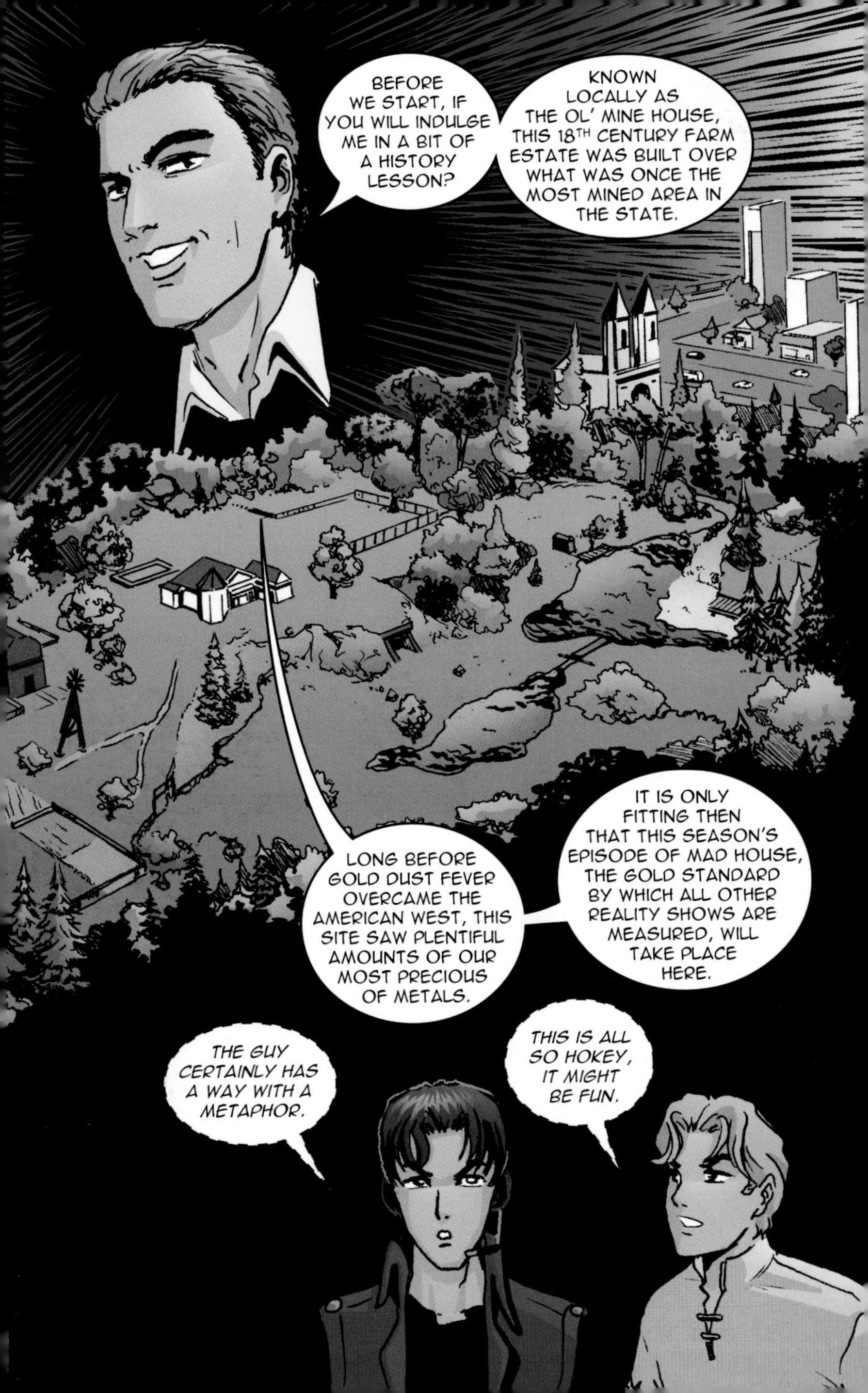
BEFORE WE START, IF YOU WILL INDULGE ME IN A BIT OF A HISTORY LESSON?
KNOWN LOCALLY AS THE OL' MINE HOUSE, THIS 18TH CENTURY FARM ESTATE WAS BUILT OVER WHAT WAS ONCE THE MOST MINED AREA IN THE STATE.
LONG BEFORE GOLD DUST FEVER OVERCAME THE AMERICAN WEST, THIS SITE SAW PLENTIFUL AMOUNTS OF OUR MOST PRECIOUS OF METALS.
IT IS ONLY FITTING THEN THAT THIS SEASON'S EPISODE OF MAD HOUSE, THE GOLD STANDARD BY WHICH ALL OTHER REALITY SHOWS ARE MEASURED, WILL TAKE PLACE HERE.
THE GUY CERTAINLY HAS A WAY WITH A METAPHOR.
THIS IS ALL SO HOKEY, IT MIGHT BE FUN.

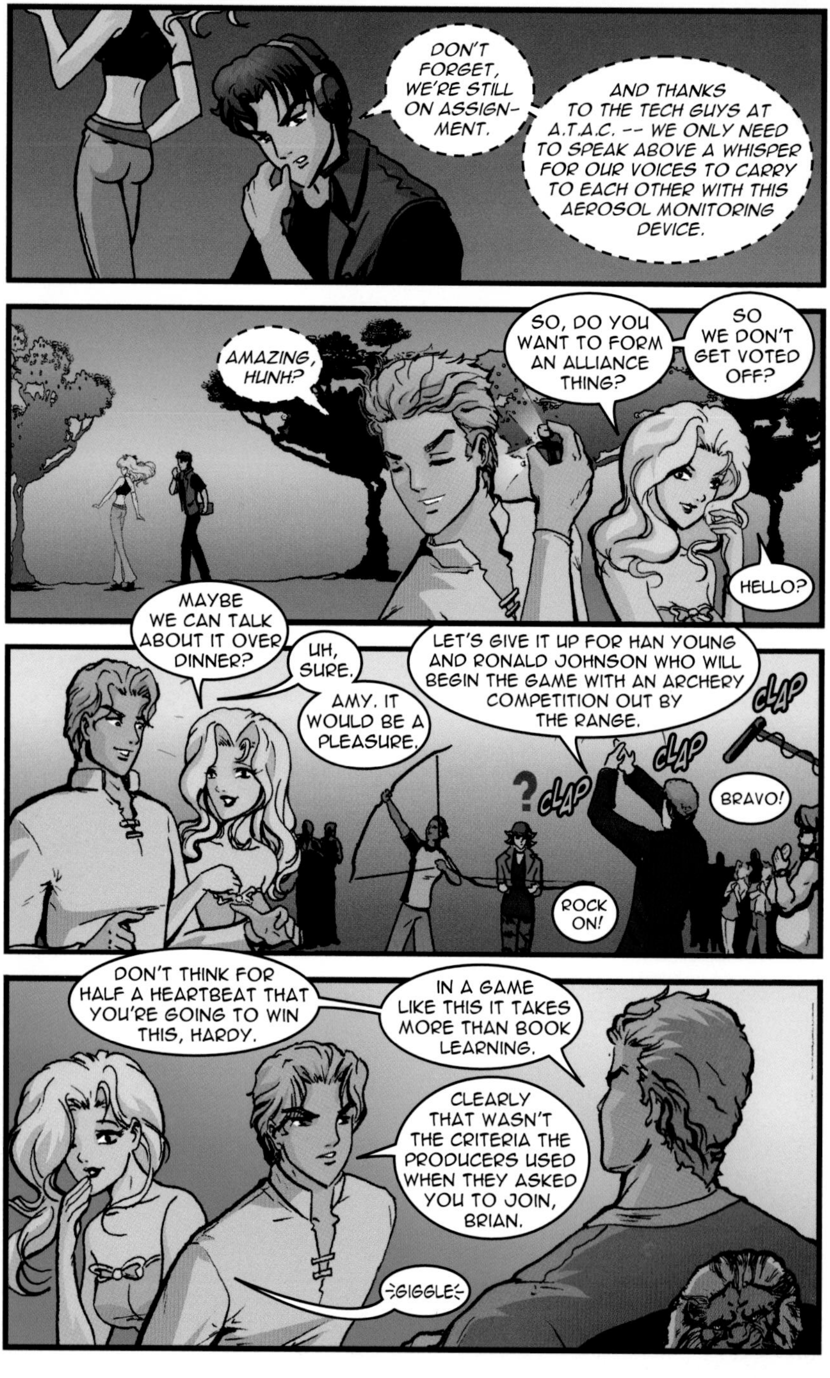
DON'T FORGET, WE'RE STILL ON ASSIGN-MENT.
AND THANKS TO THE TECH GUYS AT A.T.A.C. -- WE ONLY NEED TO SPEAK ABOVE A WHISPER FOR OUR VOICES TO CARRY TO EACH OTHER WITH THIS AEROSOL MONITORING DEVICE.
AMAZING, HUNH?
SO, DO YOU WANT TO FORM AN ALLIANCE THING?
SO WE DON'T GET VOTED OFF?
HELLO?
MAYBE WE CAN TALK ABOUT IT OVER DINNER?
UH, SURE.
AMY. IT WOULD BE A PLEASURE.
LET'S GIVE IT UP FOR HAN YOUNG AND RONALD JOHNSON WHO WILL BEGIN THE GAME WITH AN ARCHERY COMPETITION OUT BY THE RANGE.
CLAP
CLAP
CLAP
?
BRAVO!
ROCK ON!
DON'T THINK FOR HALF A HEARTBEAT THAT YOU'RE GOING TO WIN THIS, HARDY.
IN A GAME LIKE THIS IT TAKES MORE THAN BOOK LEARNING.
CLEARLY THAT WASN'T THE CRITERIA THE PRODUCERS USED WHEN THEY ASKED YOU TO JOIN, BRIAN.
GIGGLE

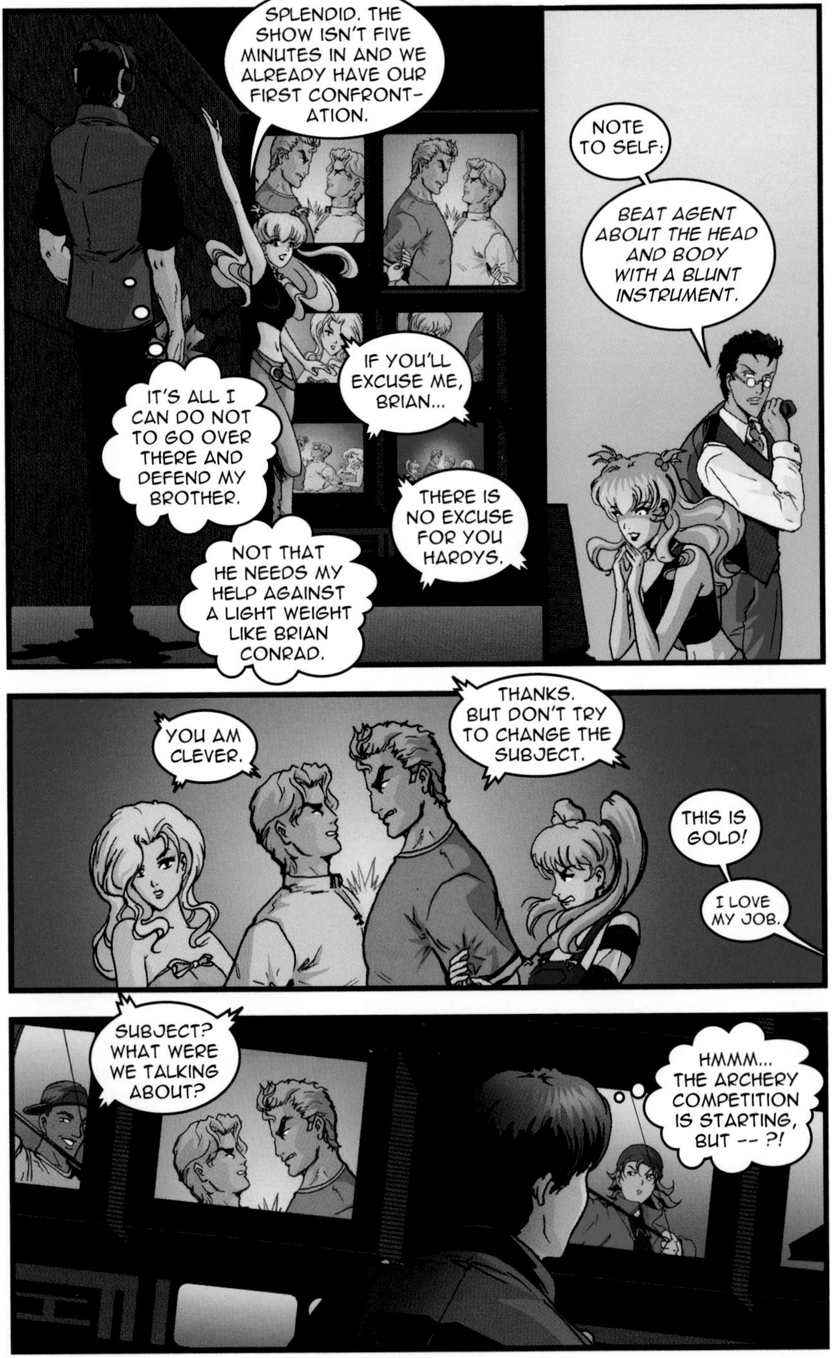

SPLENDID. THE SHOW ISN'T FIVE MINUTES IN AND WE ALREADY HAVE OUR FIRST CONFRONT-ATION.
IT'S ALL I CAN DO NOT TO GO OVER THERE AND DEFEND MY BROTHER.
NOT THAT HE NEEDS MY HELP AGAINST A LIGHT WEIGHT LIKE BRIAN CONRAD.
IF YOU'LL EXCUSE ME, BRIAN...
THERE IS NO EXCUSE FOR YOU HARDYS.
NOTE TO SELF:
BEAT AGENT ABOUT THE HEAD AND BODY WITH A BLUNT INSTRUMENT.
YOU AM CLEVER.
THANKS. BUT DON'T TRY TO CHANGE THE SUBJECT.
THIS IS GOLD!
I LOVE MY JOB.
SUBJECT? WHAT WERE WE TALKING ABOUT?
HMMM... THE ARCHERY COMPETITION IS STARTING, BUT -- ?!

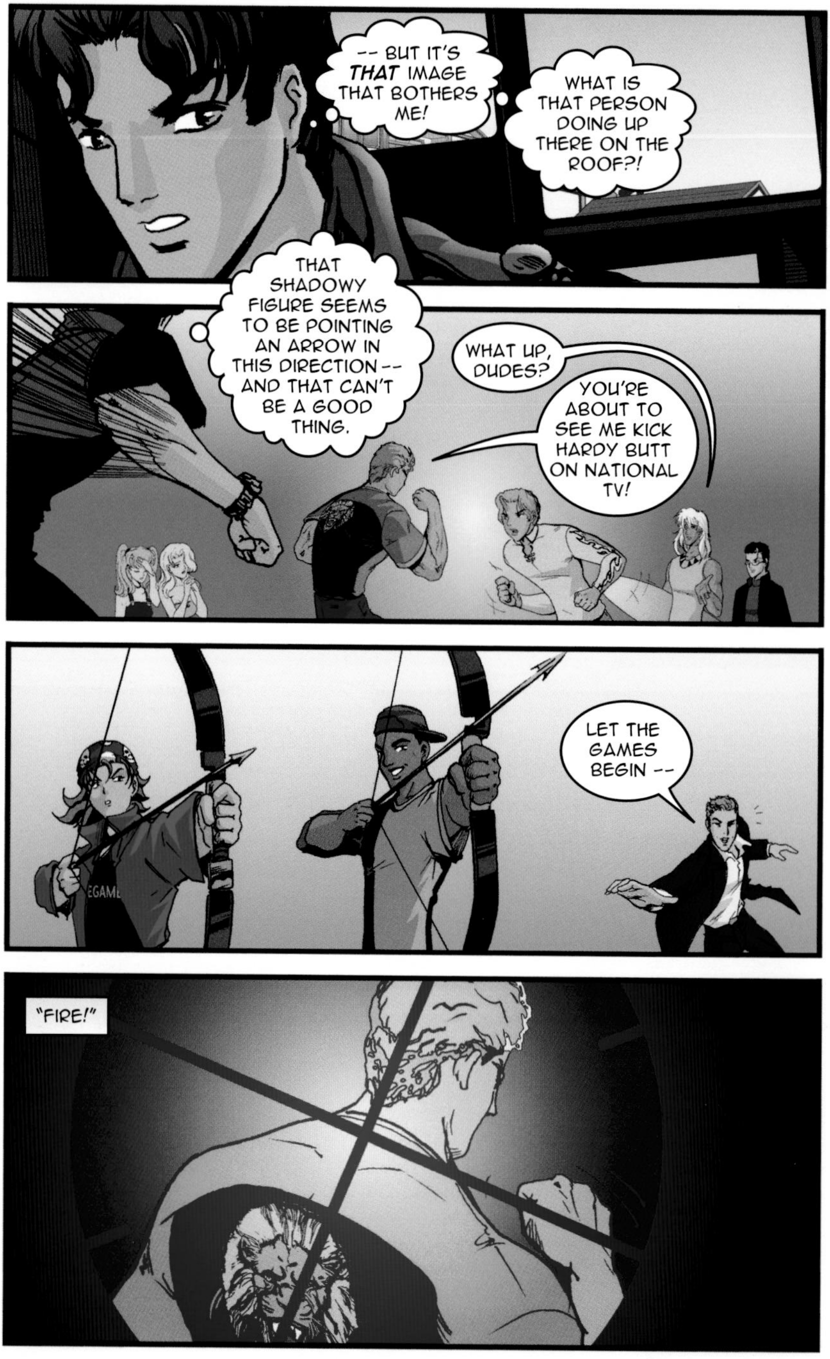
-- BUT IT'S *THAT* IMAGE THAT BOTHERS ME!
WHAT IS THAT PERSON DOING UP THERE ON THE ROOF?!
THAT SHADOWY FIGURE SEEMS TO BE POINTING AN ARROW IN THIS DIRECTION -- AND THAT CAN'T BE A GOOD THING.
WHAT UP, DUDES?
YOU'RE ABOUT TO SEE ME KICK HARDY BUTT ON NATIONAL TV!
LET THE GAMES BEGIN --
"FIRE!"

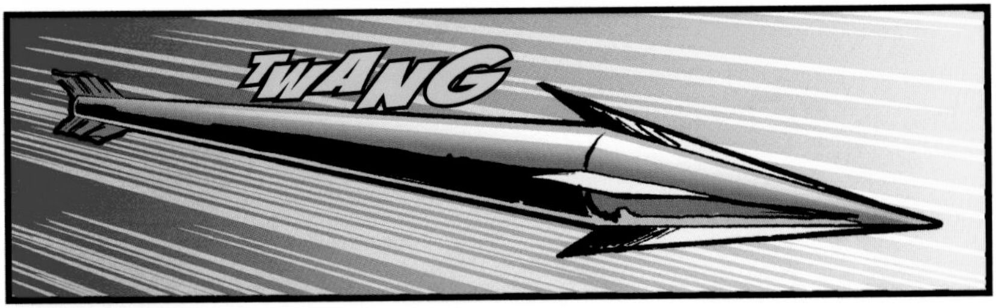
TWANG

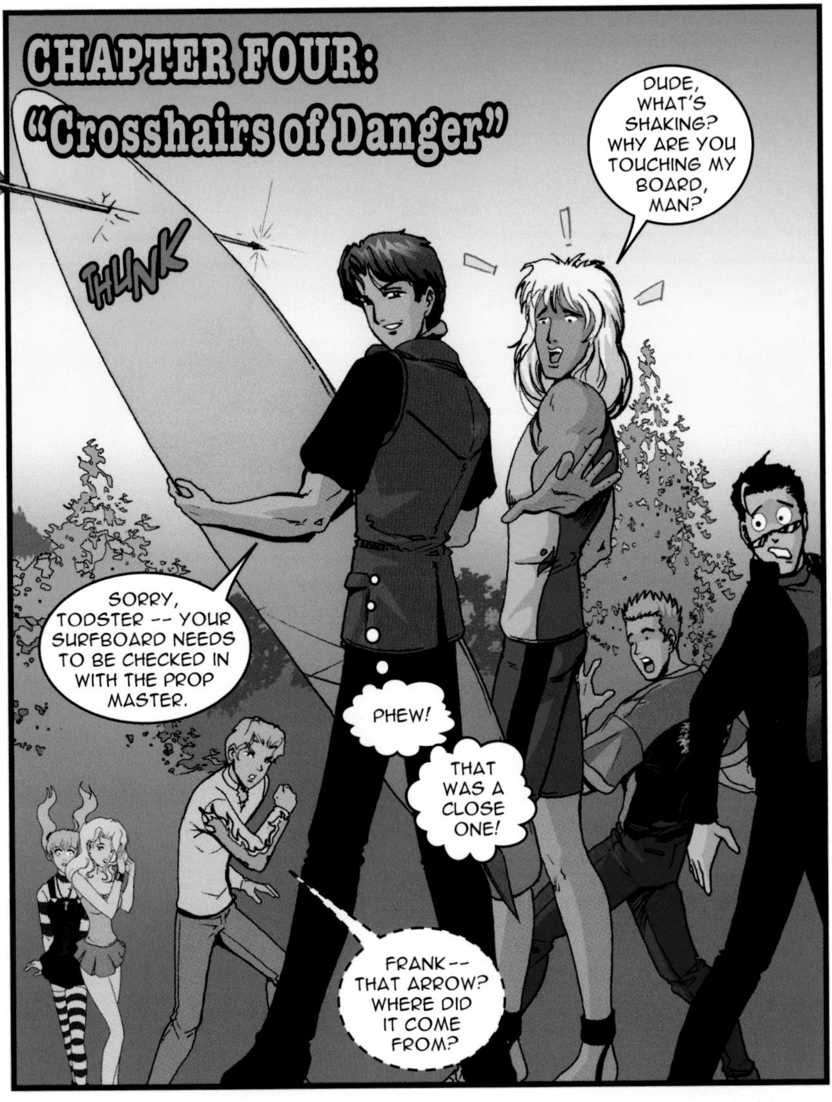
CHAPTER FOUR:
"Crosshairs of Danger"
THUNK
DUDE, WHAT'S SHAKING? WHY ARE YOU TOUCHING MY BOARD, MAN?
SORRY, TODSTER -- YOUR SURFBOARD NEEDS TO BE CHECKED IN WITH THE PROP MASTER.
PHEW!
THAT WAS A CLOSE ONE!
FRANK-- THAT ARROW? WHERE DID IT COME FROM?

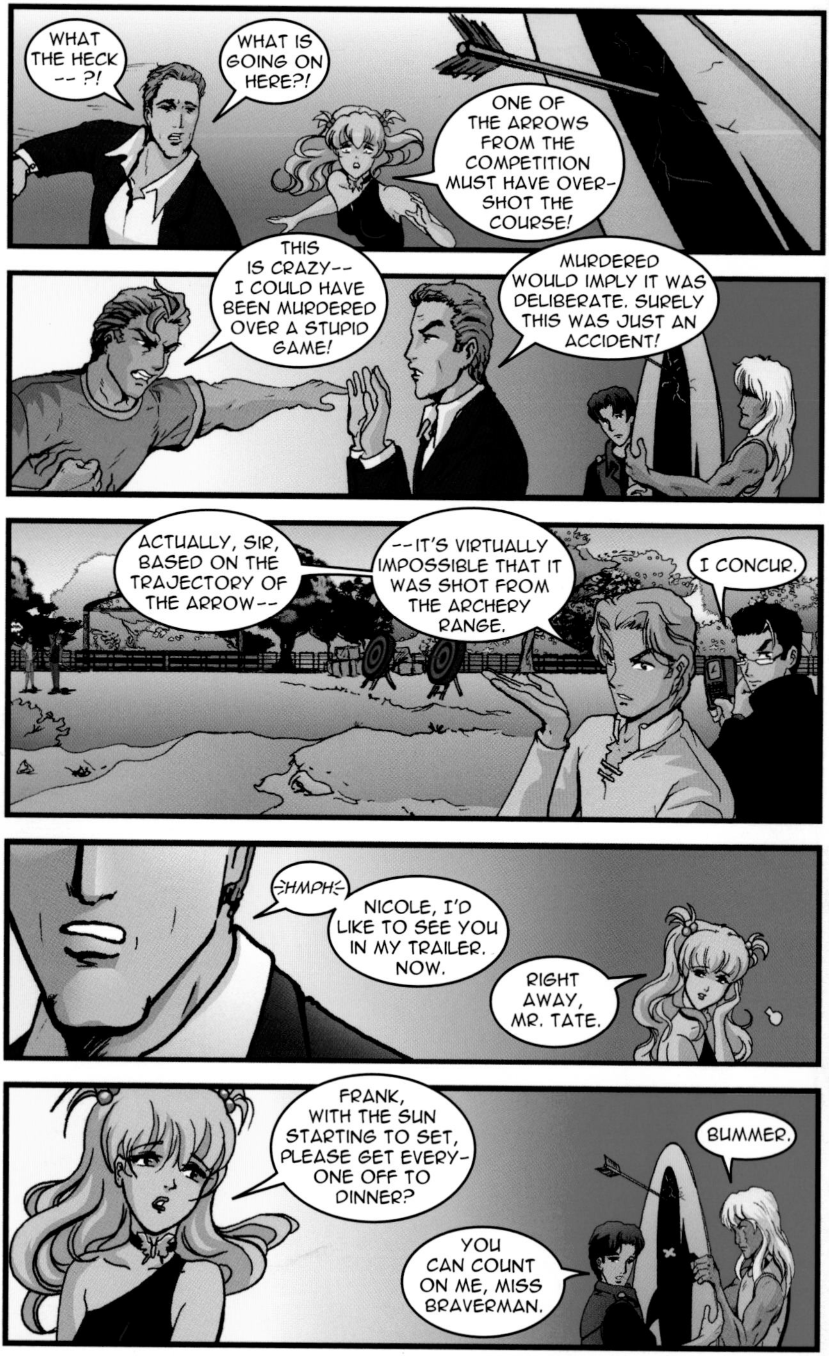
WHAT THE HECK -- ?!
WHAT IS GOING ON HERE?!
ONE OF THE ARROWS FROM THE COMPETITION MUST HAVE OVER-SHOT THE COURSE!
THIS IS CRAZY-- I COULD HAVE BEEN MURDERED OVER A STUPID GAME!
MURDERED WOULD IMPLY IT WAS DELIBERATE. SURELY THIS WAS JUST AN ACCIDENT!
ACTUALLY, SIR, BASED ON THE TRAJECTORY OF THE ARROW--
--IT'S VIRTUALLY IMPOSSIBLE THAT IT WAS SHOT FROM THE ARCHERY RANGE.
I CONCUR.
HMPH
NICOLE, I'D LIKE TO SEE YOU IN MY TRAILER. NOW.
RIGHT AWAY, MR. TATE.
FRANK, WITH THE SUN STARTING TO SET, PLEASE GET EVERY-ONE OFF TO DINNER?
BUMMER.
YOU CAN COUNT ON ME, MISS BRAVERMAN.

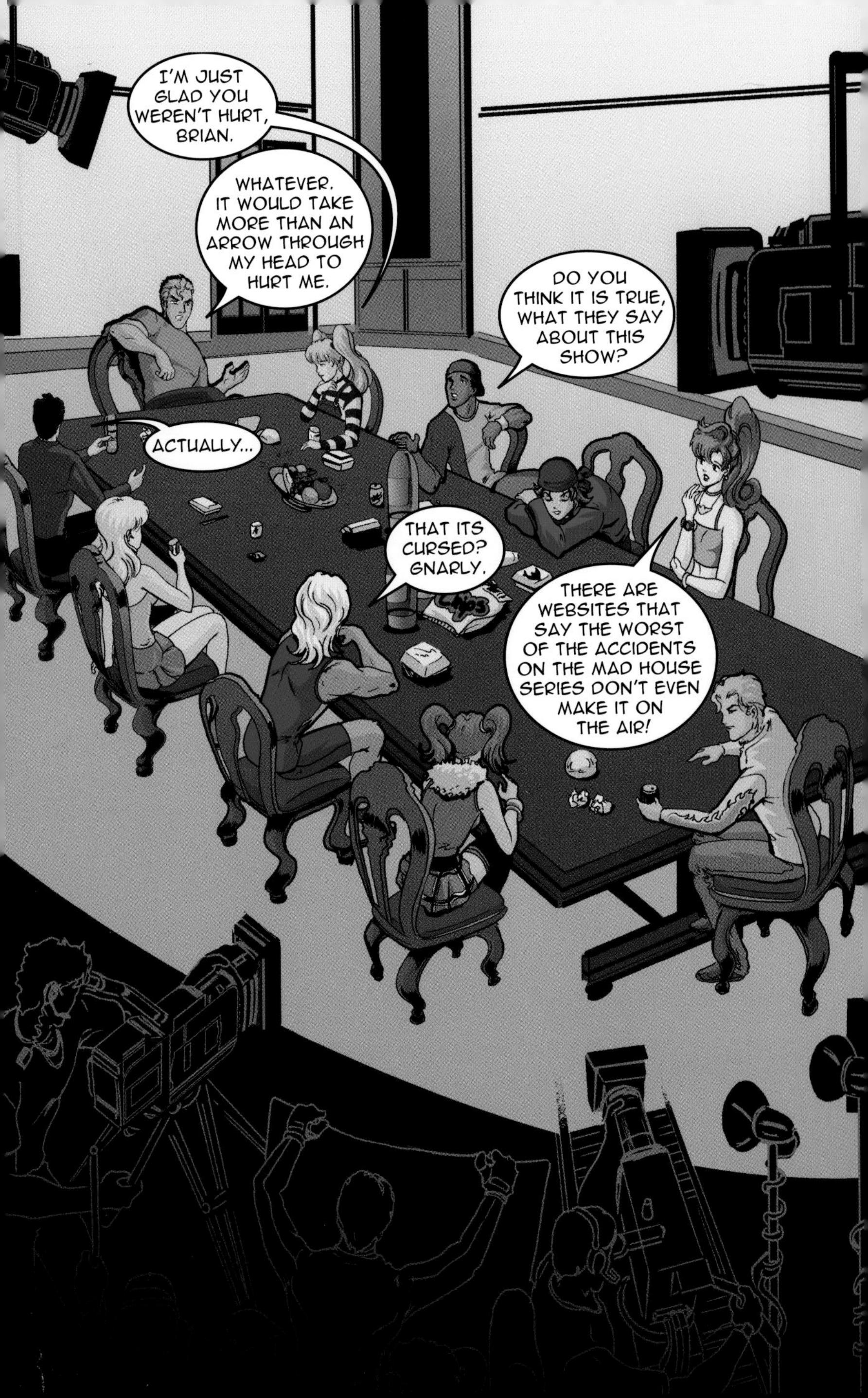
I'M JUST GLAD YOU WEREN'T HURT, BRIAN.
WHATEVER. IT WOULD TAKE MORE THAN AN ARROW THROUGH MY HEAD TO HURT ME.
DO YOU THINK IT IS TRUE, WHAT THEY SAY ABOUT THIS SHOW?
ACTUALLY...
THAT ITS CURSED? GNARLY.
THERE ARE WEBSITES THAT SAY THE WORST OF THE ACCIDENTS ON THE MAD HOUSE SERIES DON'T EVEN MAKE IT ON THE AIR!

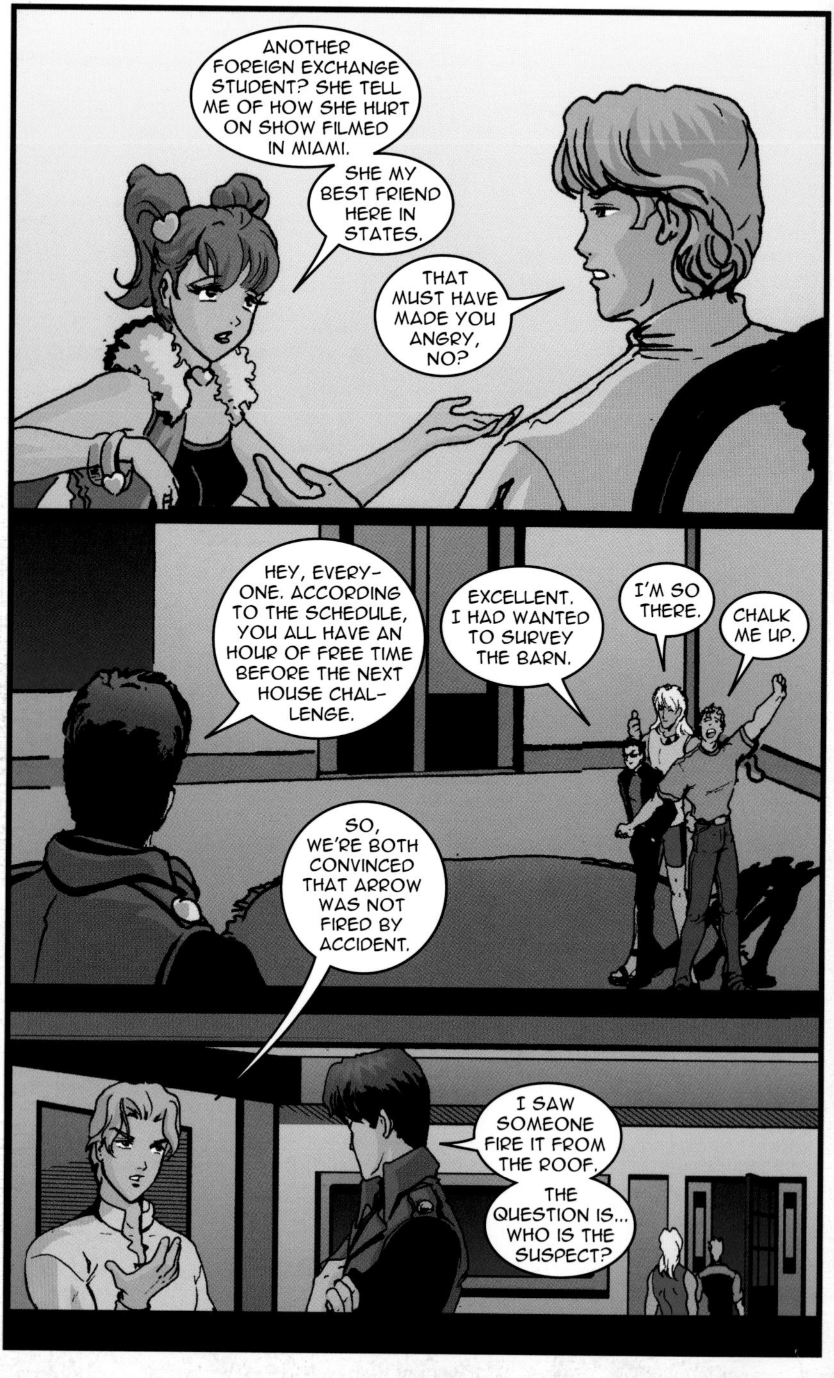
ANOTHER FOREIGN EXCHANGE STUDENT? SHE TELL ME OF HOW SHE HURT ON SHOW FILMED IN MIAMI.
SHE MY BEST FRIEND HERE IN STATES.
THAT MUST HAVE MADE YOU ANGRY, NO?
HEY, EVERY-ONE. ACCORDING TO THE SCHEDULE, YOU ALL HAVE AN HOUR OF FREE TIME BEFORE THE NEXT HOUSE CHAL-LENGE.
EXCELLENT. I HAD WANTED TO SURVEY THE BARN.
I'M SO THERE.
CHALK ME UP.
SO, WE'RE BOTH CONVINCED THAT ARROW WAS NOT FIRED BY ACCIDENT.
I SAW SOMEONE FIRE IT FROM THE ROOF.
THE QUESTION IS... WHO IS THE SUSPECT?

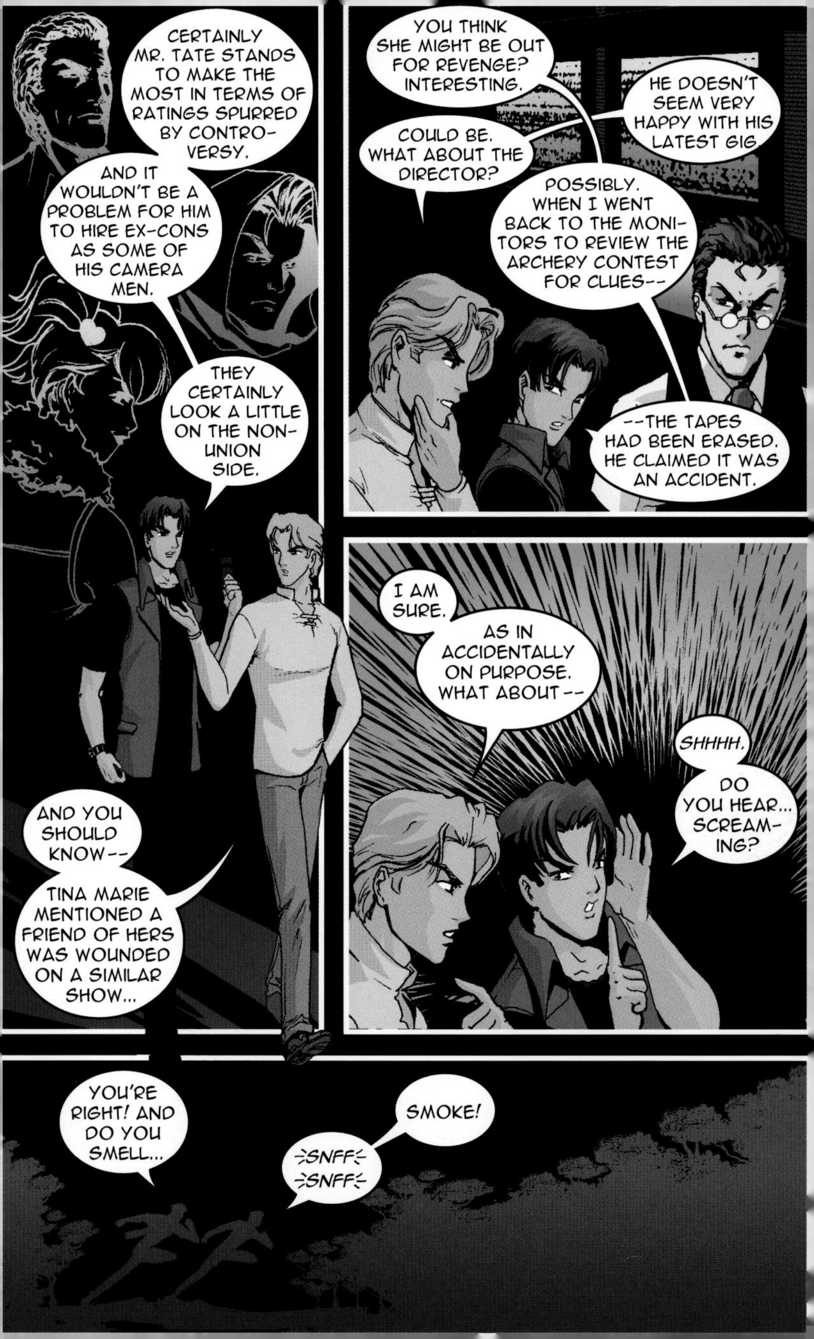
CERTAINLY MR. TATE STANDS TO MAKE THE MOST IN TERMS OF RATINGS SPURRED BY CONTRO-VERSY.
AND IT WOULDN'T BE A PROBLEM FOR HIM TO HIRE EX-CONS AS SOME OF HIS CAMERA MEN.
THEY CERTAINLY LOOK A LITTLE ON THE NON-UNION SIDE.
AND YOU SHOULD KNOW--
TINA MARIE MENTIONED A FRIEND OF HERS WAS WOUNDED ON A SIMILAR SHOW...
YOU THINK SHE MIGHT BE OUT FOR REVENGE? INTERESTING.
COULD BE. WHAT ABOUT THE DIRECTOR?
HE DOESN'T SEEM VERY HAPPY WITH HIS LATEST GIG.
POSSIBLY. WHEN I WENT BACK TO THE MONI-TORS TO REVIEW THE ARCHERY CONTEST FOR CLUES--
--THE TAPES HAD BEEN ERASED. HE CLAIMED IT WAS AN ACCIDENT.
I AM SURE.
AS IN ACCIDENTALLY ON PURPOSE. WHAT ABOUT--
SHHHH.
DO YOU HEAR... SCREAM-ING?
YOU'RE RIGHT! AND DO YOU SMELL...
SMOKE!
SNFF
SNFF

CHAPTER FIVE:
"The Heat is On!"

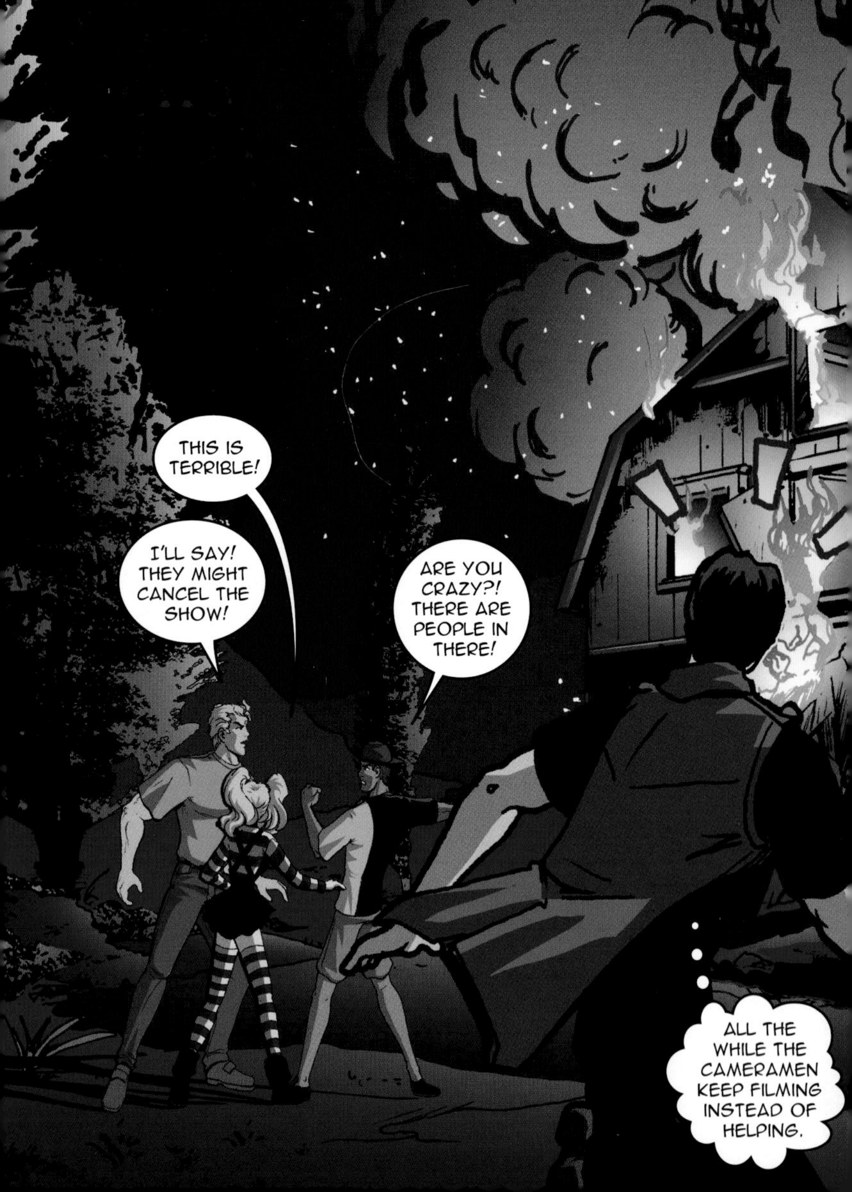

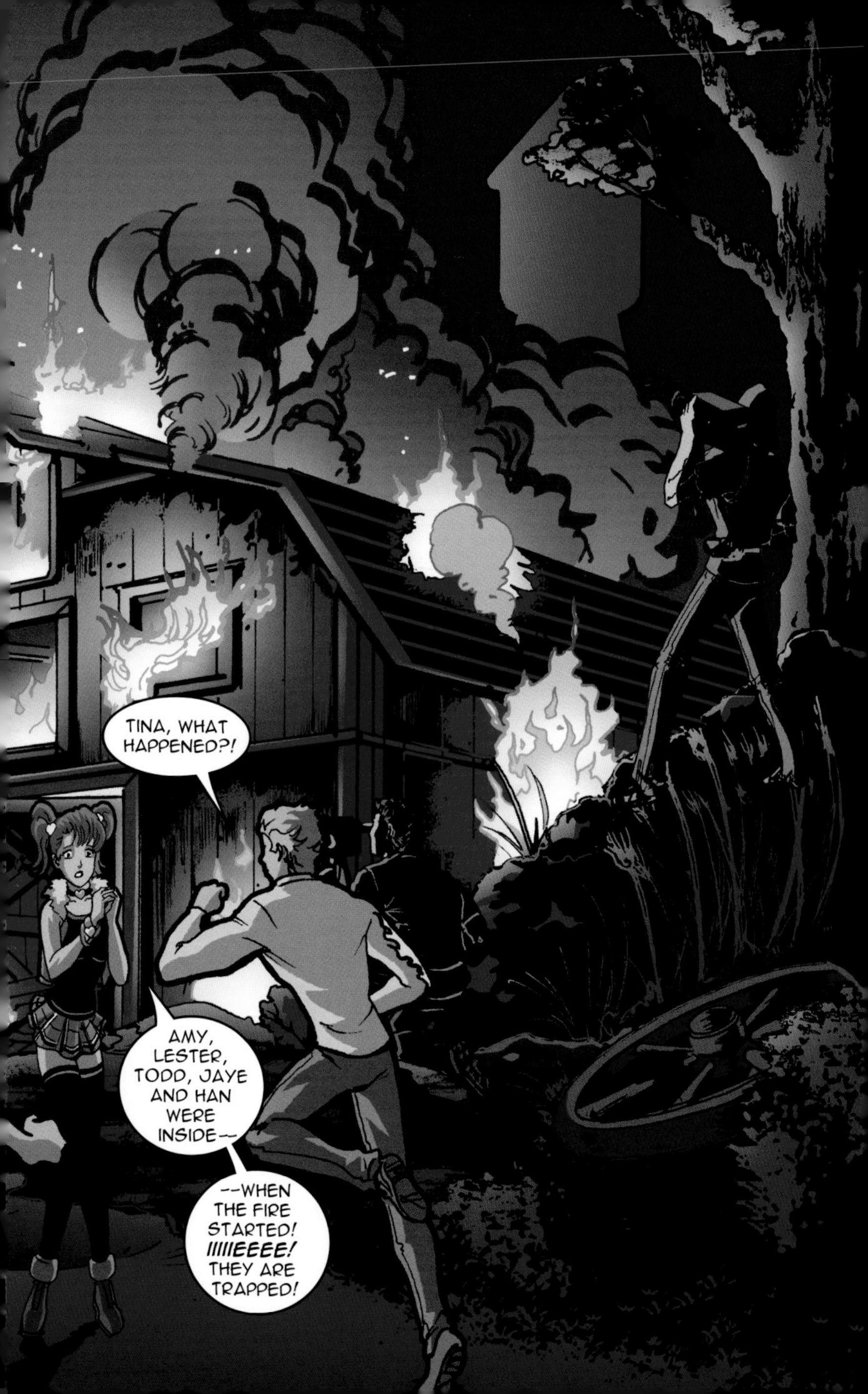
TINA, WHAT HAPPENED?!
AMY, LESTER, TODD, JAYE AND HAN WERE INSIDE--
--WHEN THE FIRE STARTED! IIIIIEEEE! THEY ARE TRAPPED!

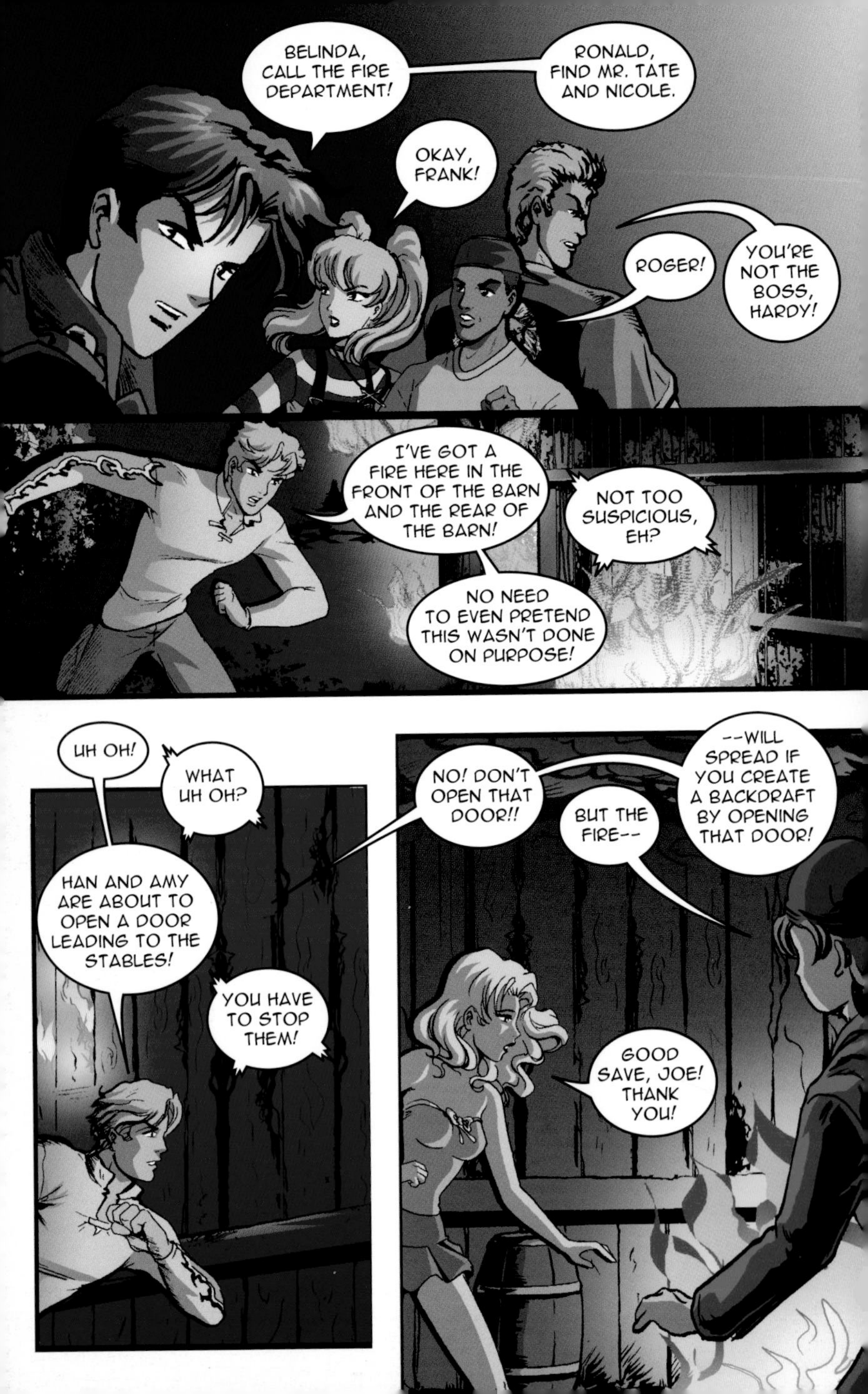
BELINDA, CALL THE FIRE DEPARTMENT!
RONALD, FIND MR. TATE AND NICOLE.
OKAY, FRANK!
ROGER!
YOU'RE NOT THE BOSS, HARDY!
I'VE GOT A FIRE HERE IN THE FRONT OF THE BARN AND THE REAR OF THE BARN!
NOT TOO SUSPICIOUS, EH?
NO NEED TO EVEN PRETEND THIS WASN'T DONE ON PURPOSE!
UH OH!
WHAT UH OH?
HAN AND AMY ARE ABOUT TO OPEN A DOOR LEADING TO THE STABLES!
YOU HAVE TO STOP THEM!
NO! DON'T OPEN THAT DOOR!!
BUT THE FIRE--
--WILL SPREAD IF YOU CREATE A BACKDRAFT BY OPENING THAT DOOR!
GOOD SAVE, JOE! THANK YOU!

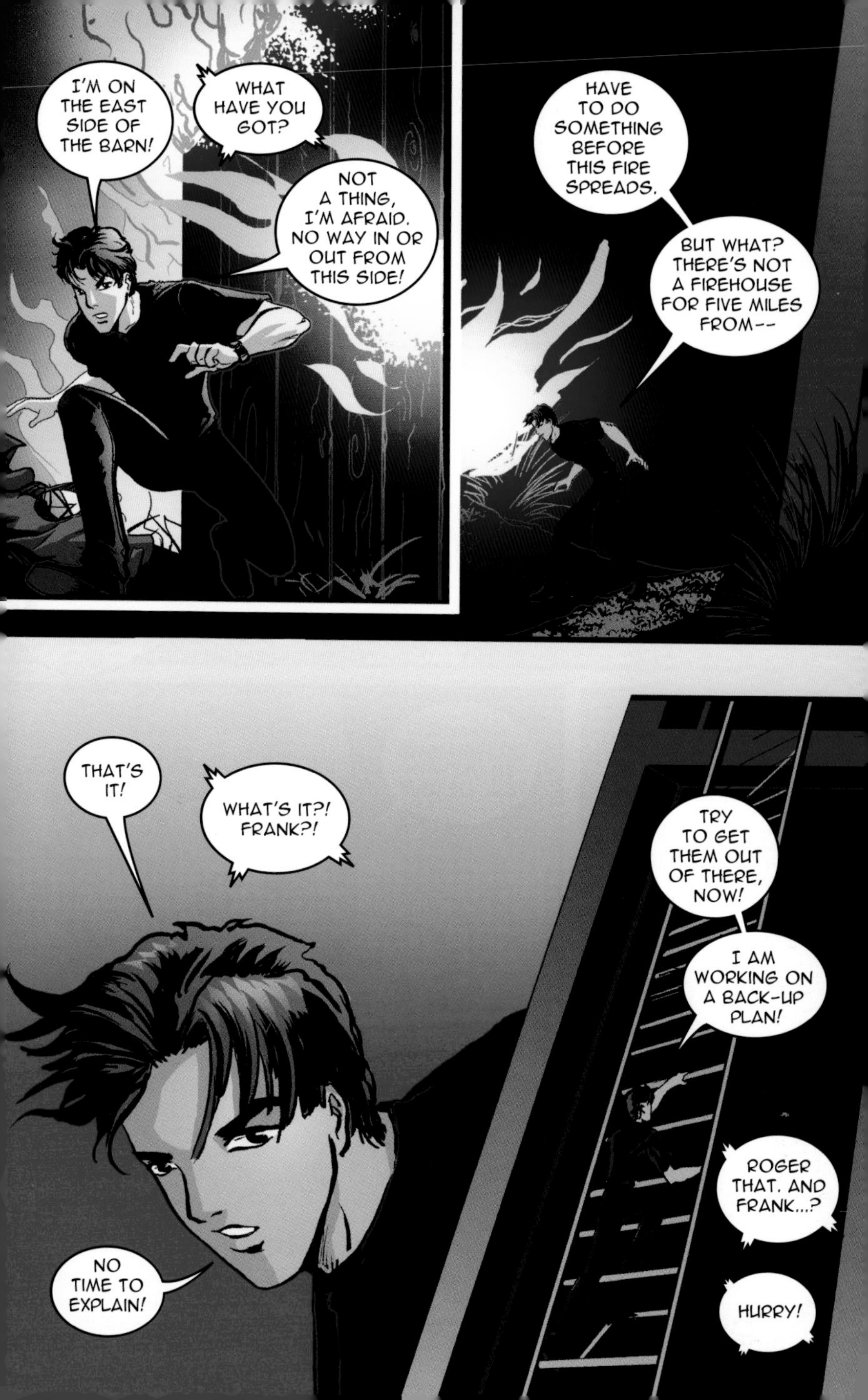
I'M ON THE EAST SIDE OF THE BARN!
WHAT HAVE YOU GOT?
NOT A THING, I'M AFRAID. NO WAY IN OR OUT FROM THIS SIDE!
HAVE TO DO SOMETHING BEFORE THIS FIRE SPREADS.
BUT WHAT? THERE'S NOT A FIREHOUSE FOR FIVE MILES FROM--
THAT'S IT!
WHAT'S IT?! FRANK?!
TRY TO GET THEM OUT OF THERE, NOW!
I AM WORKING ON A BACK-UP PLAN!
ROGER THAT. AND FRANK...?
NO TIME TO EXPLAIN!
HURRY!

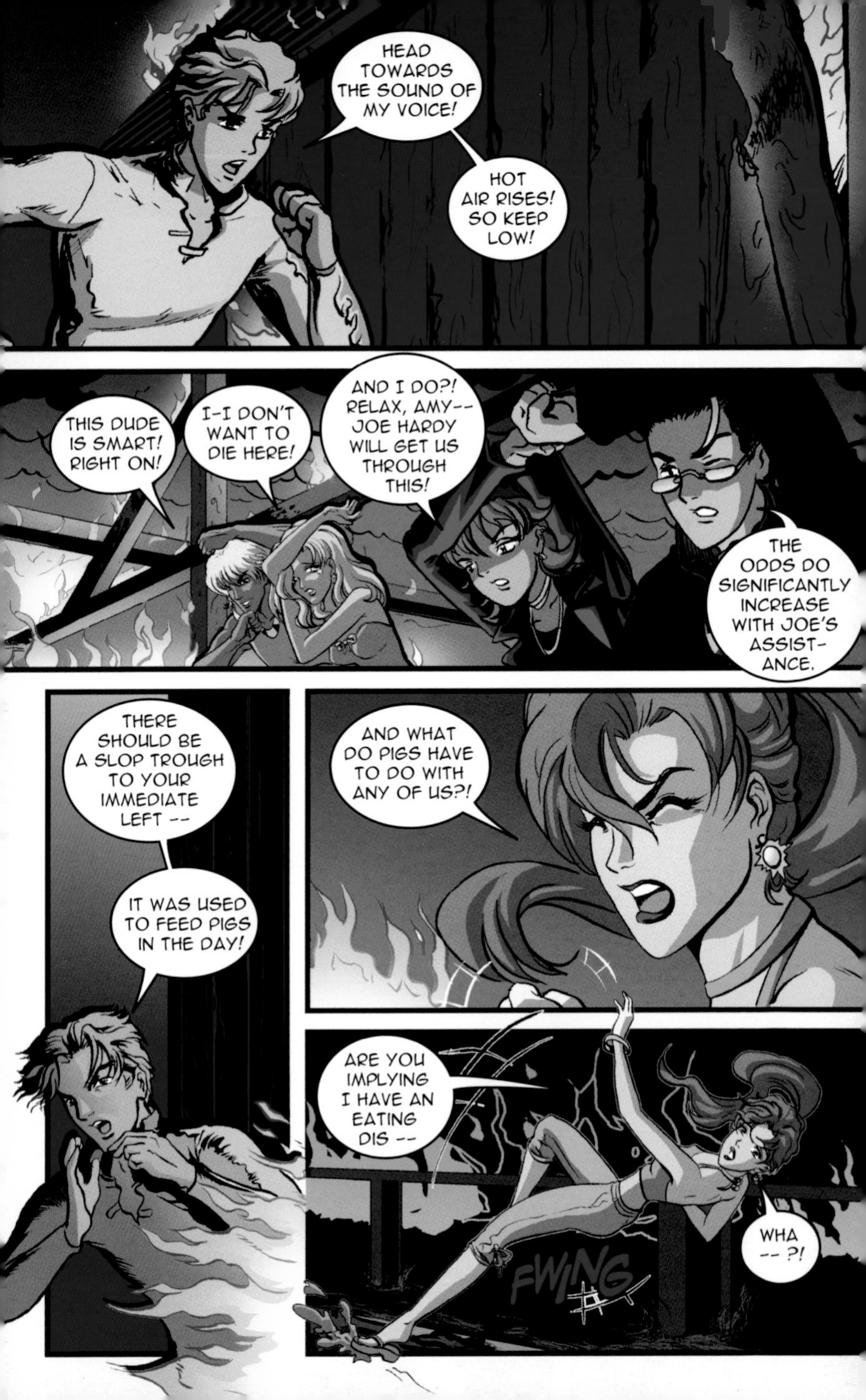

HEAD TOWARDS THE SOUND OF MY VOICE!
HOT AIR RISES! SO KEEP LOW!
THIS DUDE IS SMART! RIGHT ON!
I-I DON'T WANT TO DIE HERE!
AND I DO?! RELAX, AMY-- JOE HARDY WILL GET US THROUGH THIS!
THE ODDS DO SIGNIFICANTLY INCREASE WITH JOE'S ASSIST-ANCE.
THERE SHOULD BE A SLOP TROUGH TO YOUR IMMEDIATE LEFT --
IT WAS USED TO FEED PIGS IN THE DAY!
AND WHAT DO PIGS HAVE TO DO WITH ANY OF US?!
ARE YOU IMPLYING I HAVE AN EATING DIS --
WHA -- ?!
FWING

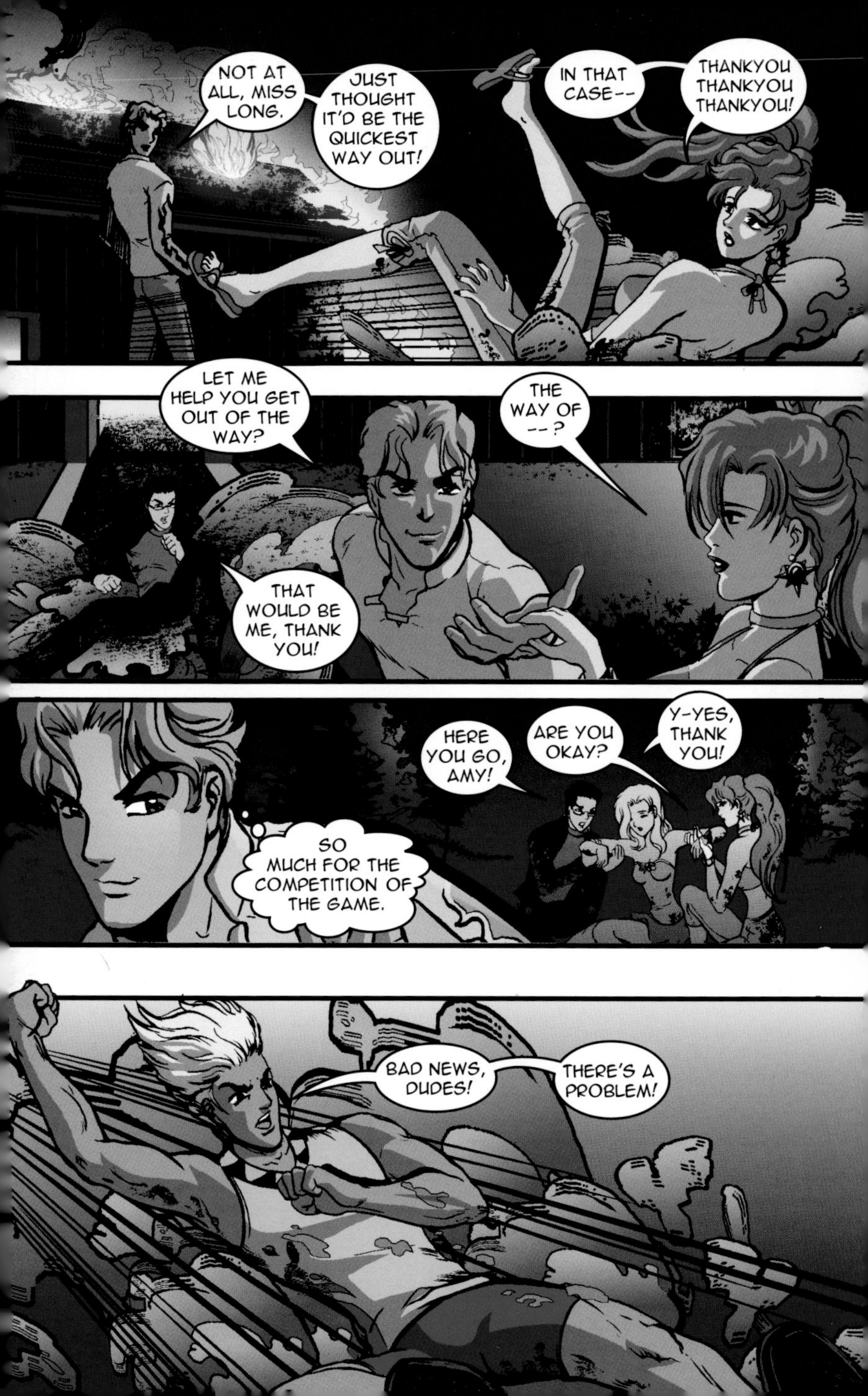
NOT AT ALL, MISS LONG.
JUST THOUGHT IT'D BE THE QUICKEST WAY OUT!
IN THAT CASE--
THANKYOU THANKYOU THANKYOU!
LET ME HELP YOU GET OUT OF THE WAY?
THE WAY OF --?
THAT WOULD BE ME, THANK YOU!
SO MUCH FOR THE COMPETITION OF THE GAME.
HERE YOU GO, AMY!
ARE YOU OKAY?
Y-YES, THANK YOU!
BAD NEWS, DUDES!
THERE'S A PROBLEM!

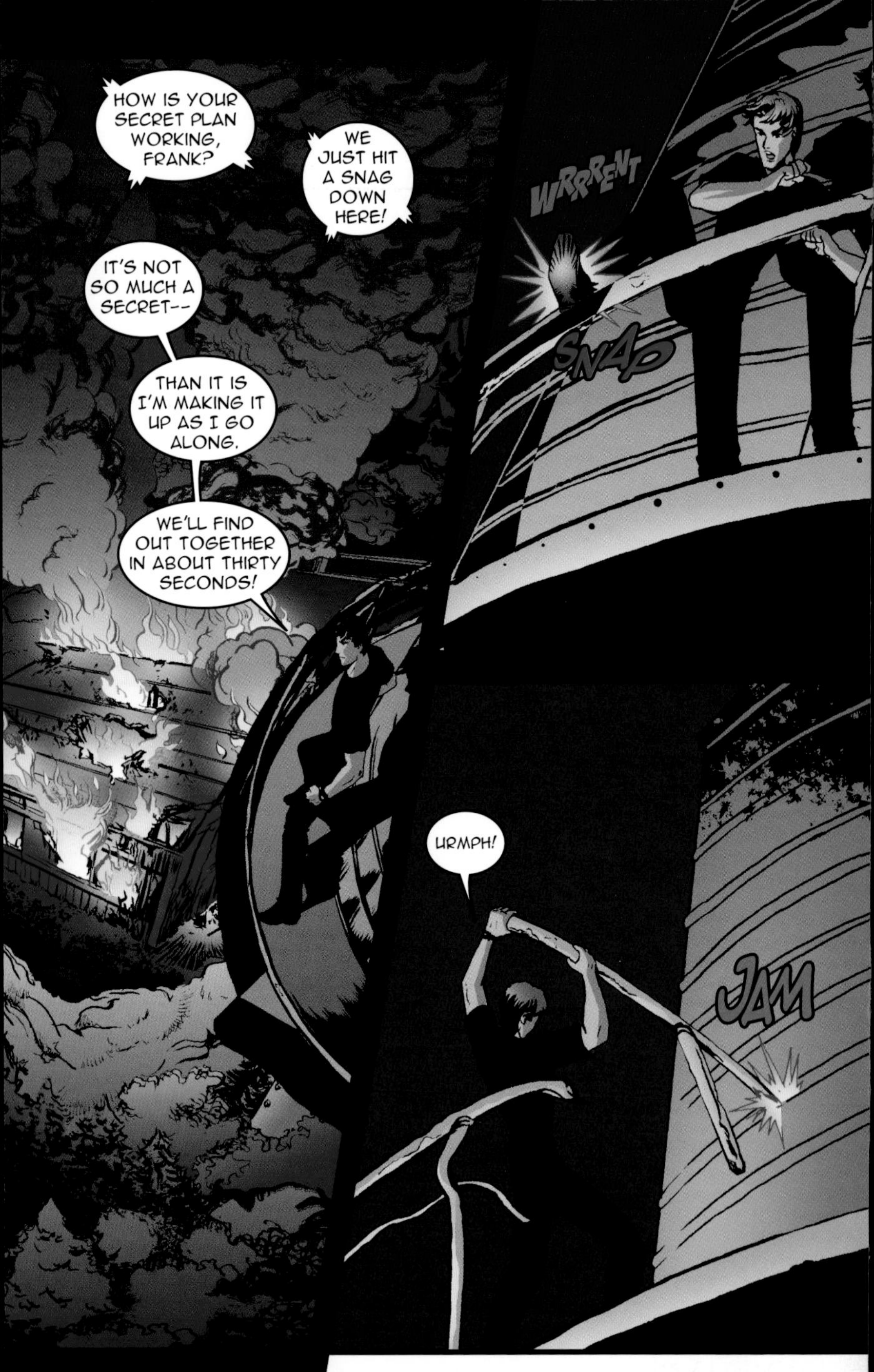
HOW IS YOUR SECRET PLAN WORKING, FRANK?
WE JUST HIT A SNAG DOWN HERE!
IT'S NOT SO MUCH A SECRET--
THAN IT IS I'M MAKING IT UP AS I GO ALONG.
WE'LL FIND OUT TOGETHER IN ABOUT THIRTY SECONDS!
WRRRENT
SNAP
URMPH!
JAM

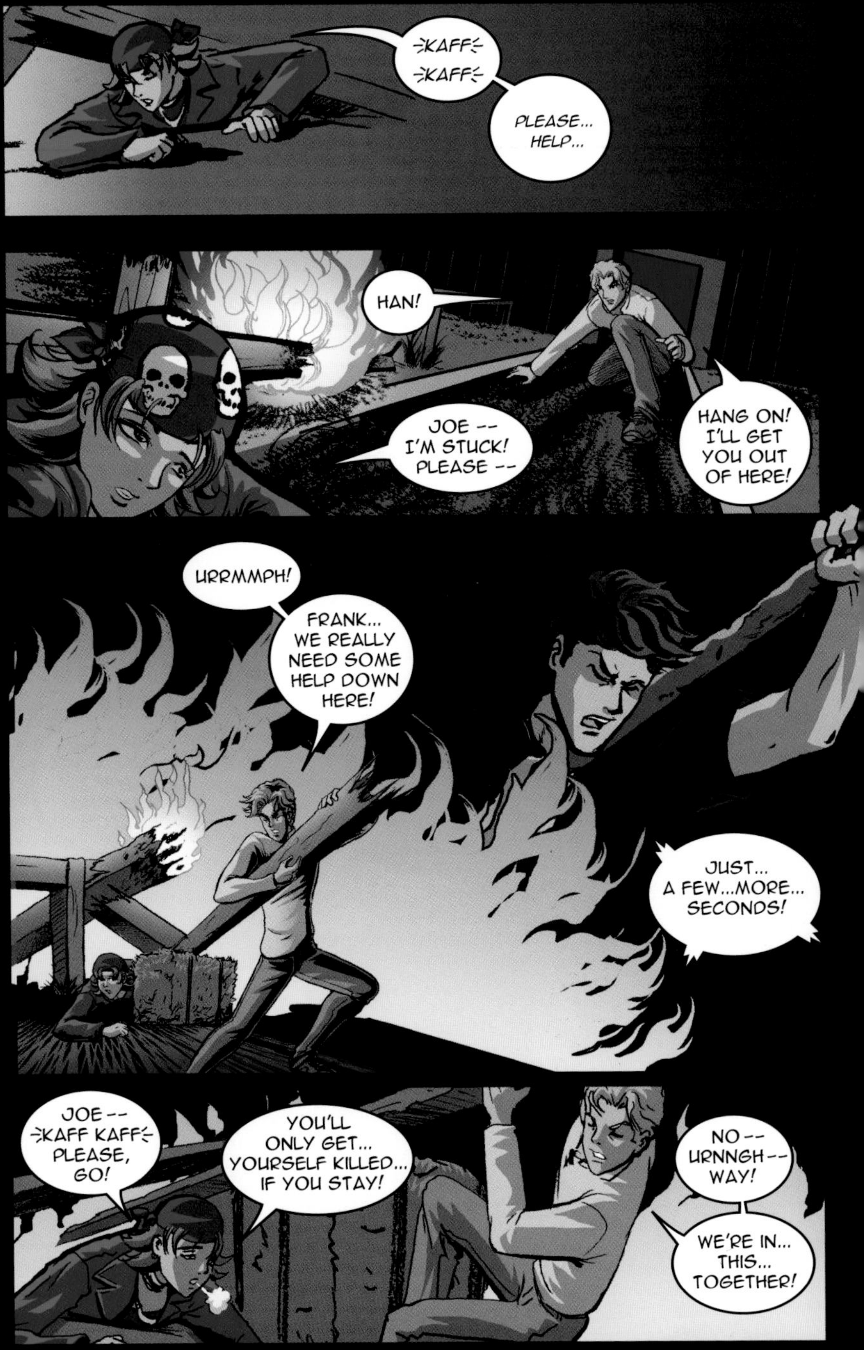

KAFF
KAFF
PLEASE... HELP...
HAN!
JOE -- I'M STUCK! PLEASE --
HANG ON! I'LL GET YOU OUT OF HERE!
URRMMPH!
FRANK... WE REALLY NEED SOME HELP DOWN HERE!
JUST... A FEW...MORE... SECONDS!
JOE -- KAFF KAFF PLEASE, GO!
YOU'LL ONLY GET... YOURSELF KILLED... IF YOU STAY!
NO -- URNNGH -- WAY!
WE'RE IN... THIS... TOGETHER!

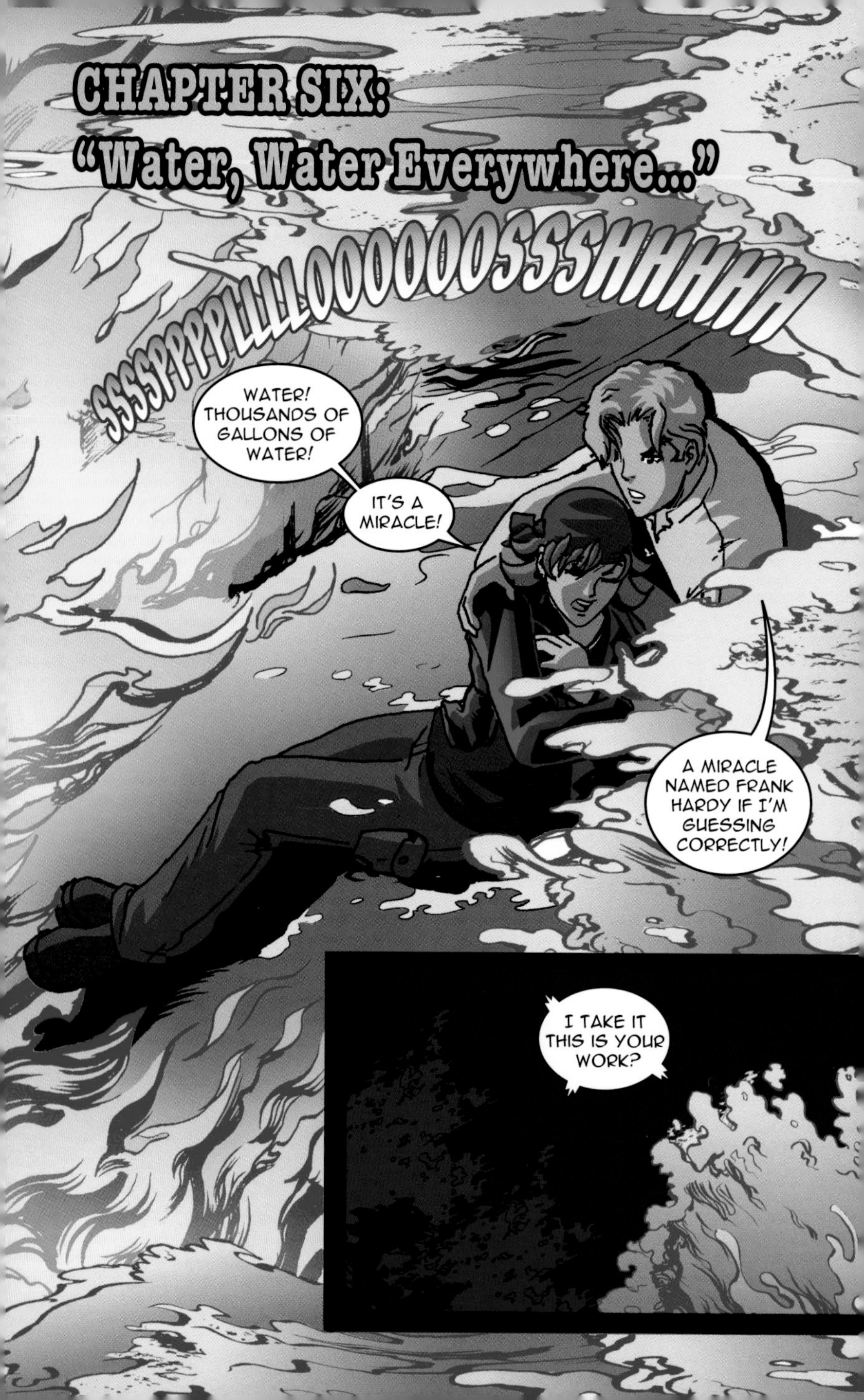
CHAPTER SIX:
"Water, Water Everywhere..."
SSSSPPPPLLLLOOOOOOOSSSSHHHHHH
WATER! THOUSANDS OF GALLONS OF WATER!
IT'S A MIRACLE!
A MIRACLE NAMED FRANK HARDY IF I'M GUESSING CORRECTLY!
I TAKE IT THIS IS YOUR WORK?

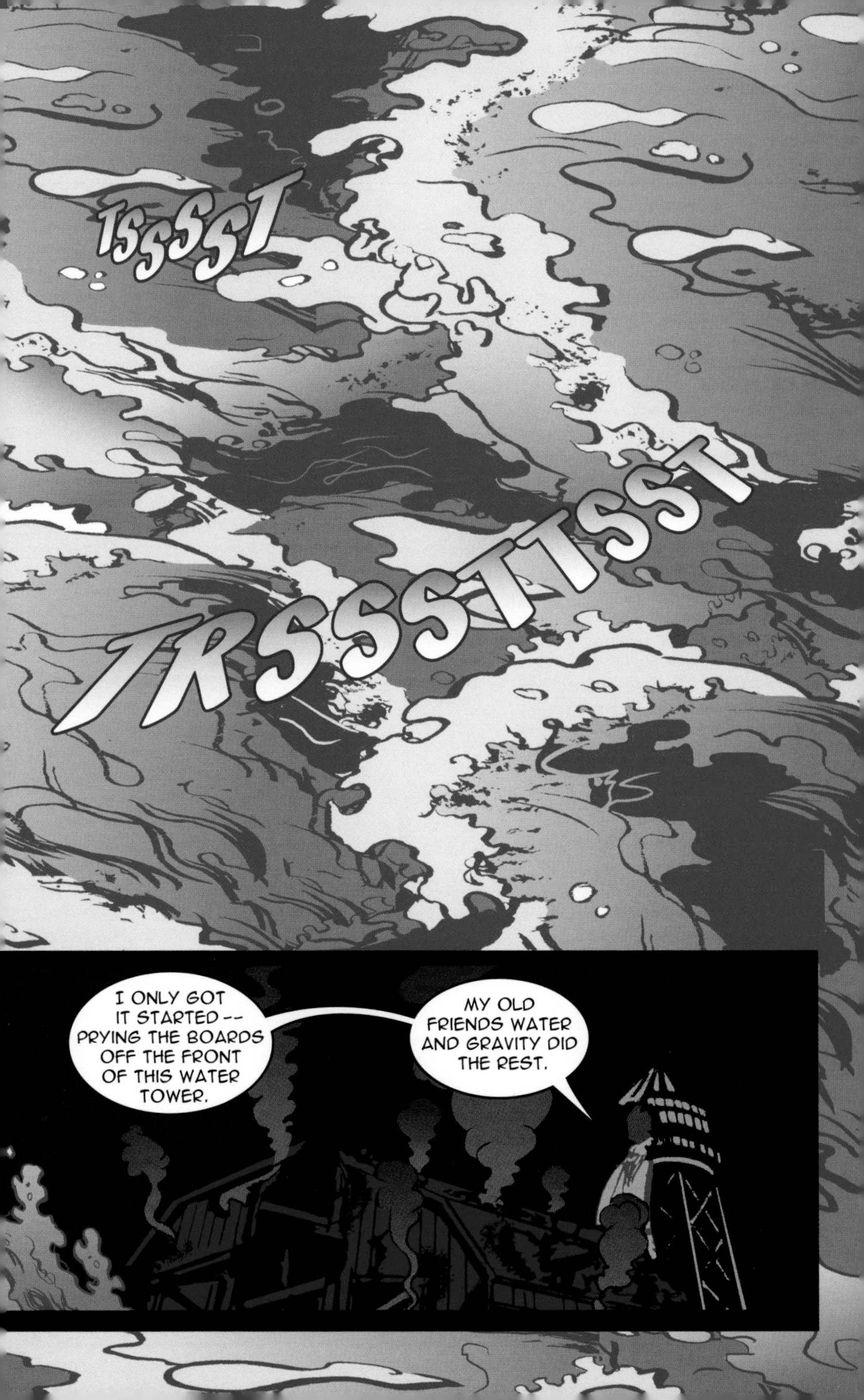
TSSSST
TRSSSTTSST
I ONLY GOT IT STARTED -- PRYING THE BOARDS OFF THE FRONT OF THIS WATER TOWER.
MY OLD FRIENDS WATER AND GRAVITY DID THE REST.

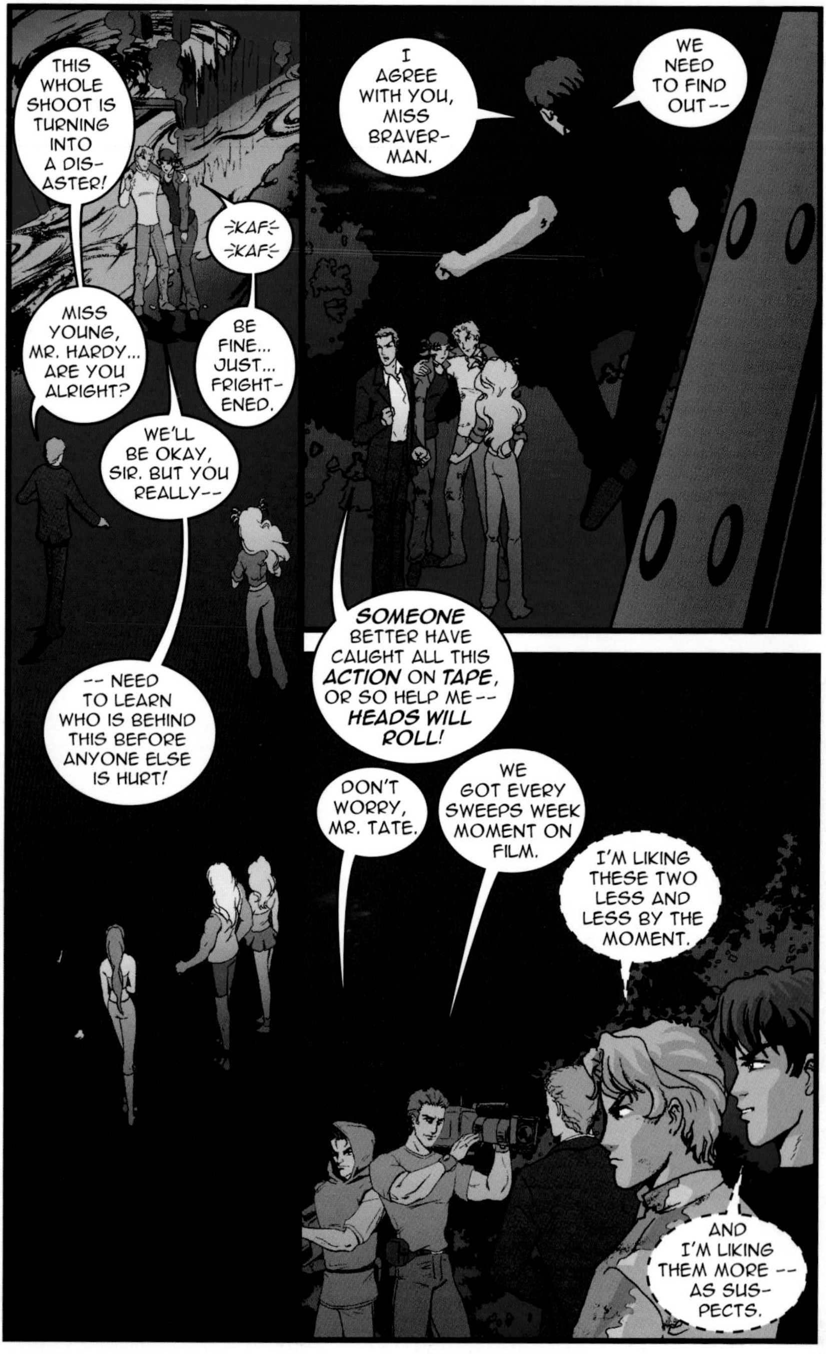
THIS WHOLE SHOOT IS TURNING INTO A DIS-ASTER!
=KAF= =KAF=
MISS YOUNG, MR. HARDY... ARE YOU ALRIGHT?
BE FINE... JUST... FRIGHT-ENED.
WE'LL BE OKAY, SIR. BUT YOU REALLY--
-- NEED TO LEARN WHO IS BEHIND THIS BEFORE ANYONE ELSE IS HURT!
I AGREE WITH YOU, MISS BRAVER-MAN.
WE NEED TO FIND OUT--
SOMEONE BETTER HAVE CAUGHT ALL THIS ACTION ON TAPE, OR SO HELP ME-- HEADS WILL ROLL!
DON'T WORRY, MR. TATE.
WE GOT EVERY SWEEPS WEEK MOMENT ON FILM.
I'M LIKING THESE TWO LESS AND LESS BY THE MOMENT.
AND I'M LIKING THEM MORE -- AS SUS-PECTS.

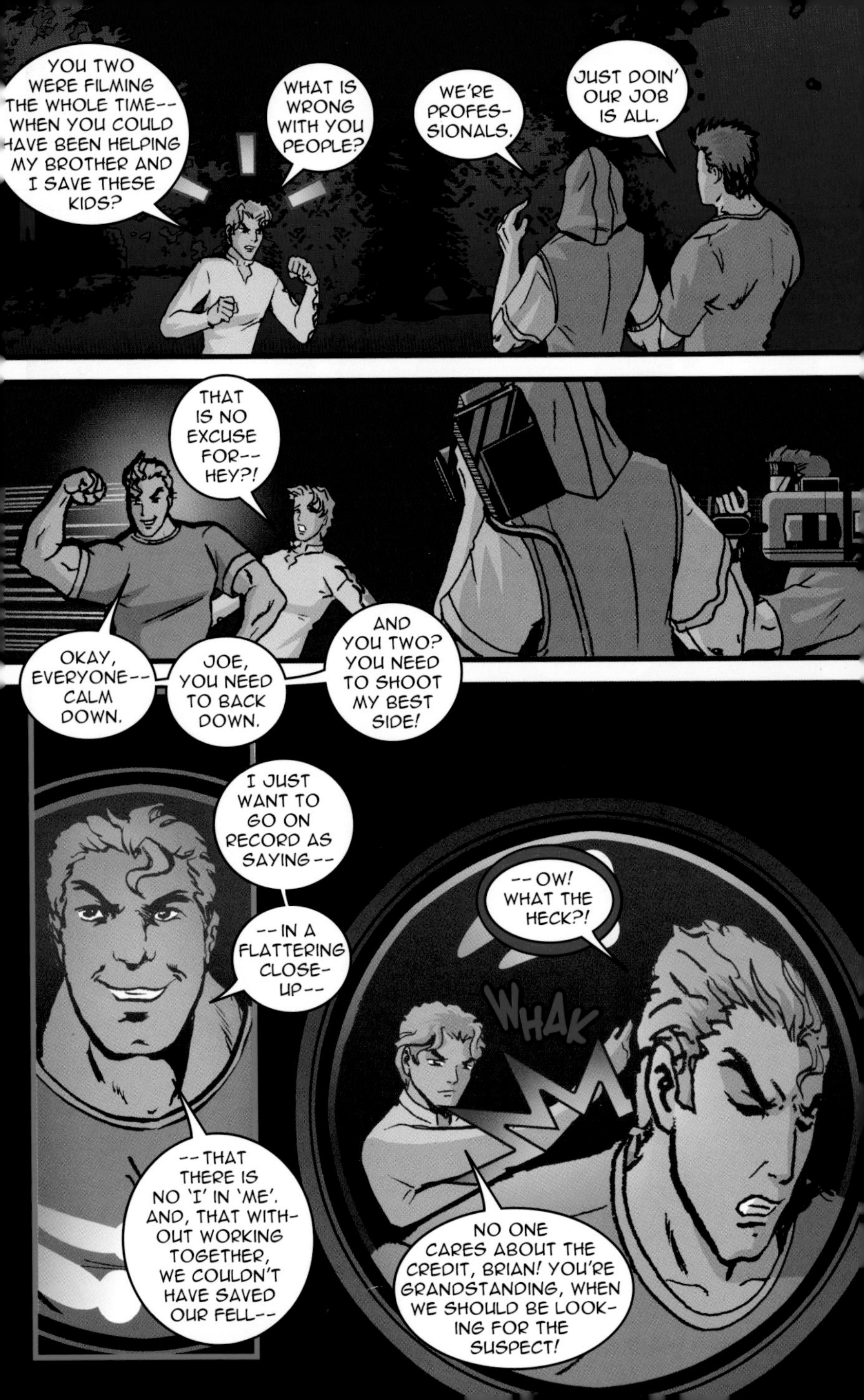
YOU TWO WERE FILMING THE WHOLE TIME-- WHEN YOU COULD HAVE BEEN HELPING MY BROTHER AND I SAVE THESE KIDS?
WHAT IS WRONG WITH YOU PEOPLE?
WE'RE PROFES-SIONALS.
JUST DOIN' OUR JOB IS ALL.
THAT IS NO EXCUSE FOR-- HEY?!
OKAY, EVERYONE-- CALM DOWN.
JOE, YOU NEED TO BACK DOWN.
AND YOU TWO? YOU NEED TO SHOOT MY BEST SIDE!
I JUST WANT TO GO ON RECORD AS SAYING--
--IN A FLATTERING CLOSE-UP--
--THAT THERE IS NO 'I' IN 'ME'. AND, THAT WITH-OUT WORKING TOGETHER, WE COULDN'T HAVE SAVED OUR FELL--
--OW! WHAT THE HECK?!
WHAK
NO ONE CARES ABOUT THE CREDIT, BRIAN! YOU'RE GRANDSTANDING, WHEN WE SHOULD BE LOOK-ING FOR THE SUSPECT!

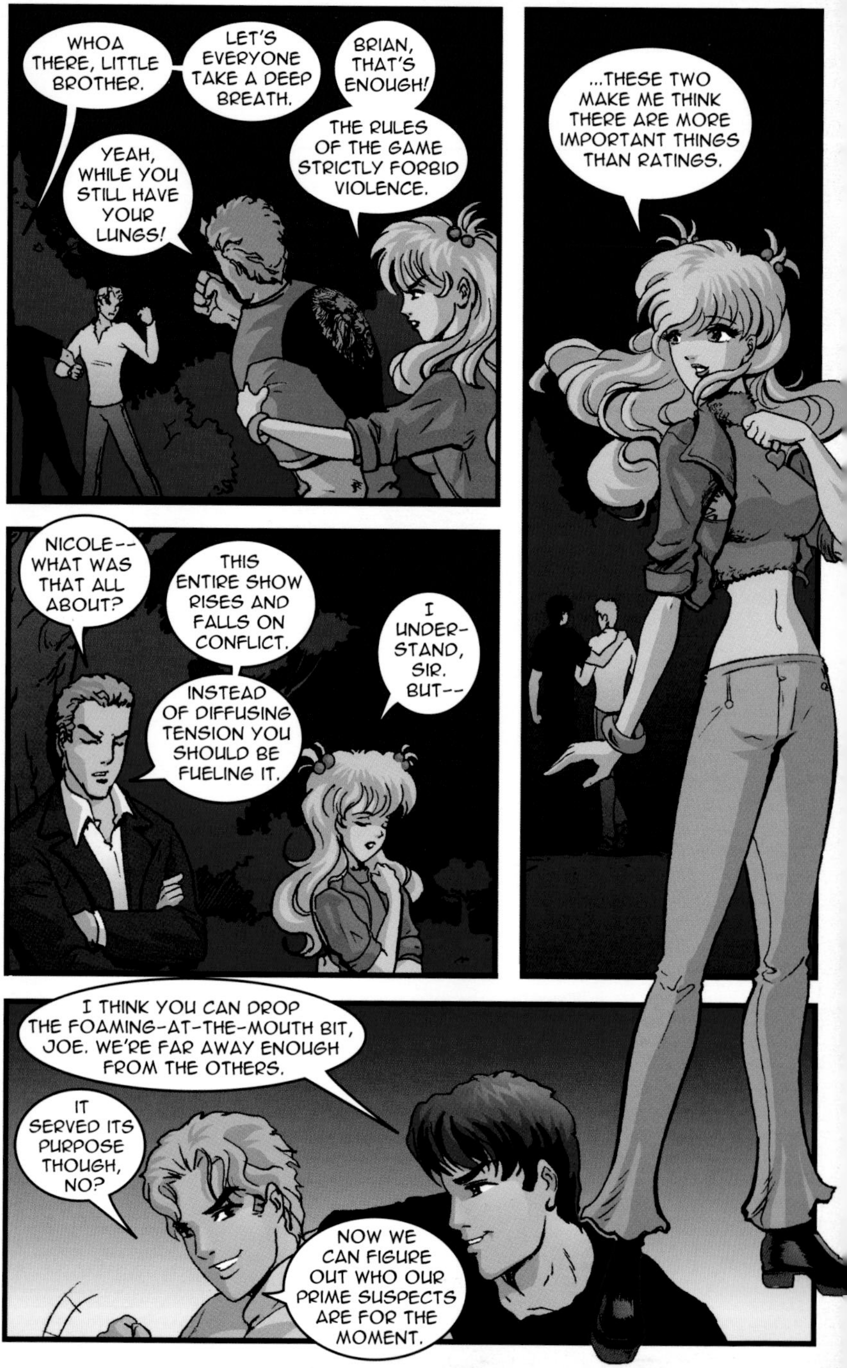
WHOA THERE, LITTLE BROTHER.
LET'S EVERYONE TAKE A DEEP BREATH.
YEAH, WHILE YOU STILL HAVE YOUR LUNGS!
BRIAN, THAT'S ENOUGH!
THE RULES OF THE GAME STRICTLY FORBID VIOLENCE.
...THESE TWO MAKE ME THINK THERE ARE MORE IMPORTANT THINGS THAN RATINGS.
NICOLE--WHAT WAS THAT ALL ABOUT?
THIS ENTIRE SHOW RISES AND FALLS ON CONFLICT.
INSTEAD OF DIFFUSING TENSION YOU SHOULD BE FUELING IT.
I UNDER-STAND, SIR. BUT--
I THINK YOU CAN DROP THE FOAMING-AT-THE-MOUTH BIT, JOE. WE'RE FAR AWAY ENOUGH FROM THE OTHERS.
IT SERVED ITS PURPOSE THOUGH, NO?
NOW WE CAN FIGURE OUT WHO OUR PRIME SUSPECTS ARE FOR THE MOMENT.

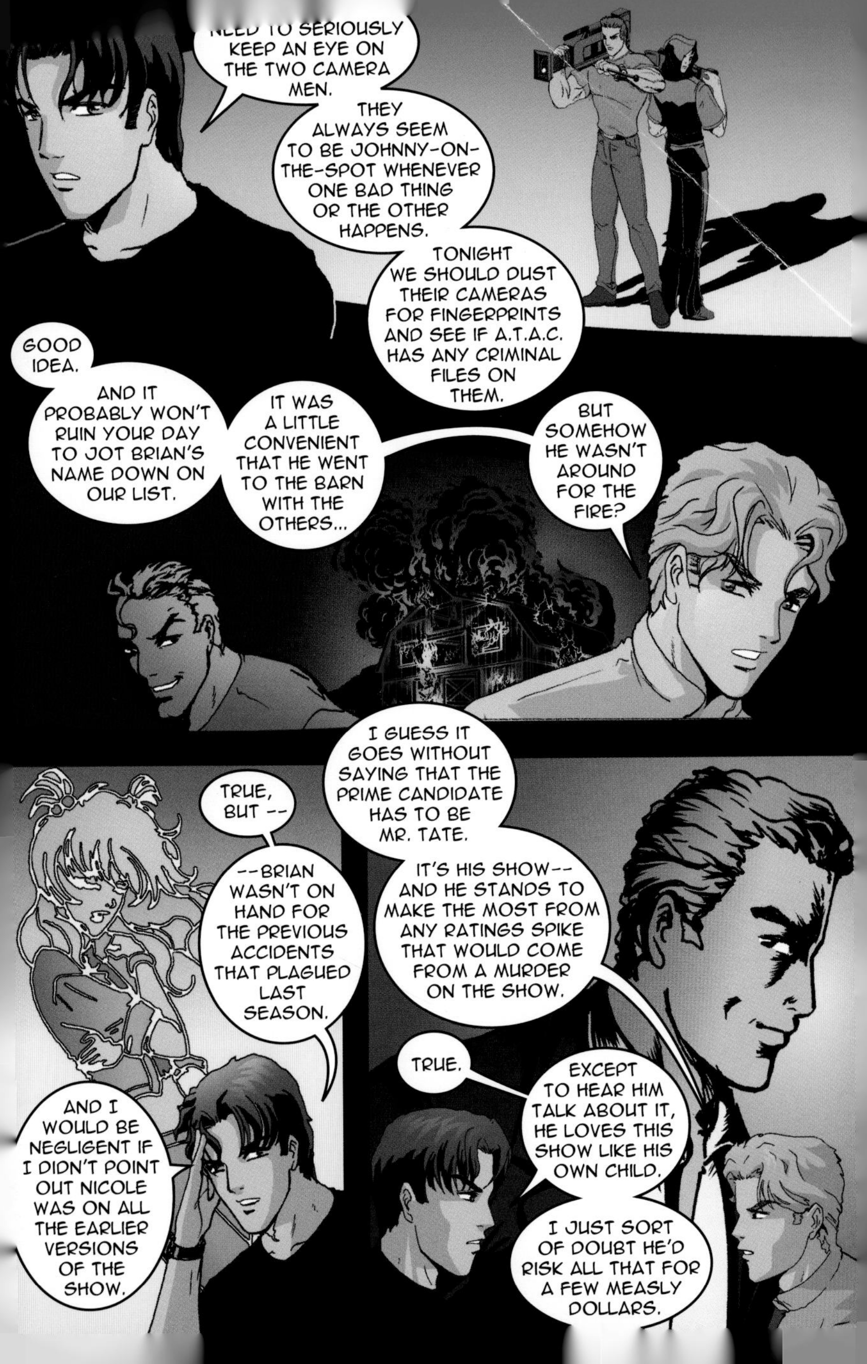
NEED TO SERIOUSLY KEEP AN EYE ON THE TWO CAMERA MEN.
THEY ALWAYS SEEM TO BE JOHNNY-ON-THE-SPOT WHENEVER ONE BAD THING OR THE OTHER HAPPENS.
TONIGHT WE SHOULD DUST THEIR CAMERAS FOR FINGERPRINTS AND SEE IF A.T.A.C. HAS ANY CRIMINAL FILES ON THEM.
GOOD IDEA.
AND IT PROBABLY WON'T RUIN YOUR DAY TO JOT BRIAN'S NAME DOWN ON OUR LIST.
IT WAS A LITTLE CONVENIENT THAT HE WENT TO THE BARN WITH THE OTHERS...
BUT SOMEHOW HE WASN'T AROUND FOR THE FIRE?
TRUE, BUT --
--BRIAN WASN'T ON HAND FOR THE PREVIOUS ACCIDENTS THAT PLAGUED LAST SEASON.
AND I WOULD BE NEGLIGENT IF I DIDN'T POINT OUT NICOLE WAS ON ALL THE EARLIER VERSIONS OF THE SHOW.
I GUESS IT GOES WITHOUT SAYING THAT THE PRIME CANDIDATE HAS TO BE MR. TATE.
IT'S HIS SHOW-- AND HE STANDS TO MAKE THE MOST FROM ANY RATINGS SPIKE THAT WOULD COME FROM A MURDER ON THE SHOW.
TRUE.
EXCEPT TO HEAR HIM TALK ABOUT IT, HE LOVES THIS SHOW LIKE HIS OWN CHILD.
I JUST SORT OF DOUBT HE'D RISK ALL THAT FOR A FEW MEASLY DOLLARS.

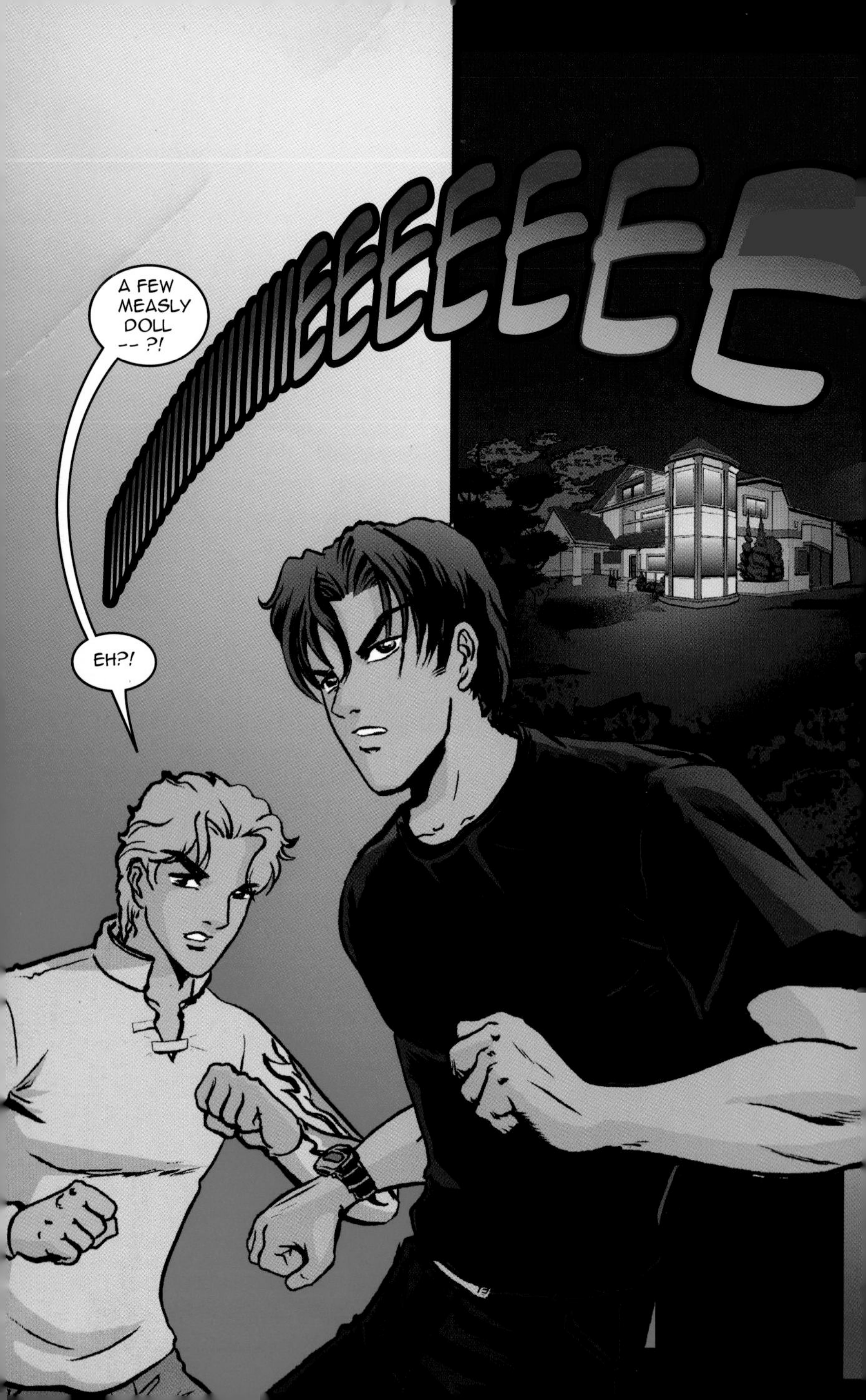
A FEW MEASLY DOLL -- ?!
EH?!
WEEEEEEEEE

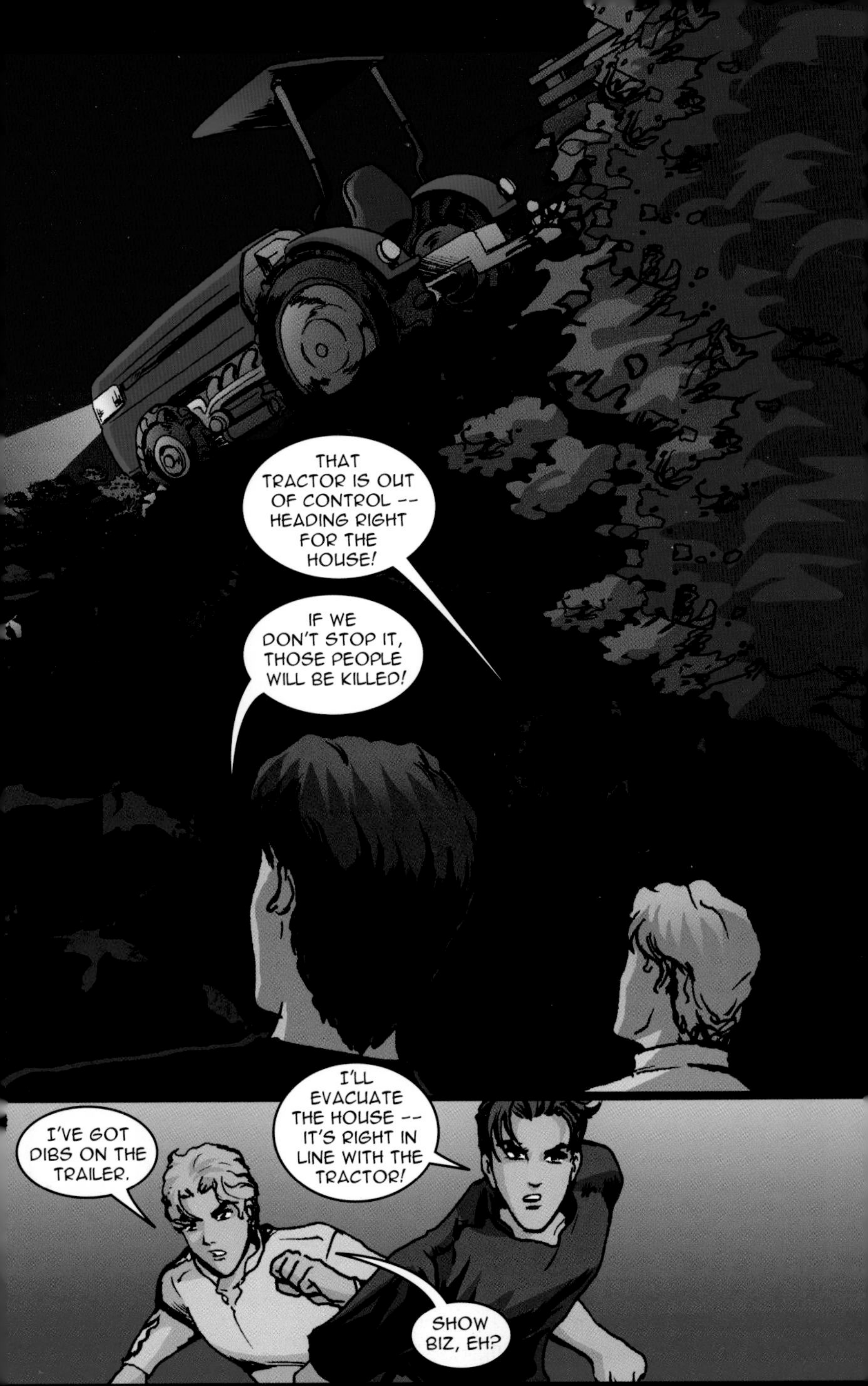
THAT TRACTOR IS OUT OF CONTROL -- HEADING RIGHT FOR THE HOUSE!
IF WE DON'T STOP IT, THOSE PEOPLE WILL BE KILLED!
I'LL EVACUATE THE HOUSE -- IT'S RIGHT IN LINE WITH THE TRACTOR!
I'VE GOT DIBS ON THE TRAILER.
SHOW BIZ, EH?

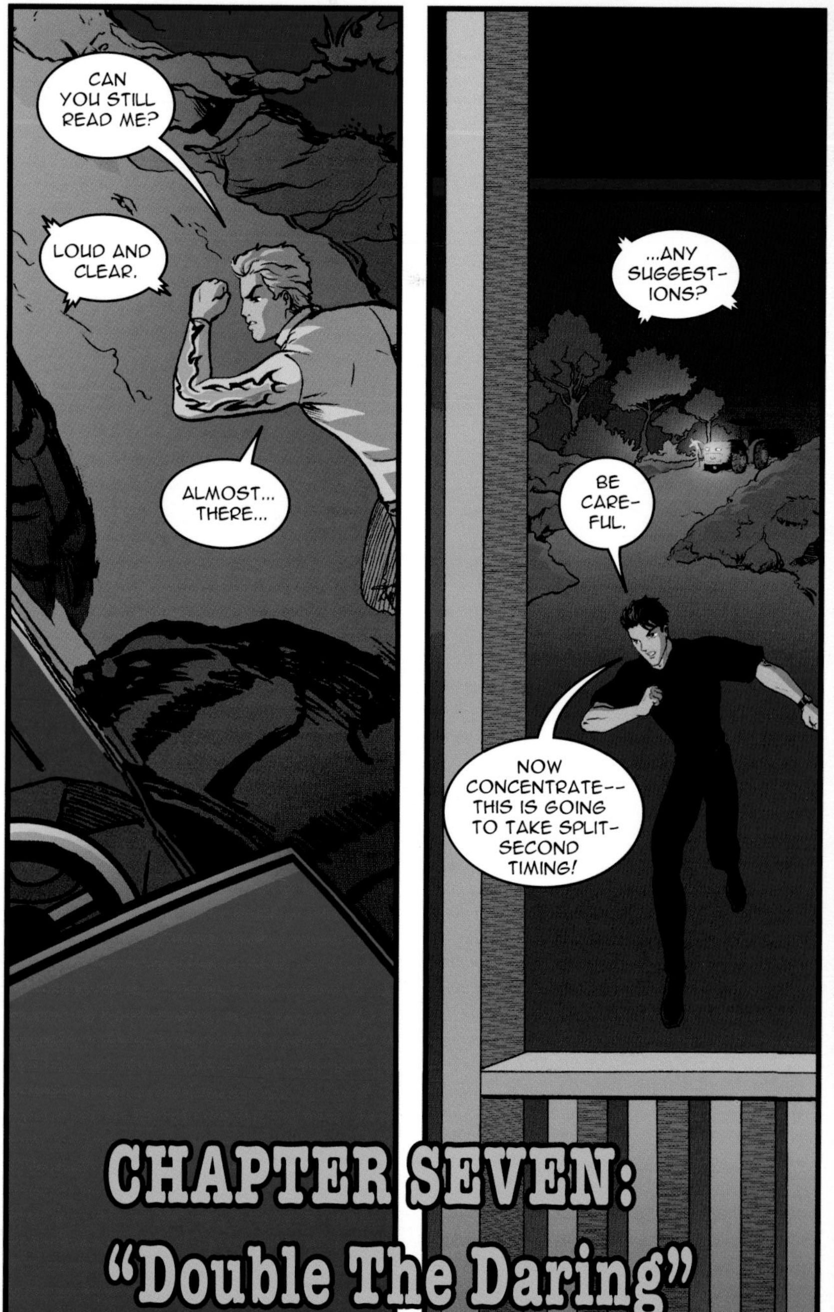
CAN YOU STILL READ ME?
LOUD AND CLEAR.
ALMOST... THERE...
...ANY SUGGEST-IONS?
BE CARE-FUL.
NOW CONCENTRATE-- THIS IS GOING TO TAKE SPLIT-SECOND TIMING!

CHAPTER SEVEN: "Double The Daring"

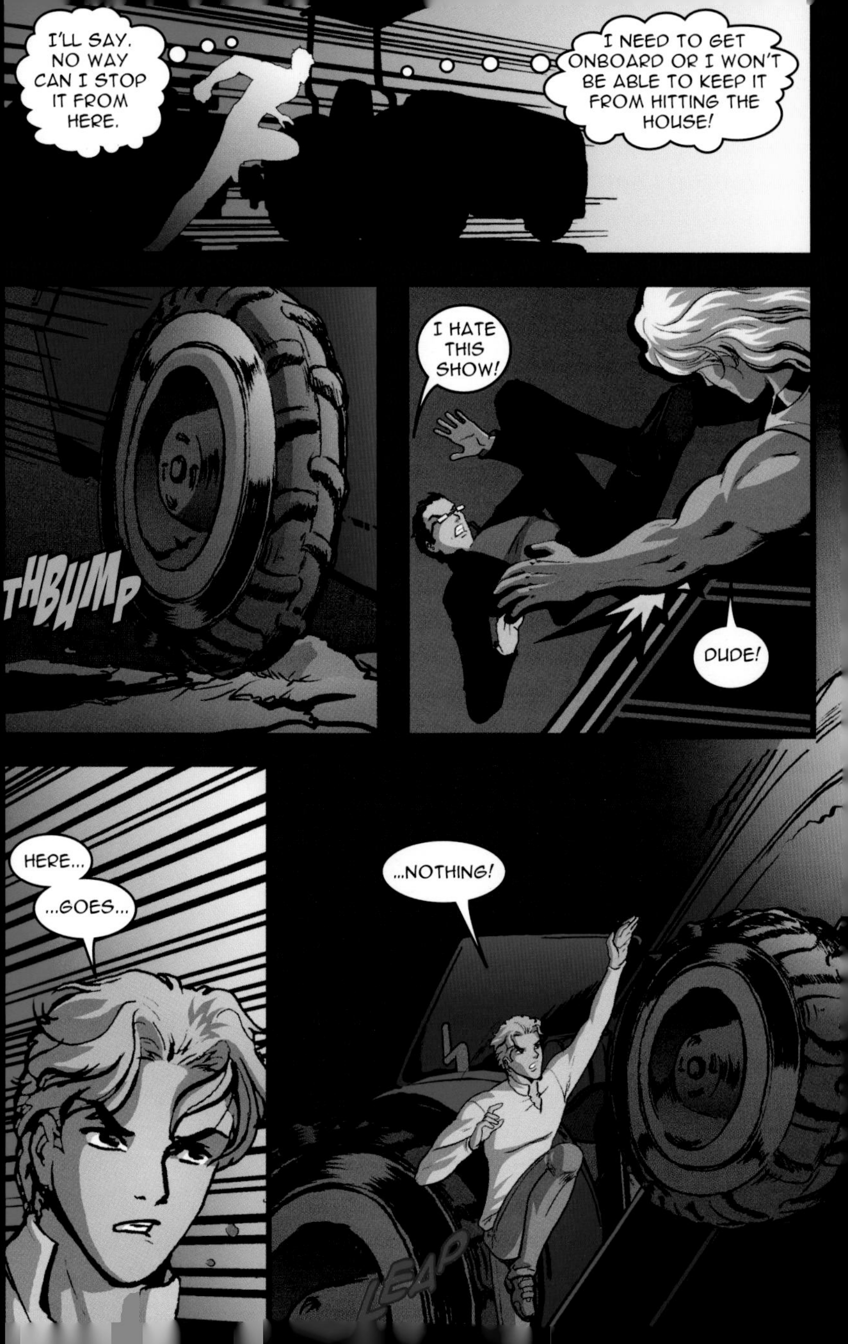
I'LL SAY. NO WAY CAN I STOP IT FROM HERE.
I NEED TO GET ONBOARD OR I WON'T BE ABLE TO KEEP IT FROM HITTING THE HOUSE!
THBUMP
I HATE THIS SHOW!
DUDE!
HERE...
...GOES...
...NOTHING!
LEAP

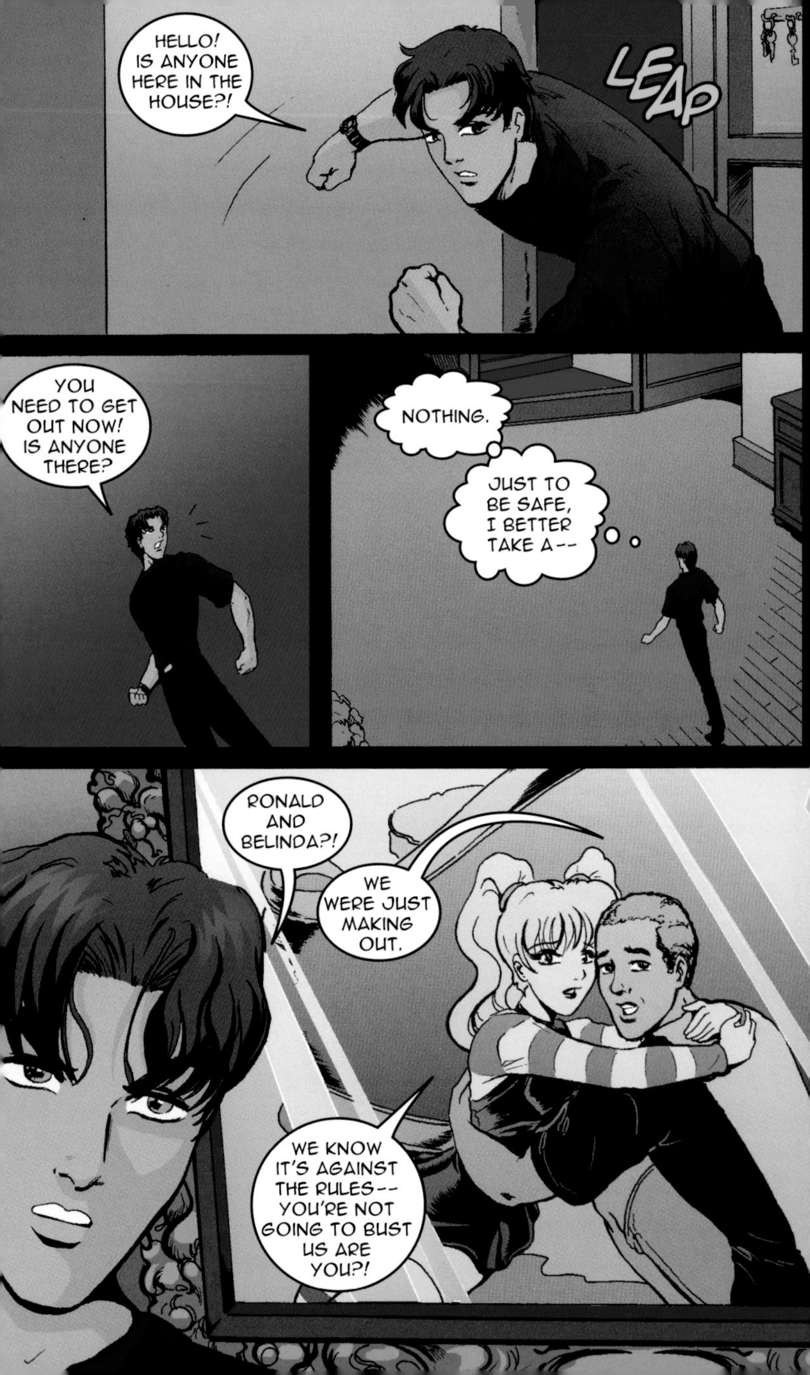
HELLO! IS ANYONE HERE IN THE HOUSE?!
LEAP
YOU NEED TO GET OUT NOW! IS ANYONE THERE?
NOTHING.
JUST TO BE SAFE, I BETTER TAKE A--
RONALD AND BELINDA?!
WE WERE JUST MAKING OUT.
WE KNOW IT'S AGAINST THE RULES-- YOU'RE NOT GOING TO BUST US ARE YOU?!

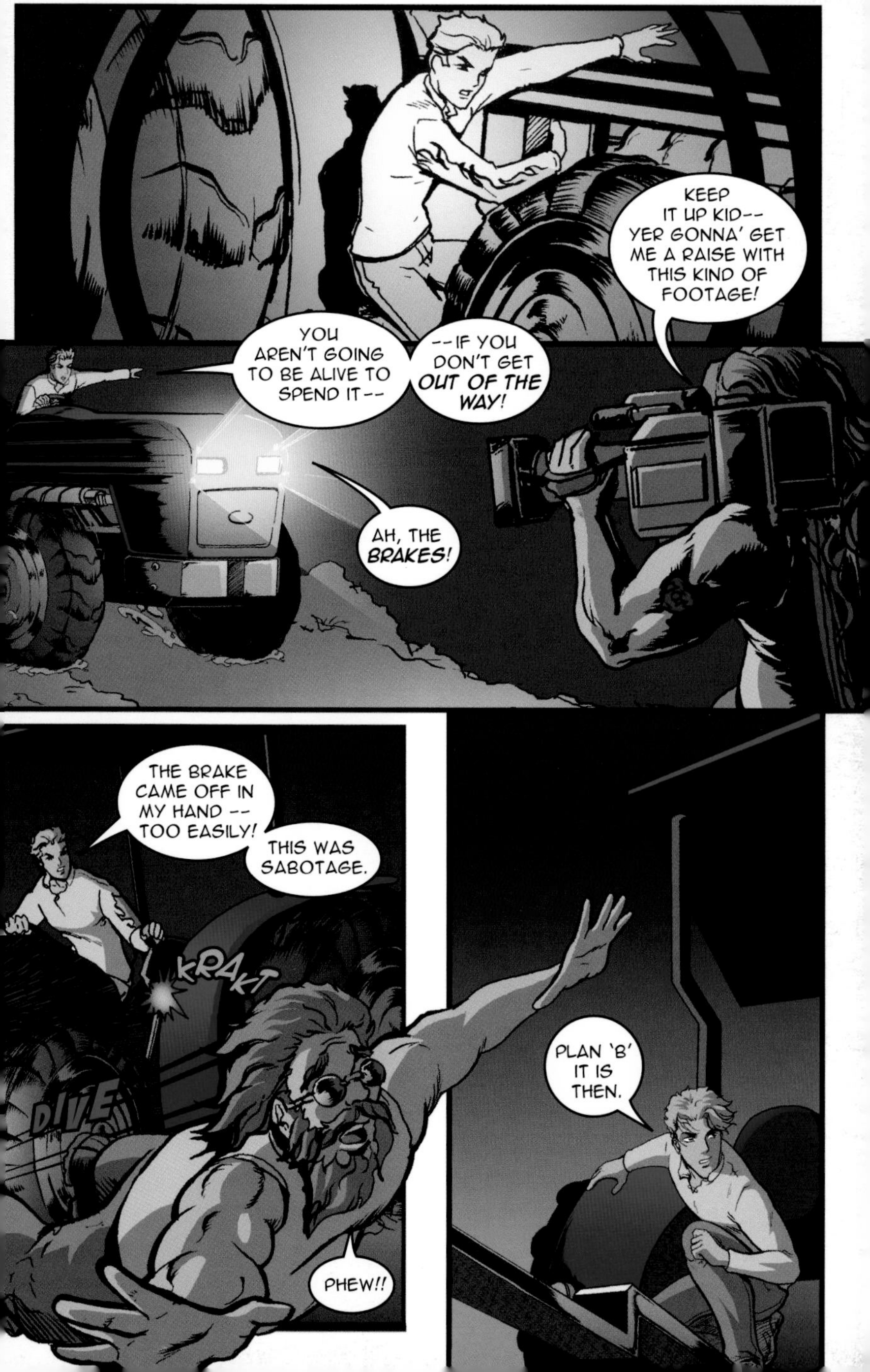
KEEP IT UP KID-- YER GONNA' GET ME A RAISE WITH THIS KIND OF FOOTAGE!
YOU AREN'T GOING TO BE ALIVE TO SPEND IT--
--IF YOU DON'T GET *OUT OF THE WAY!*
AH, THE *BRAKES!*
THE BRAKE CAME OFF IN MY HAND -- TOO EASILY!
THIS WAS SABOTAGE.
KRAKT
DIVE
PHEW!!
PLAN 'B' IT IS THEN.

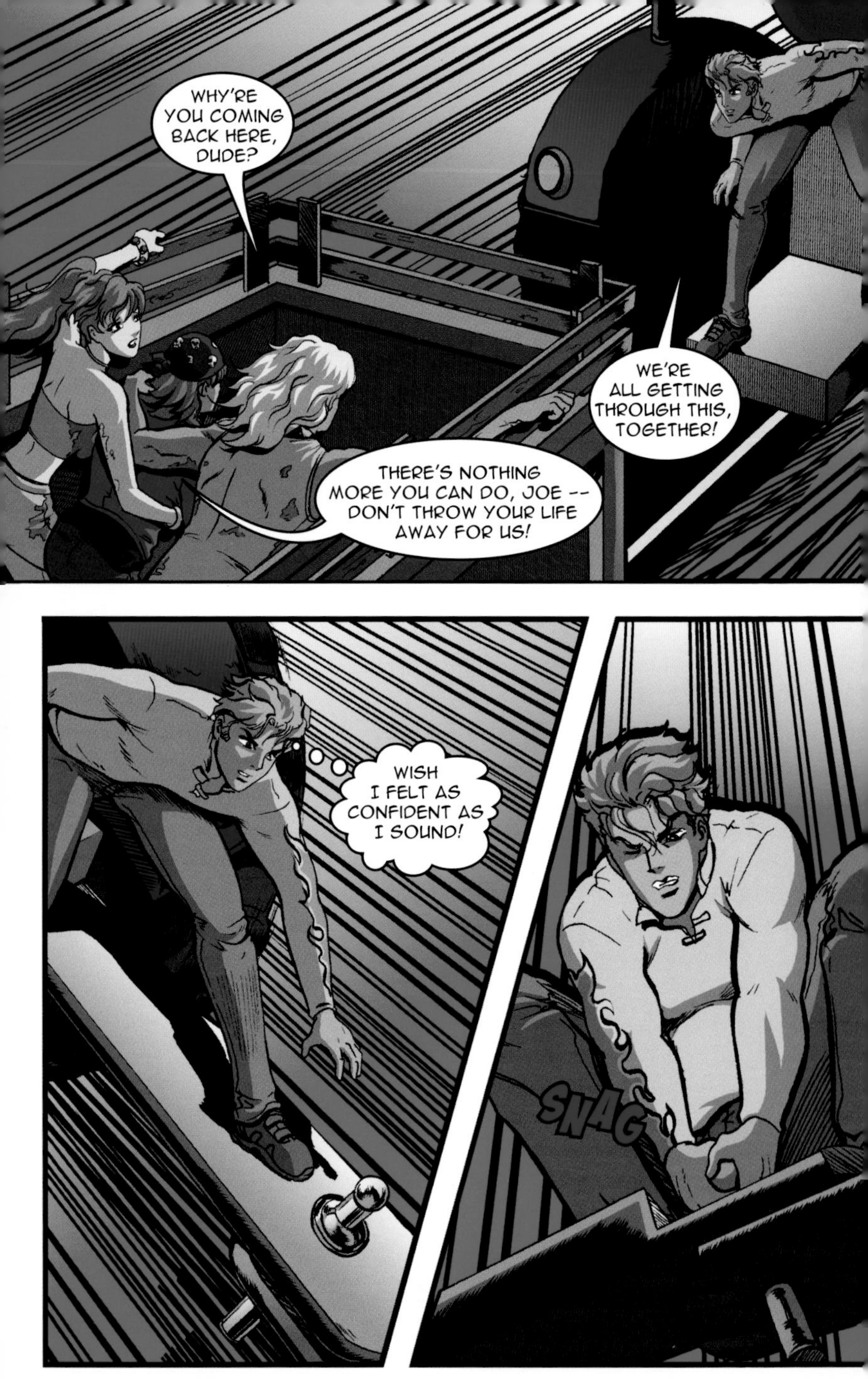
WHY'RE YOU COMING BACK HERE, DUDE?
THERE'S NOTHING MORE YOU CAN DO, JOE -- DON'T THROW YOUR LIFE AWAY FOR US!
WE'RE ALL GETTING THROUGH THIS, TOGETHER!
WISH I FELT AS CONFIDENT AS I SOUND!
SNAG

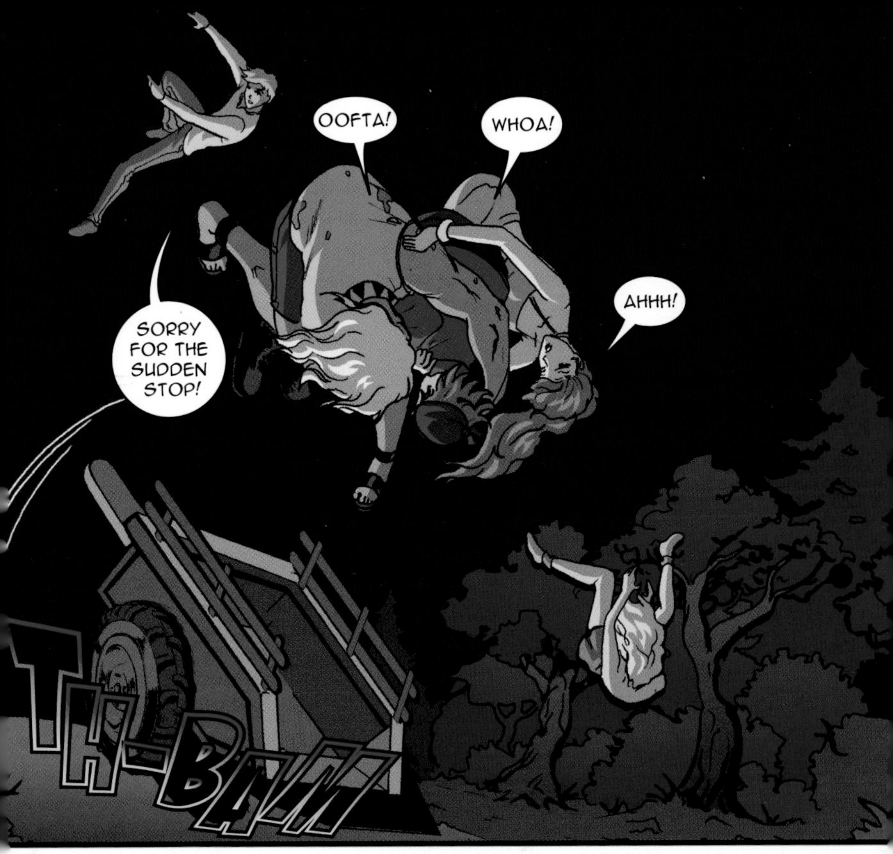
OOFTA!
WHOA!
SORRY FOR THE SUDDEN STOP!
AHHH!
TH-BAM

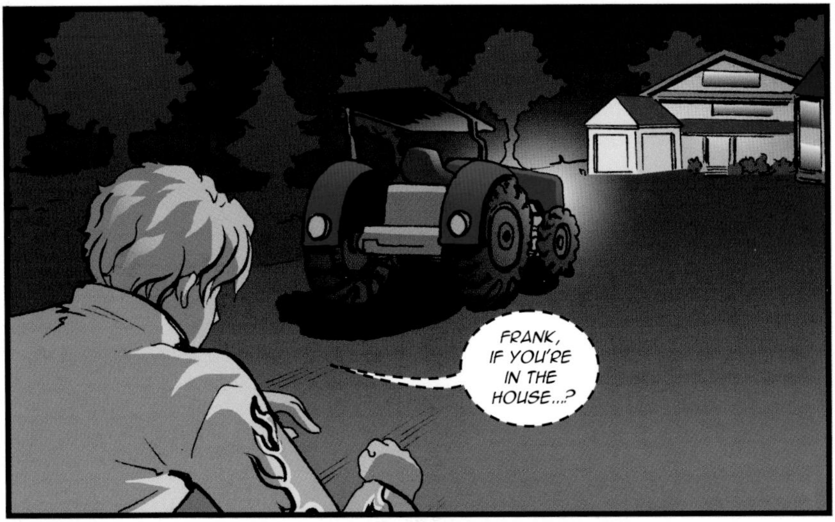
FRANK, IF YOU'RE IN THE HOUSE...?

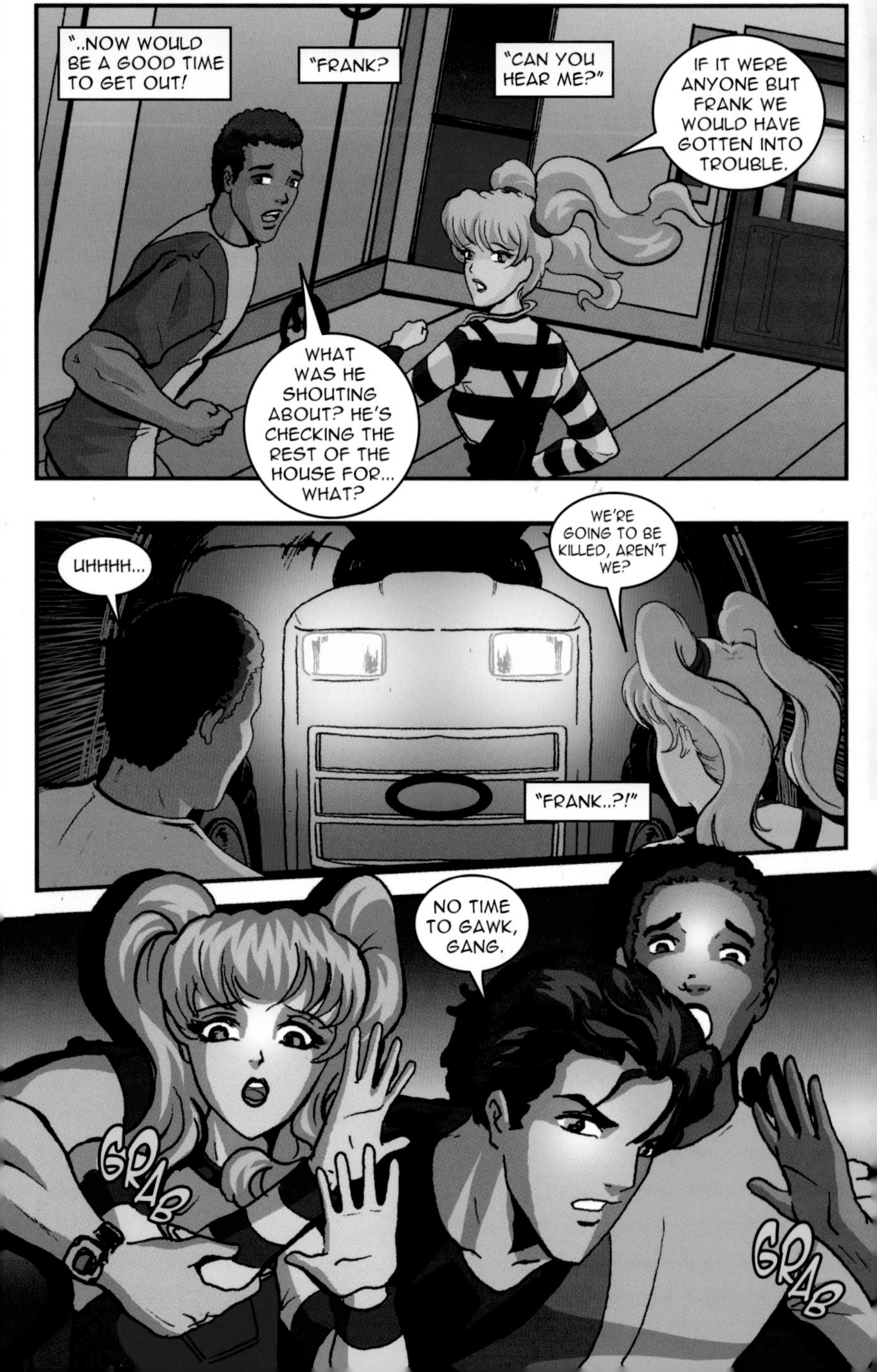
"..NOW WOULD BE A GOOD TIME TO GET OUT!
"FRANK?
"CAN YOU HEAR ME?"
IF IT WERE ANYONE BUT FRANK WE WOULD HAVE GOTTEN INTO TROUBLE.
WHAT WAS HE SHOUTING ABOUT? HE'S CHECKING THE REST OF THE HOUSE FOR... WHAT?
UHHHH...
WE'RE GOING TO BE KILLED, AREN'T WE?
"FRANK..?!"
NO TIME TO GAWK, GANG.
GRAB
GRAB

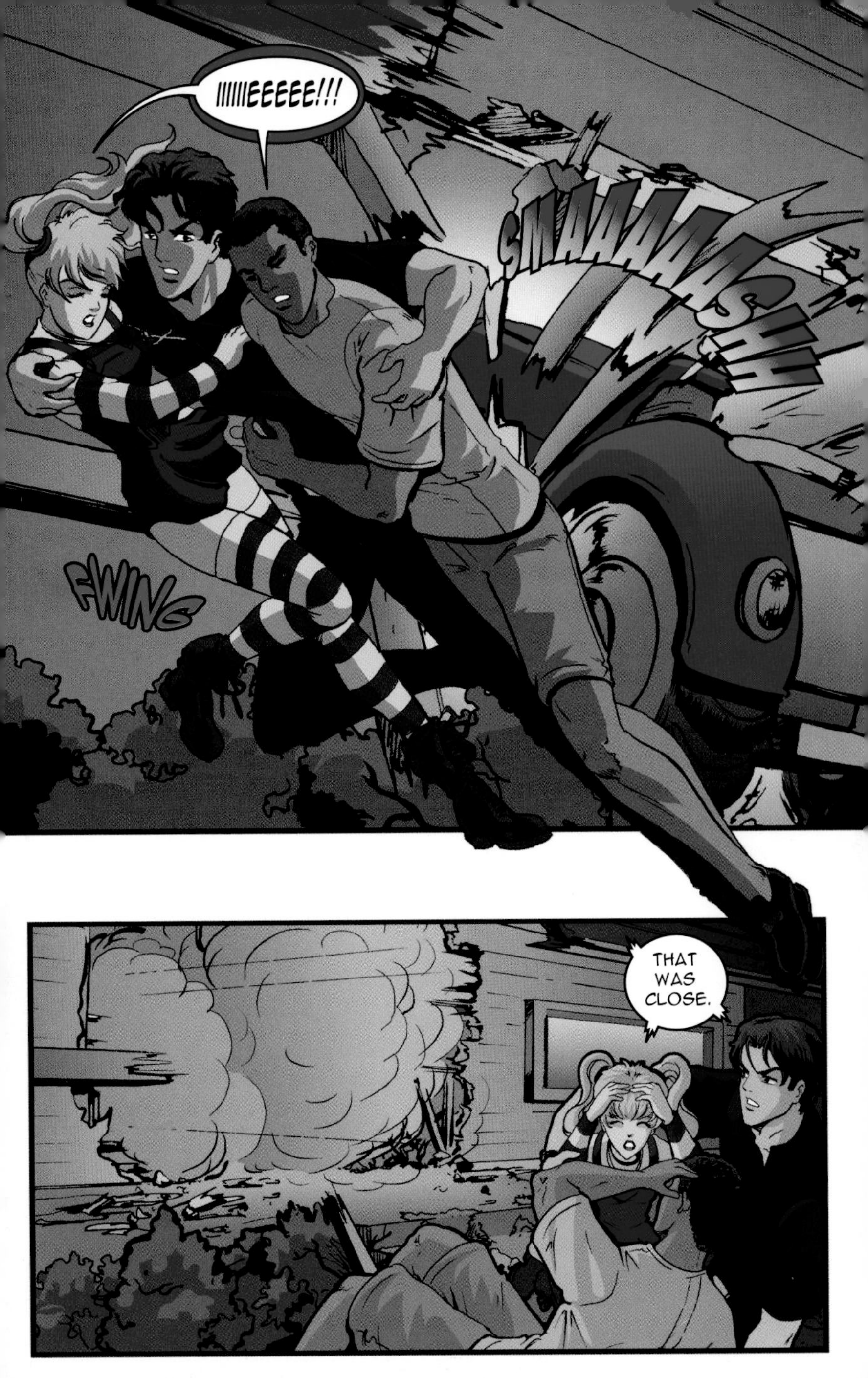
IIIIIIEEEEEE!!!
SMAAAAASHH
FWING
THAT WAS CLOSE.

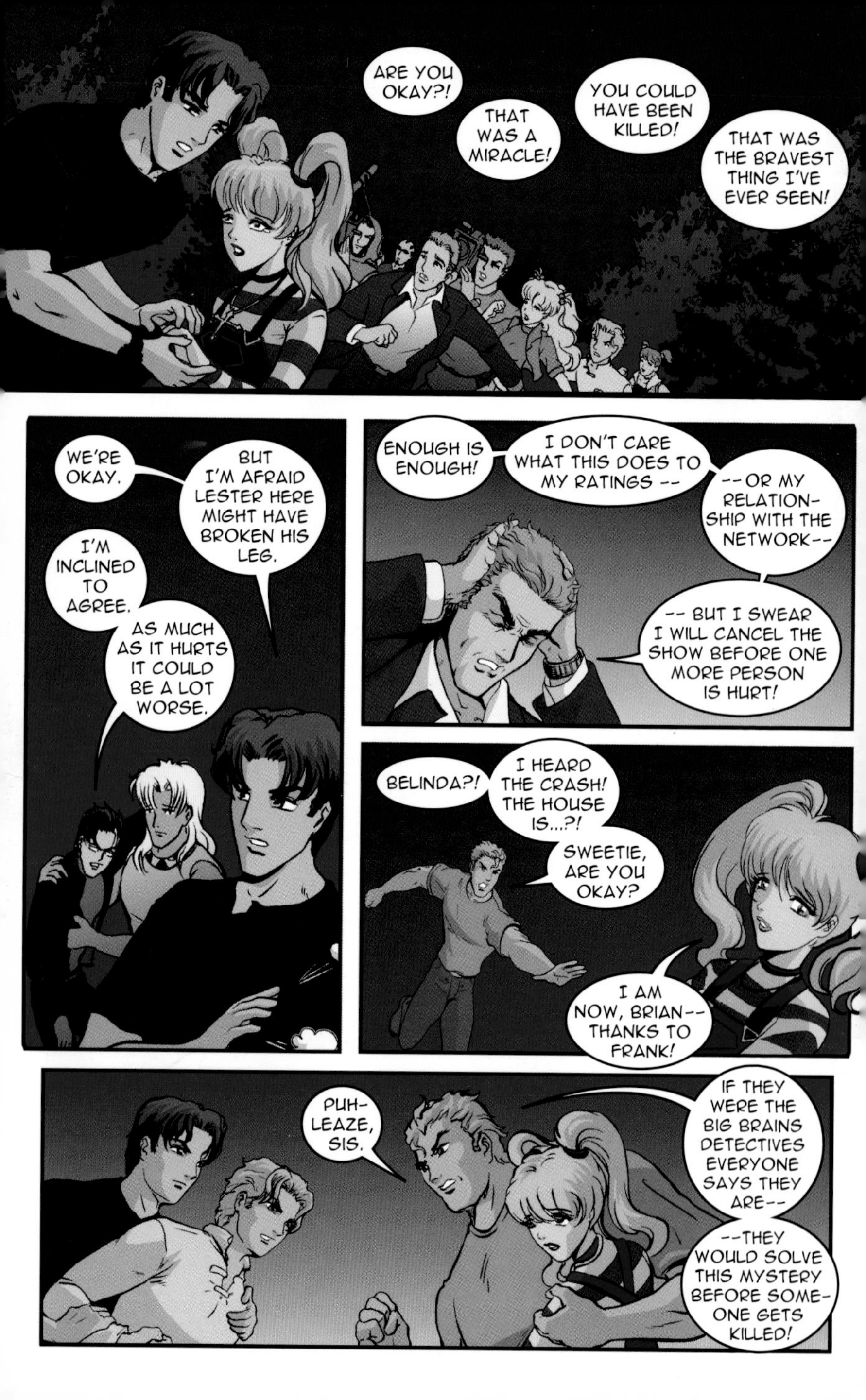
ARE YOU OKAY?!
THAT WAS A MIRACLE!
YOU COULD HAVE BEEN KILLED!
THAT WAS THE BRAVEST THING I'VE EVER SEEN!
WE'RE OKAY.
BUT I'M AFRAID LESTER HERE MIGHT HAVE BROKEN HIS LEG.
I'M INCLINED TO AGREE.
AS MUCH AS IT HURTS IT COULD BE A LOT WORSE.
ENOUGH IS ENOUGH!
I DON'T CARE WHAT THIS DOES TO MY RATINGS --
--OR MY RELATIONSHIP WITH THE NETWORK--
-- BUT I SWEAR I WILL CANCEL THE SHOW BEFORE ONE MORE PERSON IS HURT!
BELINDA?!
I HEARD THE CRASH! THE HOUSE IS...?!
SWEETIE, ARE YOU OKAY?
I AM NOW, BRIAN-- THANKS TO FRANK!
PUH-LEAZE, SIS.
IF THEY WERE THE BIG BRAINS DETECTIVES EVERYONE SAYS THEY ARE--
--THEY WOULD SOLVE THIS MYSTERY BEFORE SOMEONE GETS KILLED!

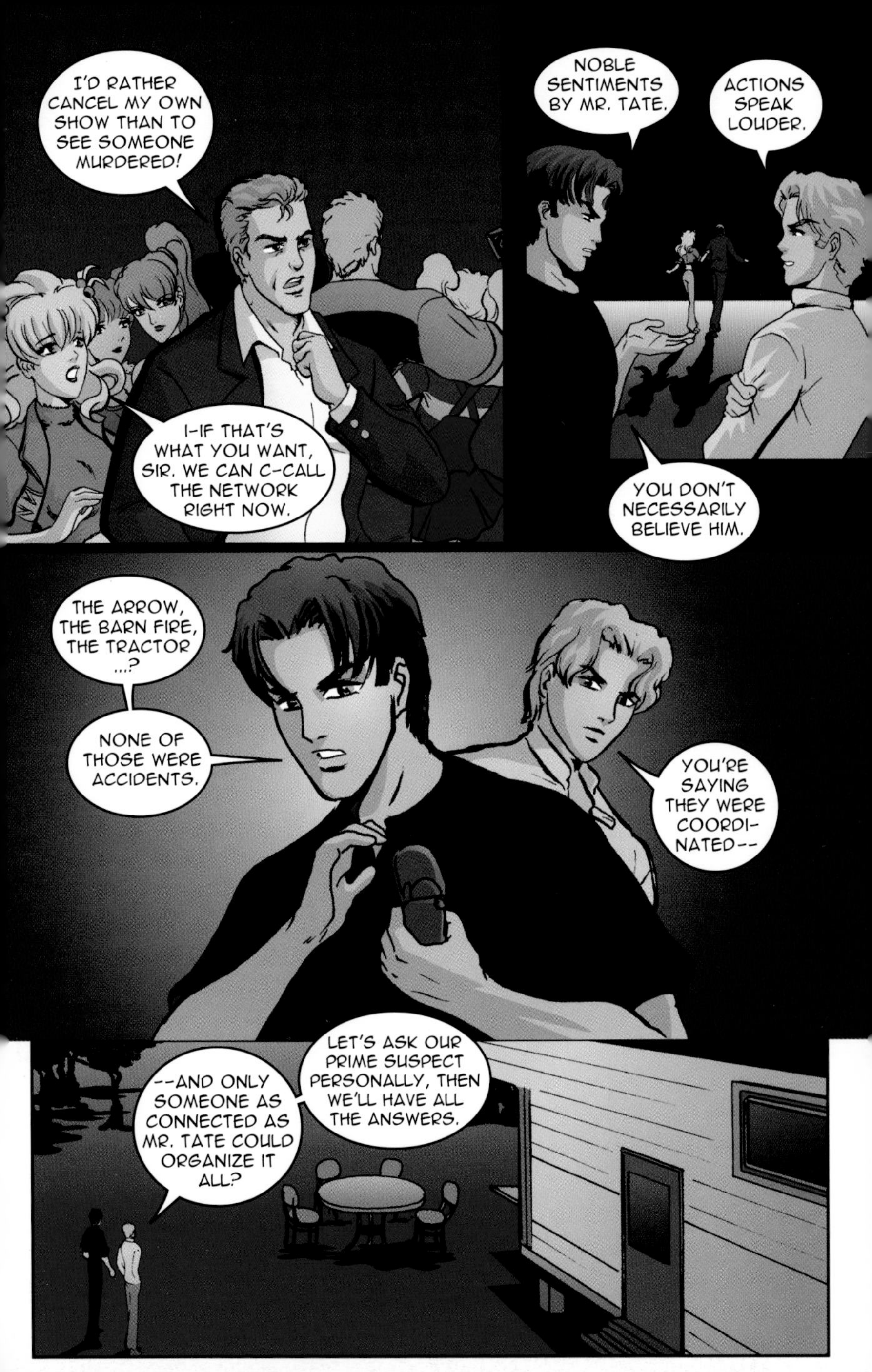
I'D RATHER CANCEL MY OWN SHOW THAN TO SEE SOMEONE MURDERED!
I-IF THAT'S WHAT YOU WANT, SIR. WE CAN C-CALL THE NETWORK RIGHT NOW.
NOBLE SENTIMENTS BY MR. TATE.
ACTIONS SPEAK LOUDER.
YOU DON'T NECESSARILY BELIEVE HIM.
THE ARROW, THE BARN FIRE, THE TRACTOR ...?
NONE OF THOSE WERE ACCIDENTS.
YOU'RE SAYING THEY WERE COORDI-NATED--
--AND ONLY SOMEONE AS CONNECTED AS MR. TATE COULD ORGANIZE IT ALL?
LET'S ASK OUR PRIME SUSPECT PERSONALLY, THEN WE'LL HAVE ALL THE ANSWERS.

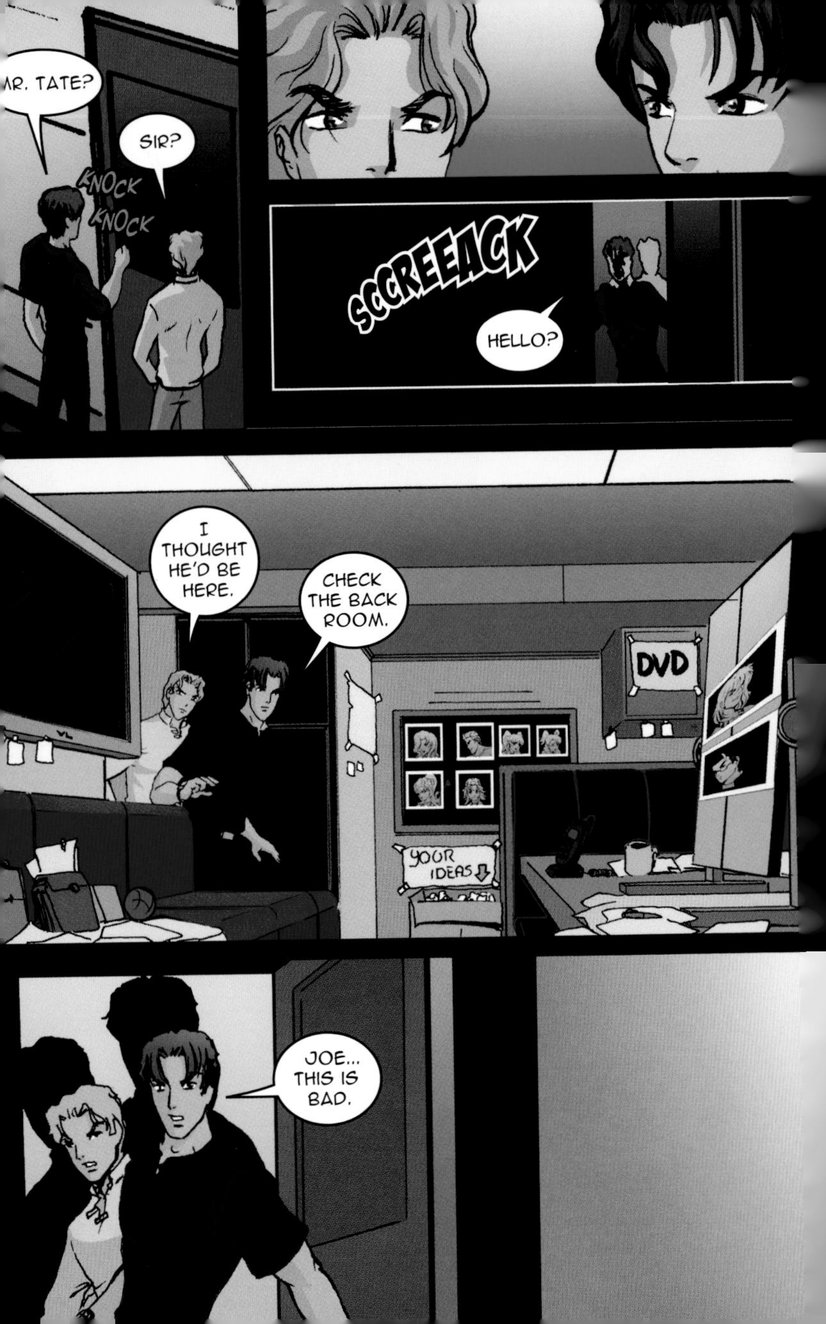
MR. TATE?
SIR?
KNOCK KNOCK
SCCREEACK
HELLO?
I THOUGHT HE'D BE HERE.
CHECK THE BACK ROOM.
DVD
YOUR IDEAS
JOE... THIS IS BAD.

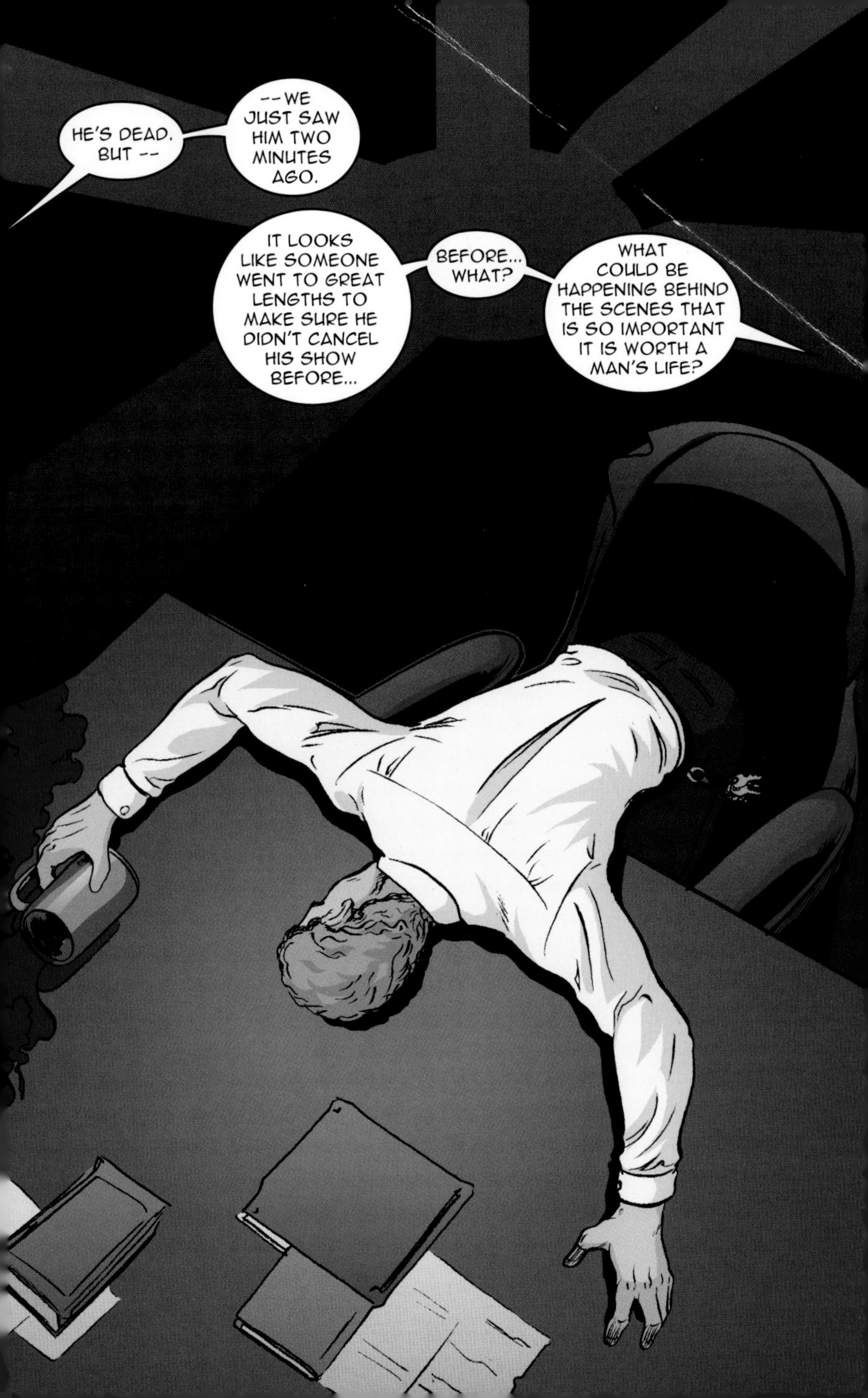
HE'S DEAD. BUT --
-- WE JUST SAW HIM TWO MINUTES AGO.
IT LOOKS LIKE SOMEONE WENT TO GREAT LENGTHS TO MAKE SURE HE DIDN'T CANCEL HIS SHOW BEFORE...
BEFORE... WHAT?
WHAT COULD BE HAPPENING BEHIND THE SCENES THAT IS SO IMPORTANT IT IS WORTH A MAN'S LIFE?

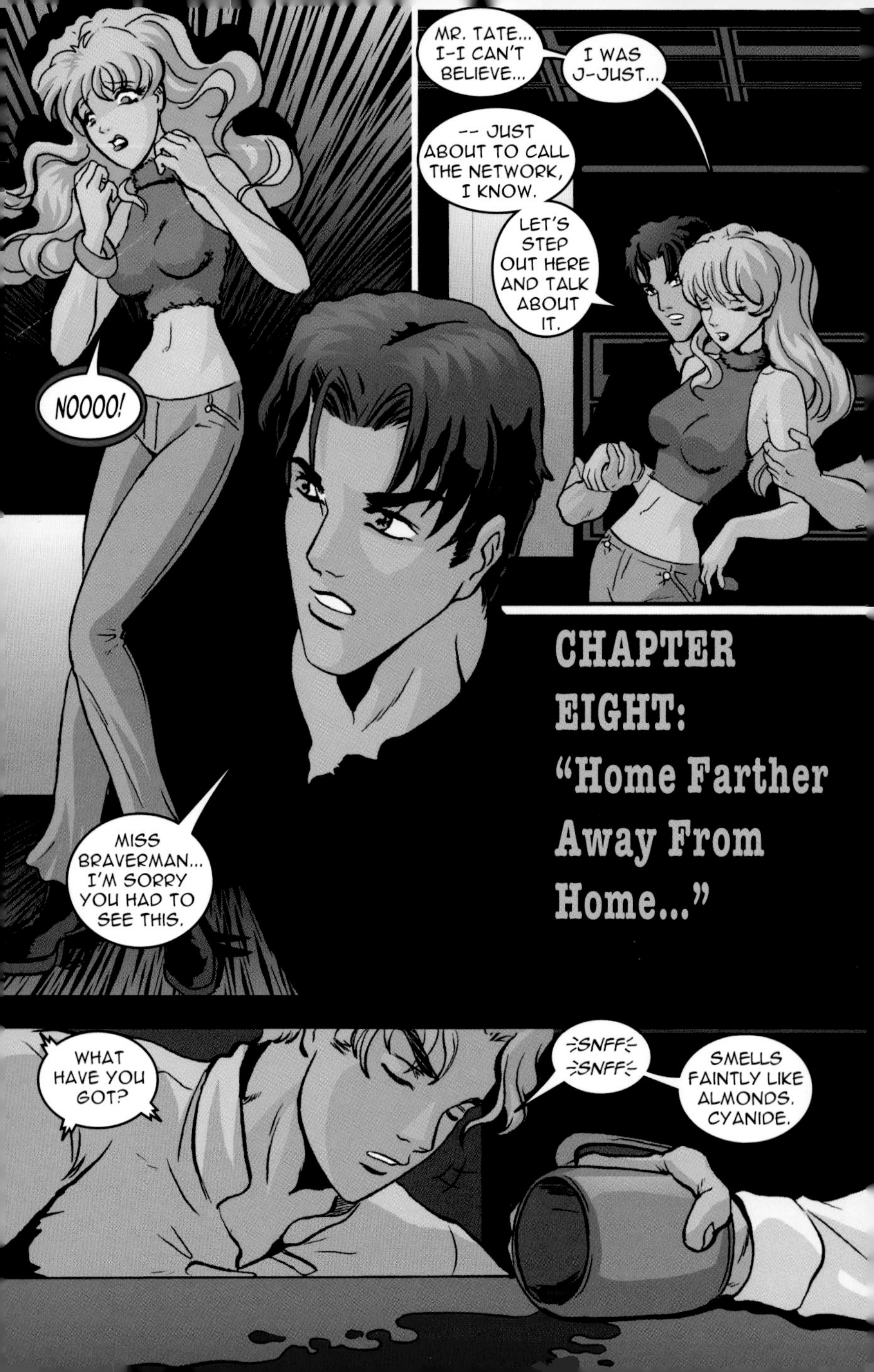
NOOOO!
MR. TATE... I-I CAN'T BELIEVE...
I WAS J-JUST...
-- JUST ABOUT TO CALL THE NETWORK, I KNOW.
LET'S STEP OUT HERE AND TALK ABOUT IT.
MISS BRAVERMAN... I'M SORRY YOU HAD TO SEE THIS.
CHAPTER EIGHT: "Home Farther Away From Home..."
WHAT HAVE YOU GOT?
SNFF SNFF
SMELLS FAINTLY LIKE ALMONDS. CYANIDE.

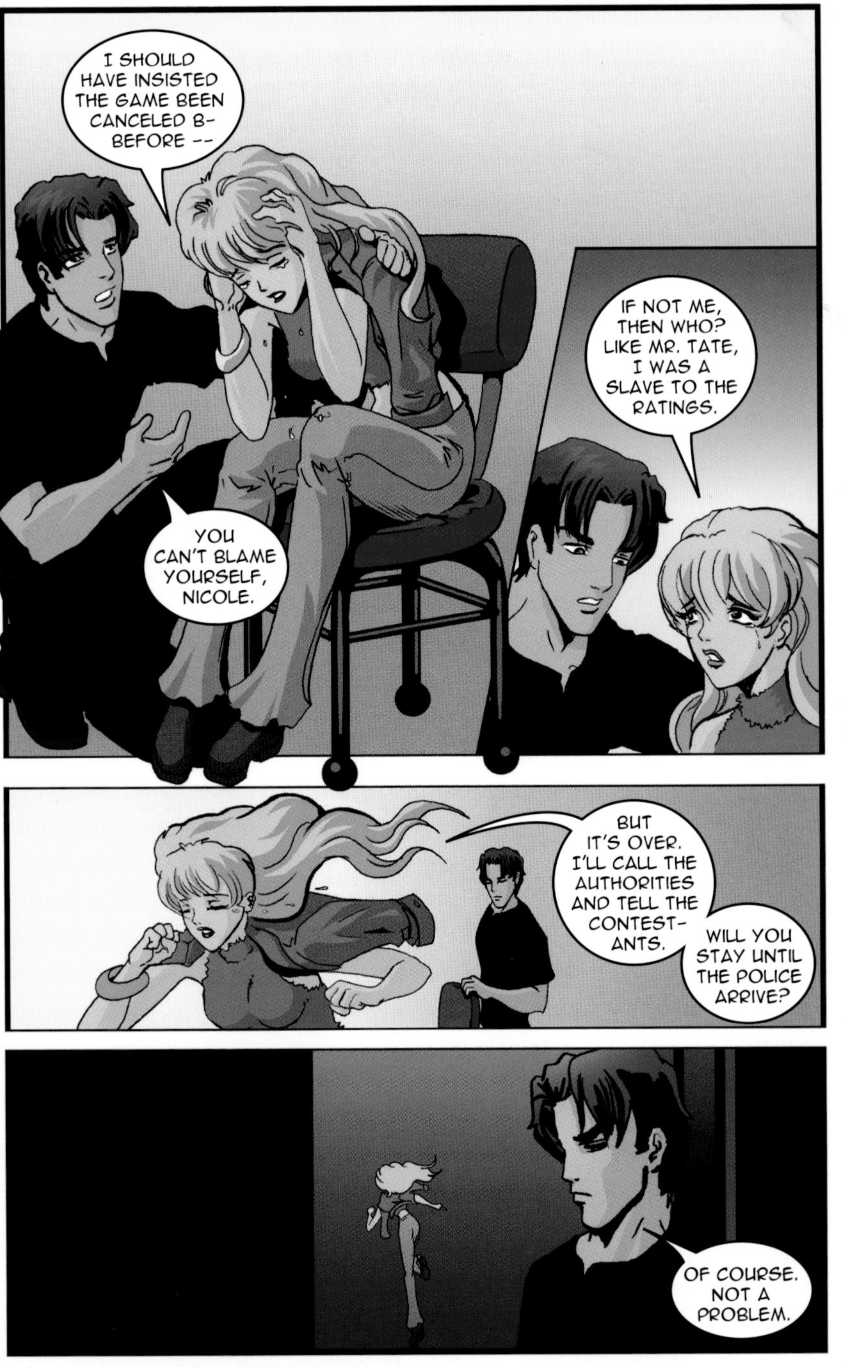
I SHOULD HAVE INSISTED THE GAME BEEN CANCELED B- BEFORE --
YOU CAN'T BLAME YOURSELF, NICOLE.
IF NOT ME, THEN WHO? LIKE MR. TATE, I WAS A SLAVE TO THE RATINGS.
BUT IT'S OVER. I'LL CALL THE AUTHORITIES AND TELL THE CONTEST-ANTS.
WILL YOU STAY UNTIL THE POLICE ARRIVE?
OF COURSE. NOT A PROBLEM.

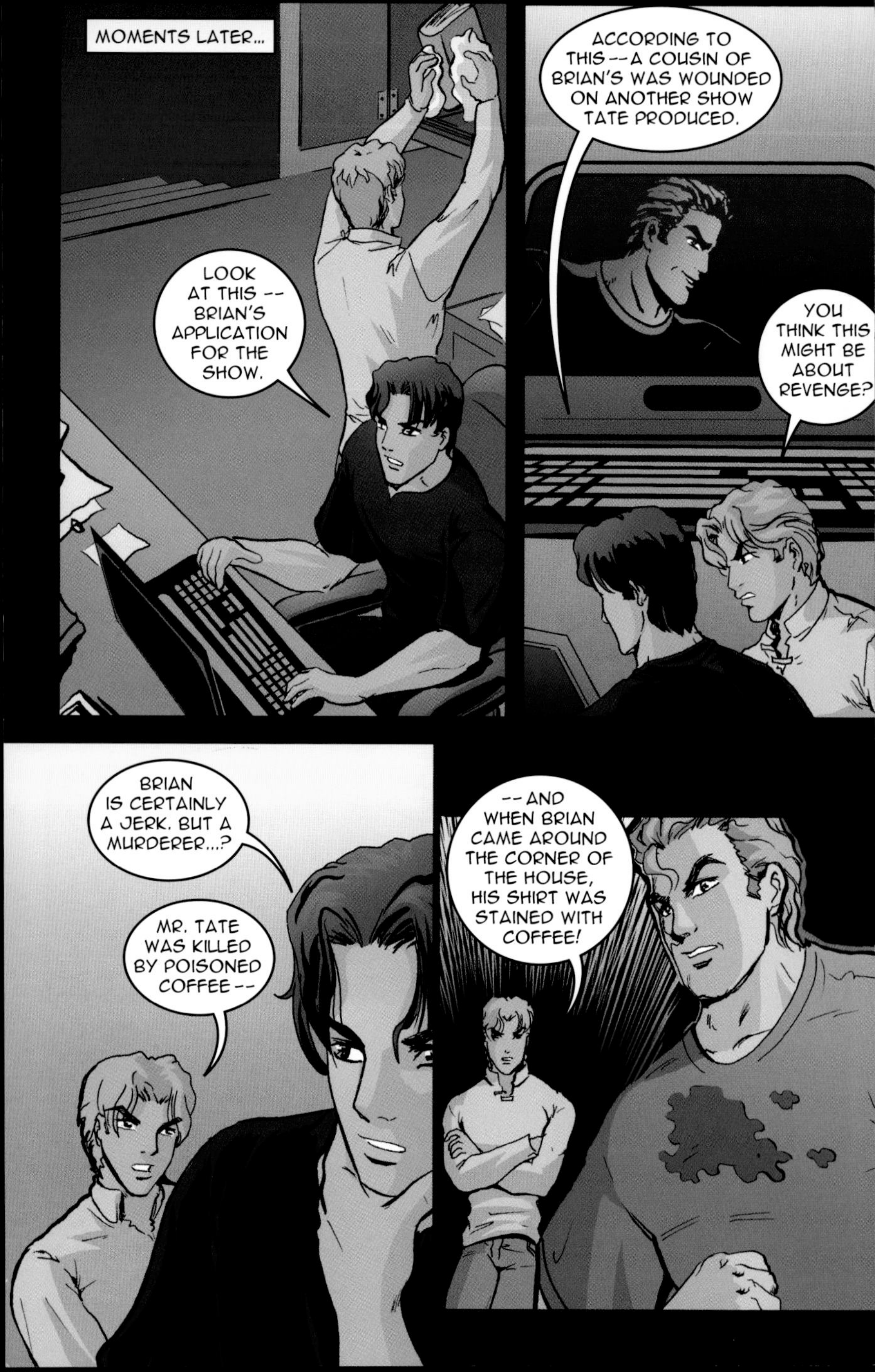
MOMENTS LATER...
LOOK AT THIS -- BRIAN'S APPLICATION FOR THE SHOW.
ACCORDING TO THIS -- A COUSIN OF BRIAN'S WAS WOUNDED ON ANOTHER SHOW TATE PRODUCED.
YOU THINK THIS MIGHT BE ABOUT REVENGE?
BRIAN IS CERTAINLY A JERK. BUT A MURDERER...?
MR. TATE WAS KILLED BY POISONED COFFEE --
-- AND WHEN BRIAN CAME AROUND THE CORNER OF THE HOUSE, HIS SHIRT WAS STAINED WITH COFFEE!

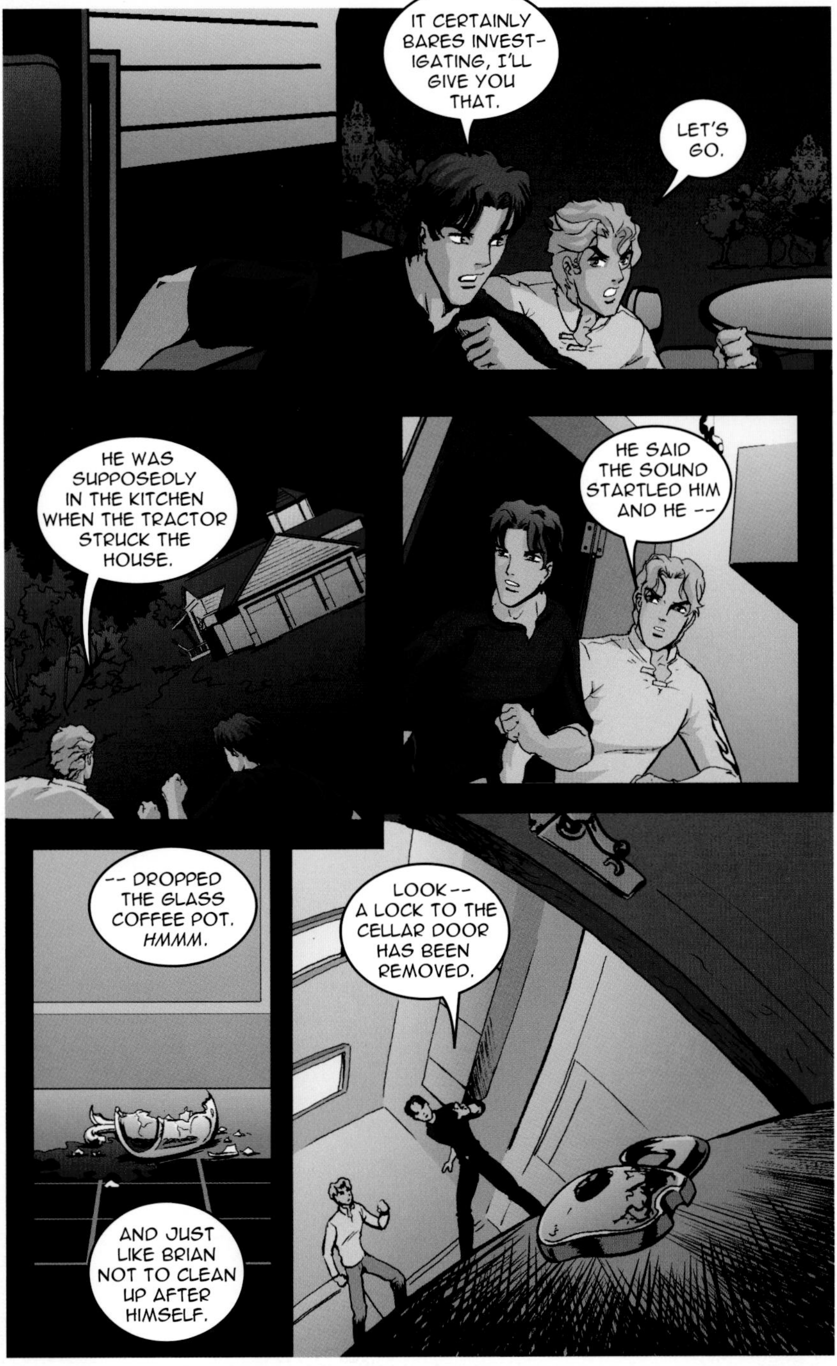
IT CERTAINLY BARES INVESTIGATING, I'LL GIVE YOU THAT.
LET'S GO.
HE WAS SUPPOSEDLY IN THE KITCHEN WHEN THE TRACTOR STRUCK THE HOUSE.
HE SAID THE SOUND STARTLED HIM AND HE --
-- DROPPED THE GLASS COFFEE POT. *HMMM*.
AND JUST LIKE BRIAN NOT TO CLEAN UP AFTER HIMSELF.
LOOK-- A LOCK TO THE CELLAR DOOR HAS BEEN REMOVED.

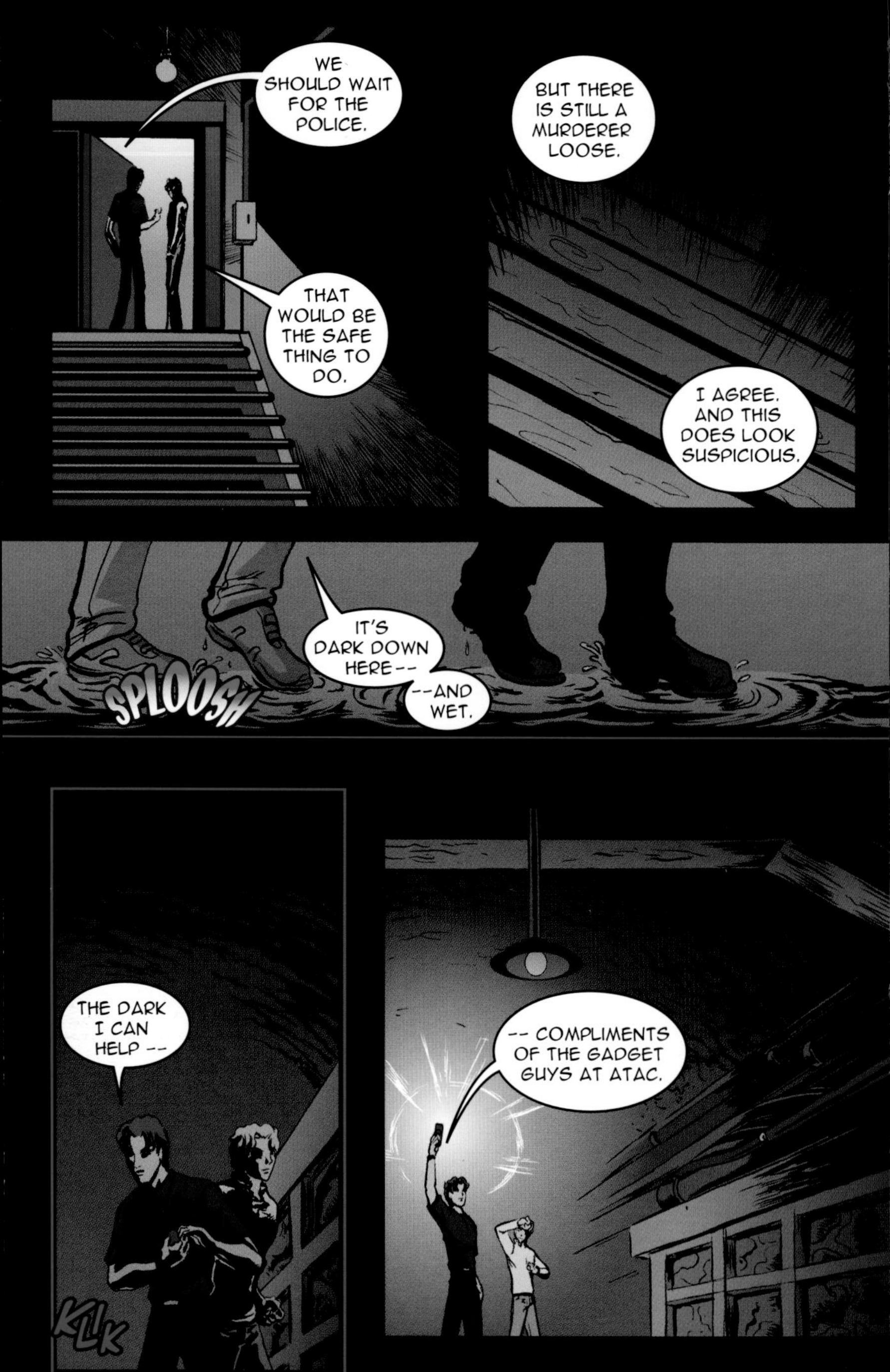
WE SHOULD WAIT FOR THE POLICE.
THAT WOULD BE THE SAFE THING TO DO.
BUT THERE IS STILL A MURDERER LOOSE.
I AGREE. AND THIS DOES LOOK SUSPICIOUS.
SPLOOSH
IT'S DARK DOWN HERE--
--AND WET.
THE DARK I CAN HELP --
KLIK
-- COMPLIMENTS OF THE GADGET GUYS AT ATAC.

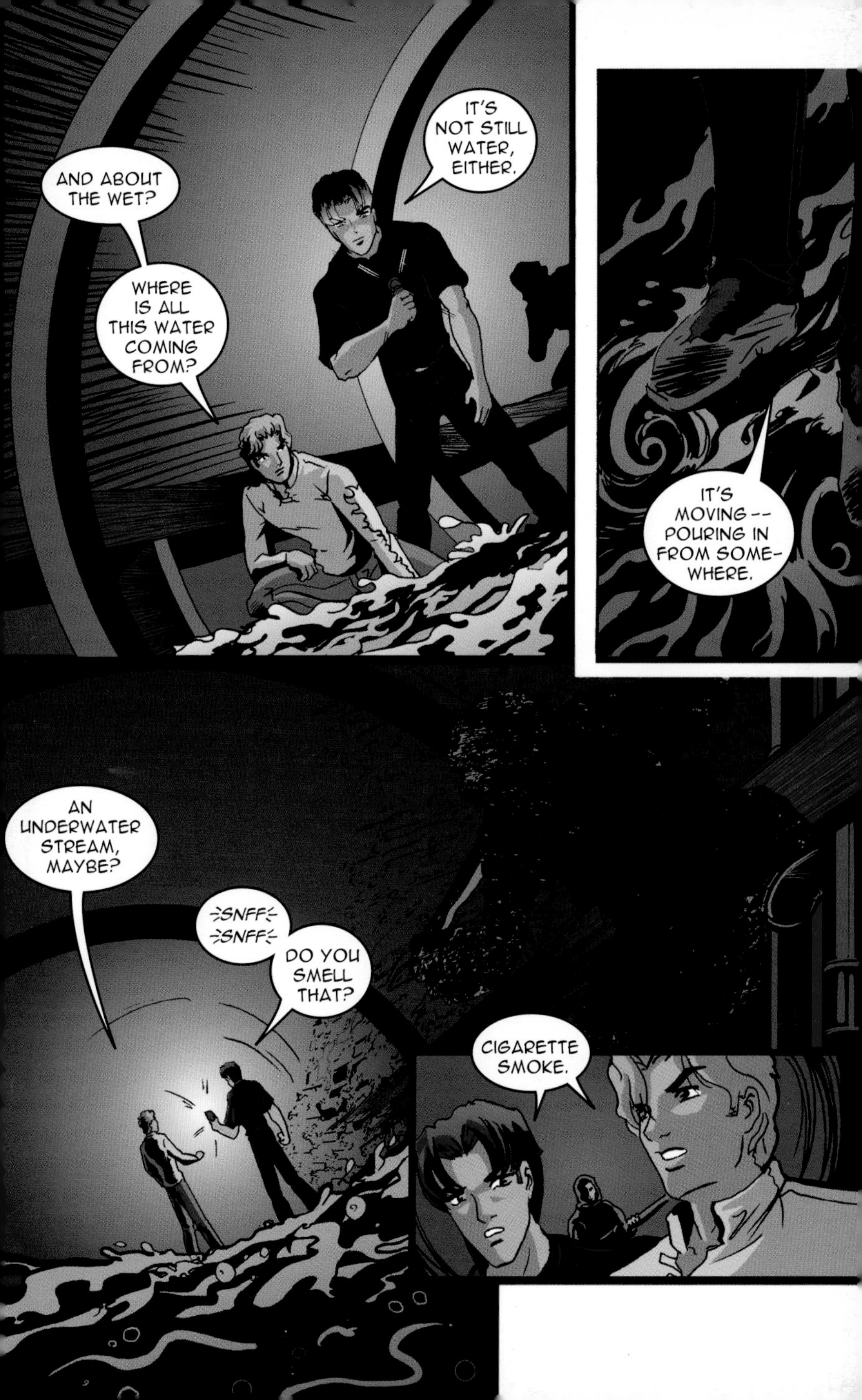
AND ABOUT THE WET?
WHERE IS ALL THIS WATER COMING FROM?
IT'S NOT STILL WATER, EITHER.
IT'S MOVING -- POURING IN FROM SOME-WHERE.
AN UNDERWATER STREAM, MAYBE?
SNFF SNFF
DO YOU SMELL THAT?
CIGARETTE SMOKE.

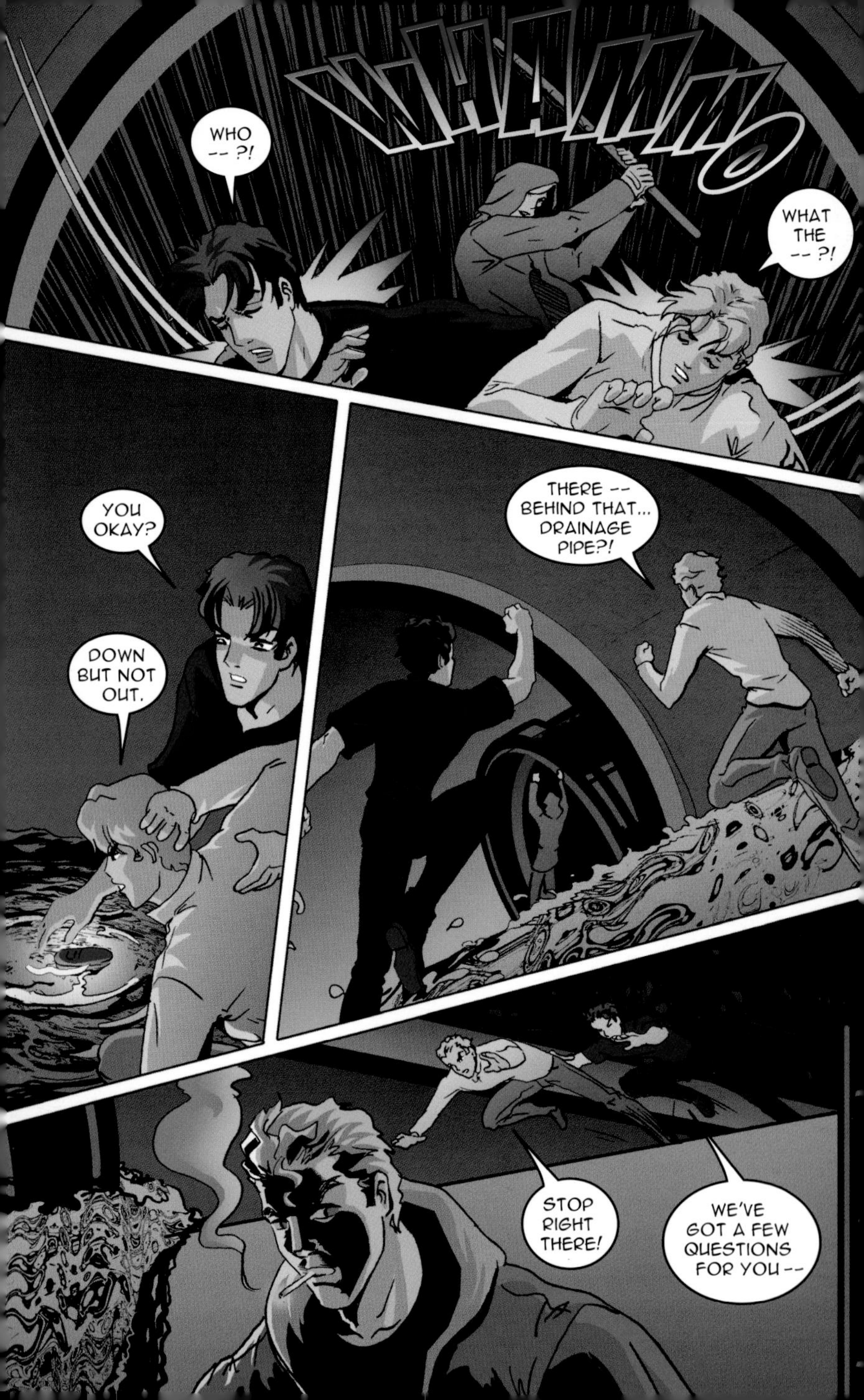
WHO -- ?!
WHAMM
WHAT THE -- ?!
YOU OKAY?
DOWN BUT NOT OUT.
THERE -- BEHIND THAT... DRAINAGE PIPE?!
STOP RIGHT THERE!
WE'VE GOT A FEW QUESTIONS FOR YOU --

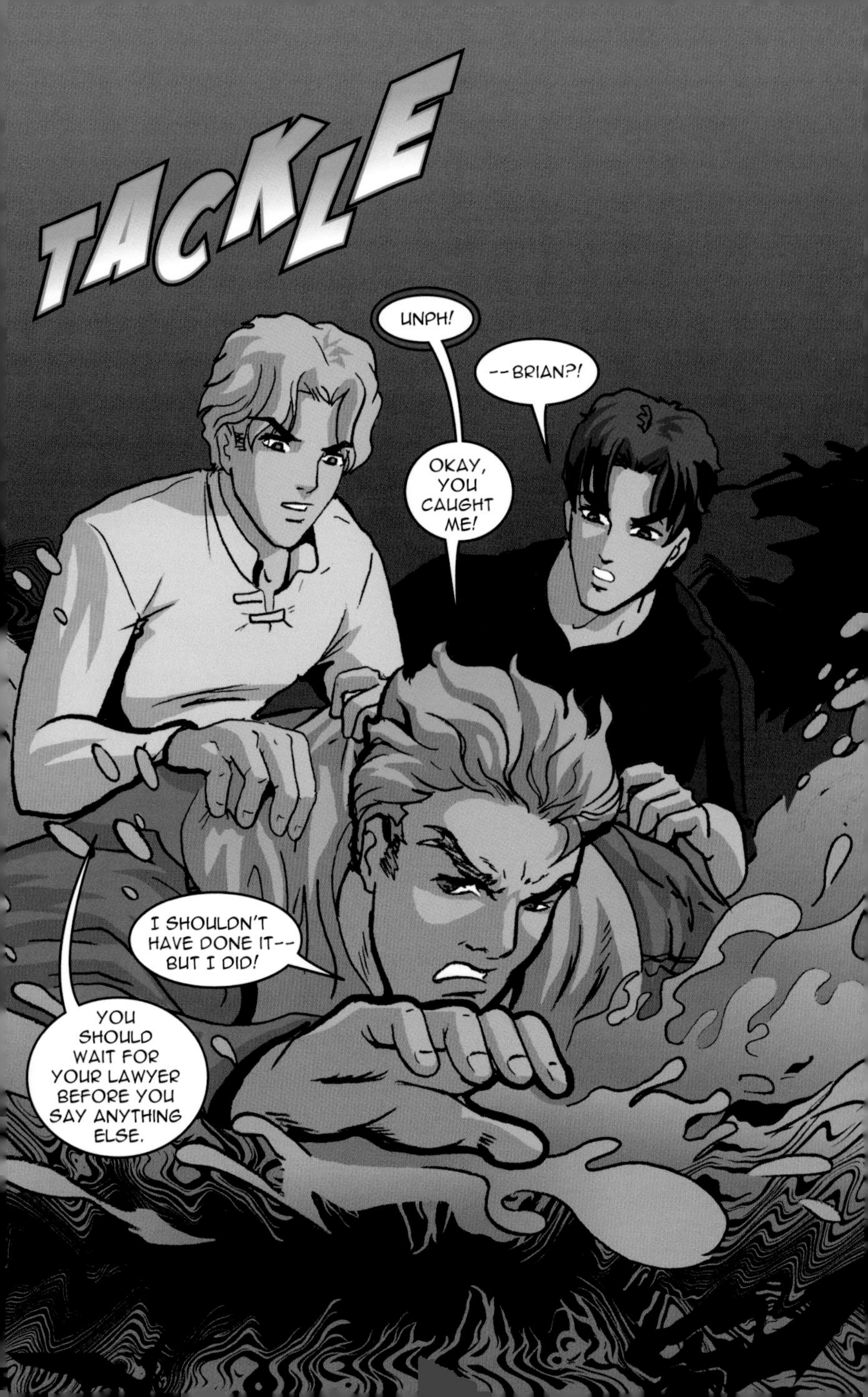
TACKLE
UNPH!
OKAY, YOU CAUGHT ME!
--BRIAN?!
I SHOULDN'T HAVE DONE IT--BUT I DID!
YOU SHOULD WAIT FOR YOUR LAWYER BEFORE YOU SAY ANYTHING ELSE.

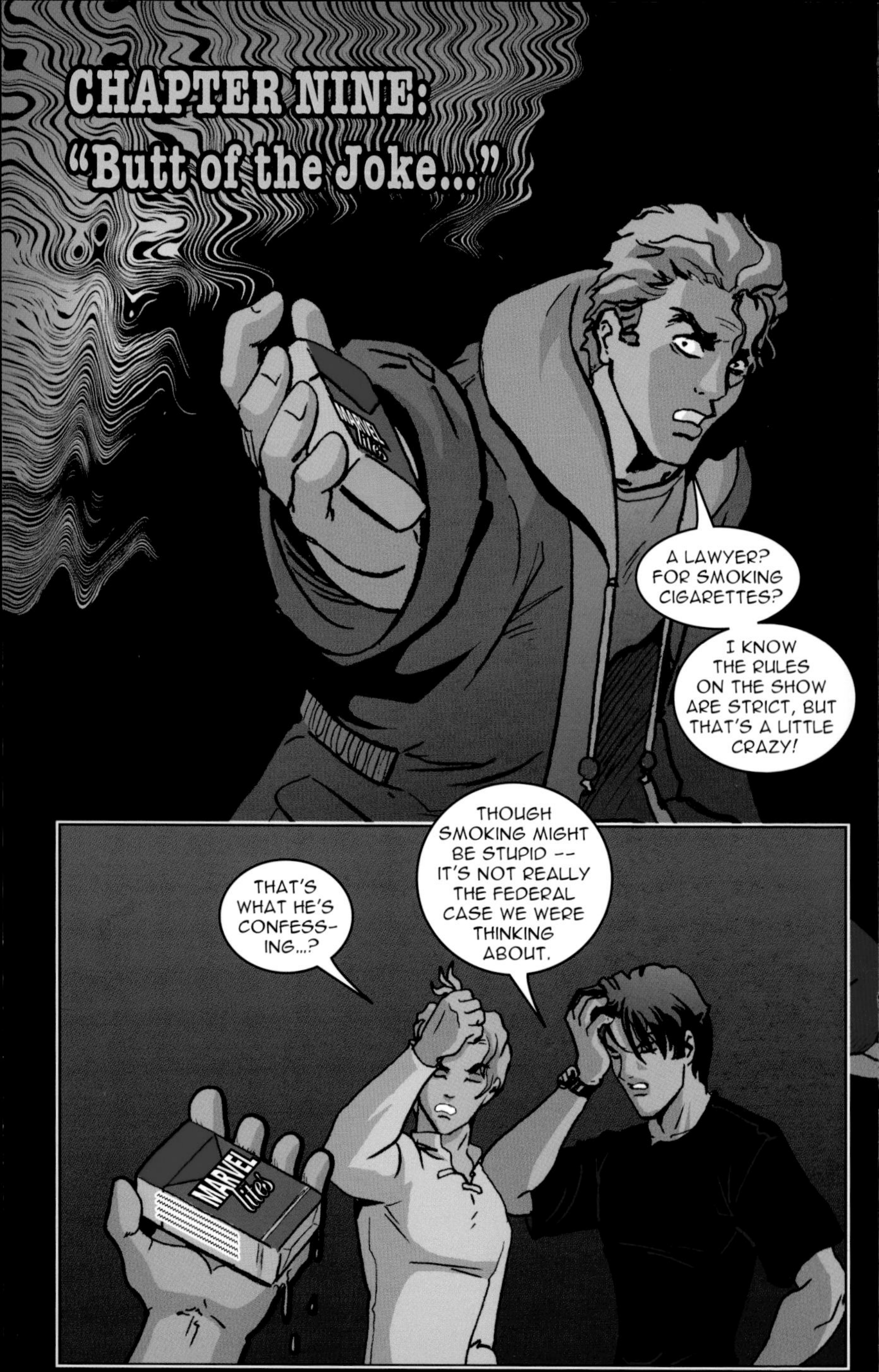
CHAPTER NINE:
"Butt of the Joke..."
MARVEL lites
A LAWYER? FOR SMOKING CIGARETTES?
I KNOW THE RULES ON THE SHOW ARE STRICT, BUT THAT'S A LITTLE CRAZY!
THAT'S WHAT HE'S CONFESS-ING...?
THOUGH SMOKING MIGHT BE STUPID -- IT'S NOT REALLY THE FEDERAL CASE WE WERE THINKING ABOUT.
MARVEL lites

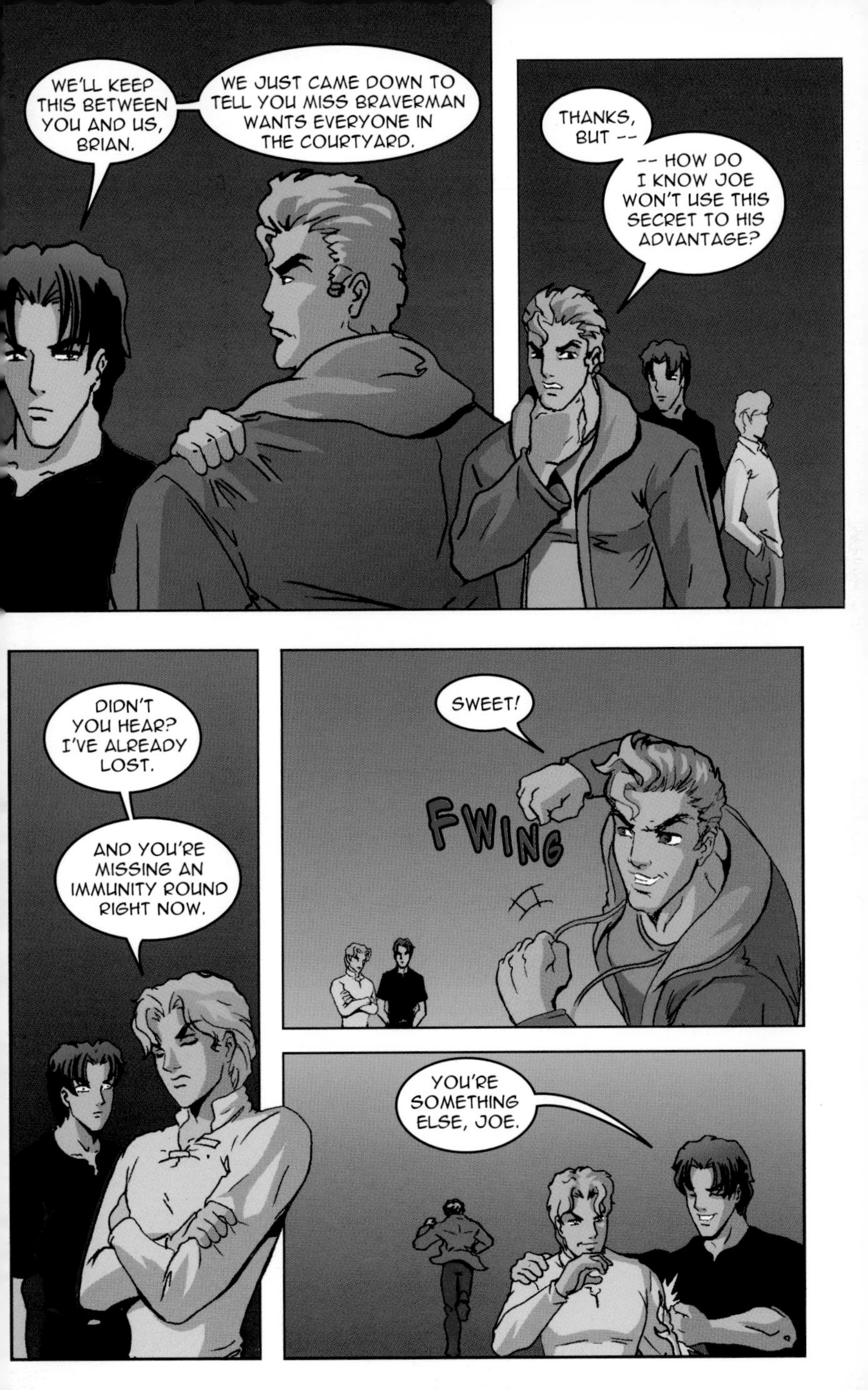
WE'LL KEEP THIS BETWEEN YOU AND US, BRIAN.
WE JUST CAME DOWN TO TELL YOU MISS BRAVERMAN WANTS EVERYONE IN THE COURTYARD.
THANKS, BUT --
-- HOW DO I KNOW JOE WON'T USE THIS SECRET TO HIS ADVANTAGE?
DIDN'T YOU HEAR? I'VE ALREADY LOST.
AND YOU'RE MISSING AN IMMUNITY ROUND RIGHT NOW.
SWEET!
FWING
YOU'RE SOMETHING ELSE, JOE.

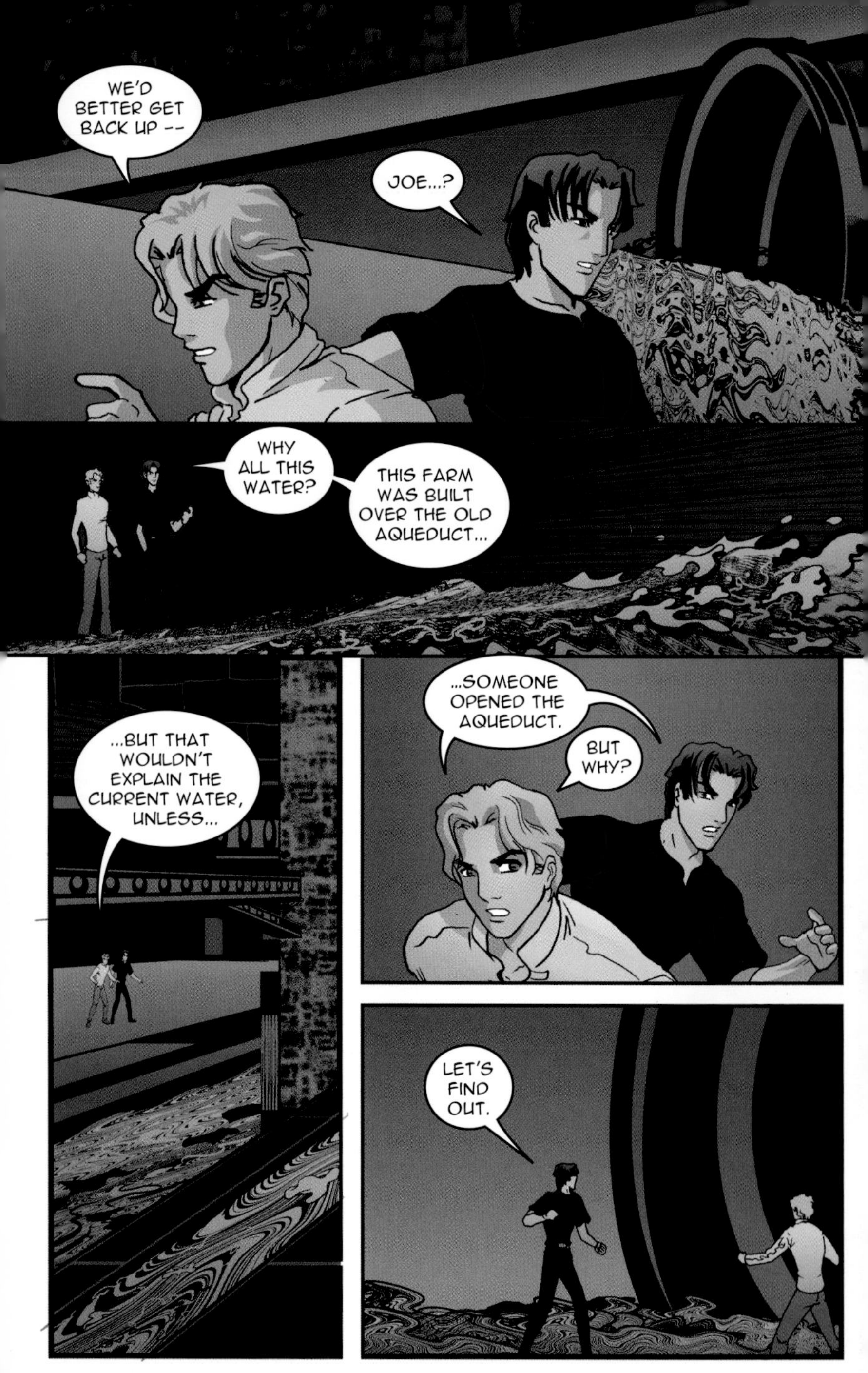
WE'D BETTER GET BACK UP --
JOE...?
WHY ALL THIS WATER?
THIS FARM WAS BUILT OVER THE OLD AQUEDUCT...
...BUT THAT WOULDN'T EXPLAIN THE CURRENT WATER, UNLESS...
...SOMEONE OPENED THE AQUEDUCT.
BUT WHY?
LET'S FIND OUT.

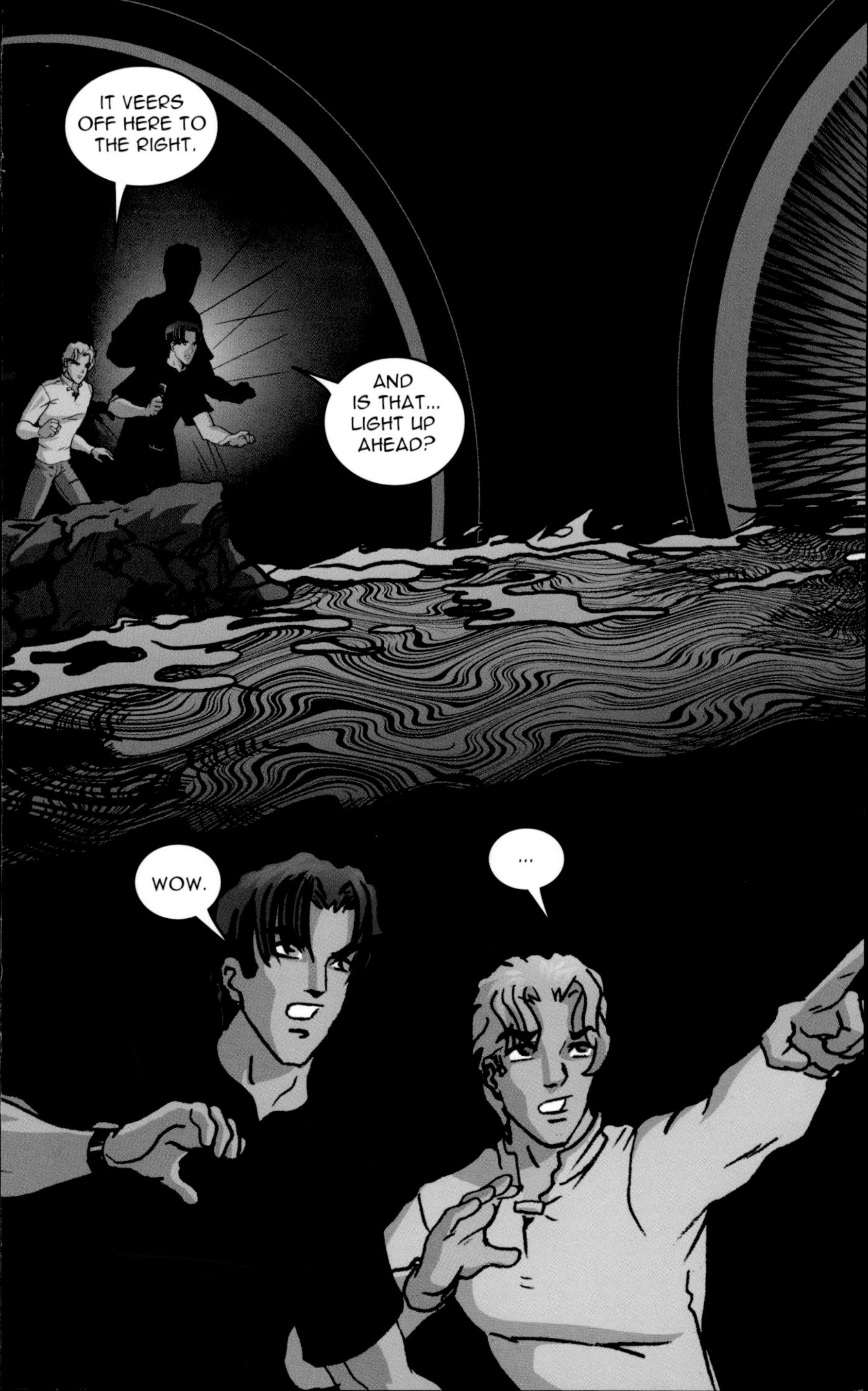
IT VEERS OFF HERE TO THE RIGHT.
AND IS THAT... LIGHT UP AHEAD?
WOW.
...

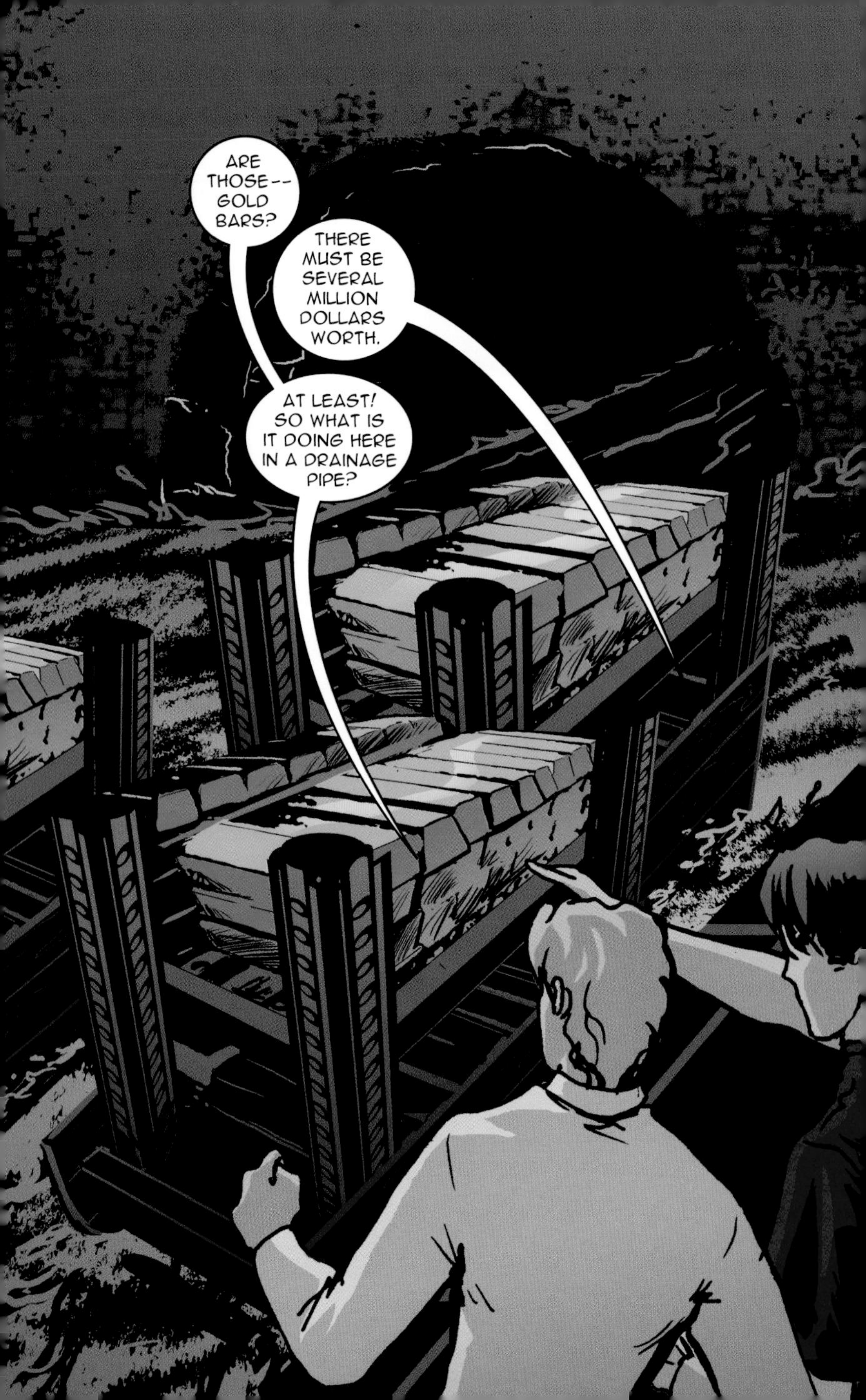
ARE THOSE--GOLD BARS?
THERE MUST BE SEVERAL MILLION DOLLARS WORTH.
AT LEAST! SO WHAT IS IT DOING HERE IN A DRAINAGE PIPE?

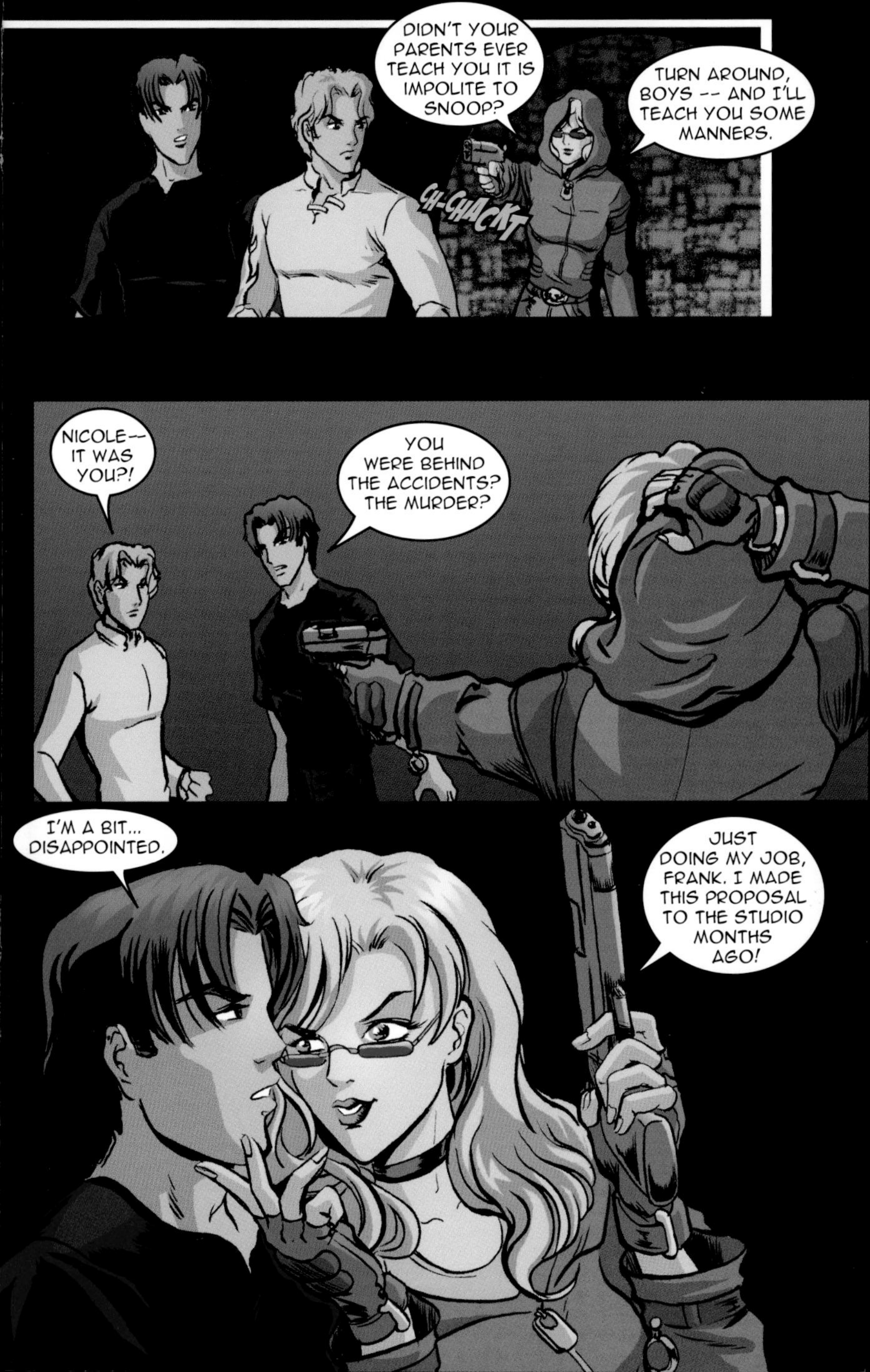
DIDN'T YOUR PARENTS EVER TEACH YOU IT IS IMPOLITE TO SNOOP?
TURN AROUND, BOYS -- AND I'LL TEACH YOU SOME MANNERS.
CH-CHACKT
NICOLE-- IT WAS YOU?!
YOU WERE BEHIND THE ACCIDENTS? THE MURDER?
I'M A BIT... DISAPPOINTED.
JUST DOING MY JOB, FRANK. I MADE THIS PROPOSAL TO THE STUDIO MONTHS AGO!

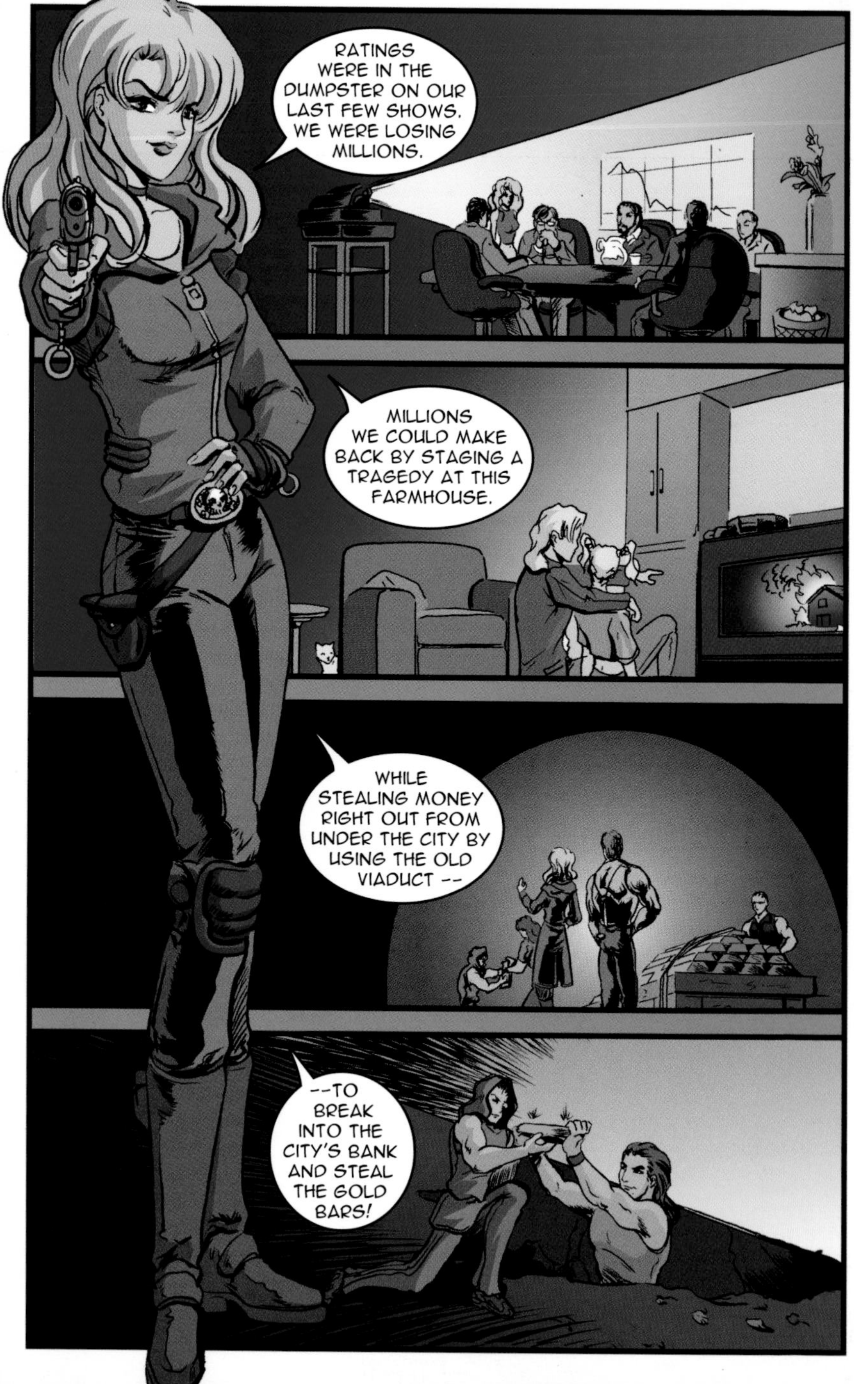
RATINGS WERE IN THE DUMPSTER ON OUR LAST FEW SHOWS. WE WERE LOSING MILLIONS.
MILLIONS WE COULD MAKE BACK BY STAGING A TRAGEDY AT THIS FARMHOUSE.
WHILE STEALING MONEY RIGHT OUT FROM UNDER THE CITY BY USING THE OLD VIADUCT --
--TO BREAK INTO THE CITY'S BANK AND STEAL THE GOLD BARS!

CHAPTER TEN:
"Bringing Down The House"

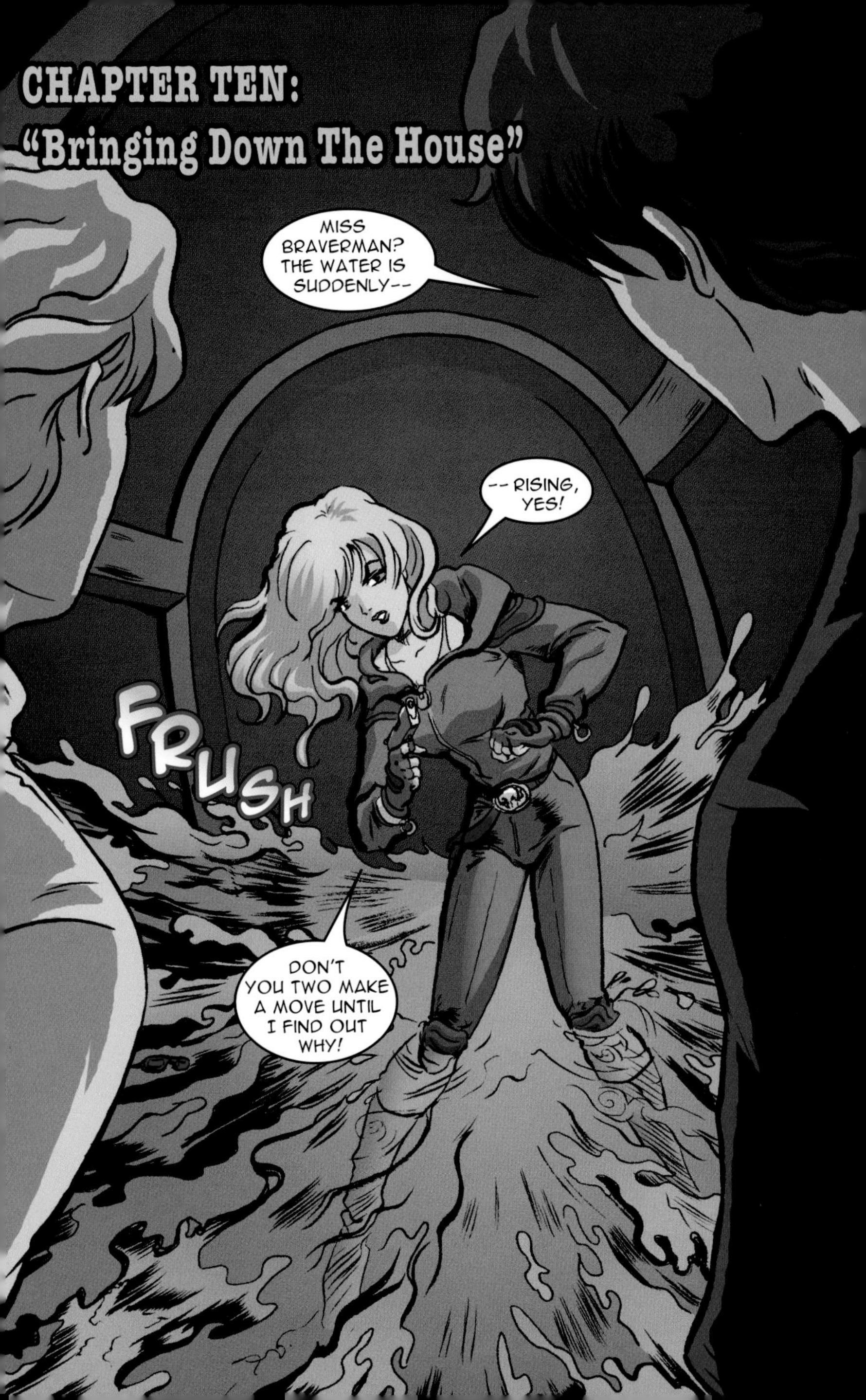

MISS BRAVERMAN? THE WATER IS SUDDENLY--
--RISING, YES!
FRUSH
DON'T YOU TWO MAKE A MOVE UNTIL I FIND OUT WHY!

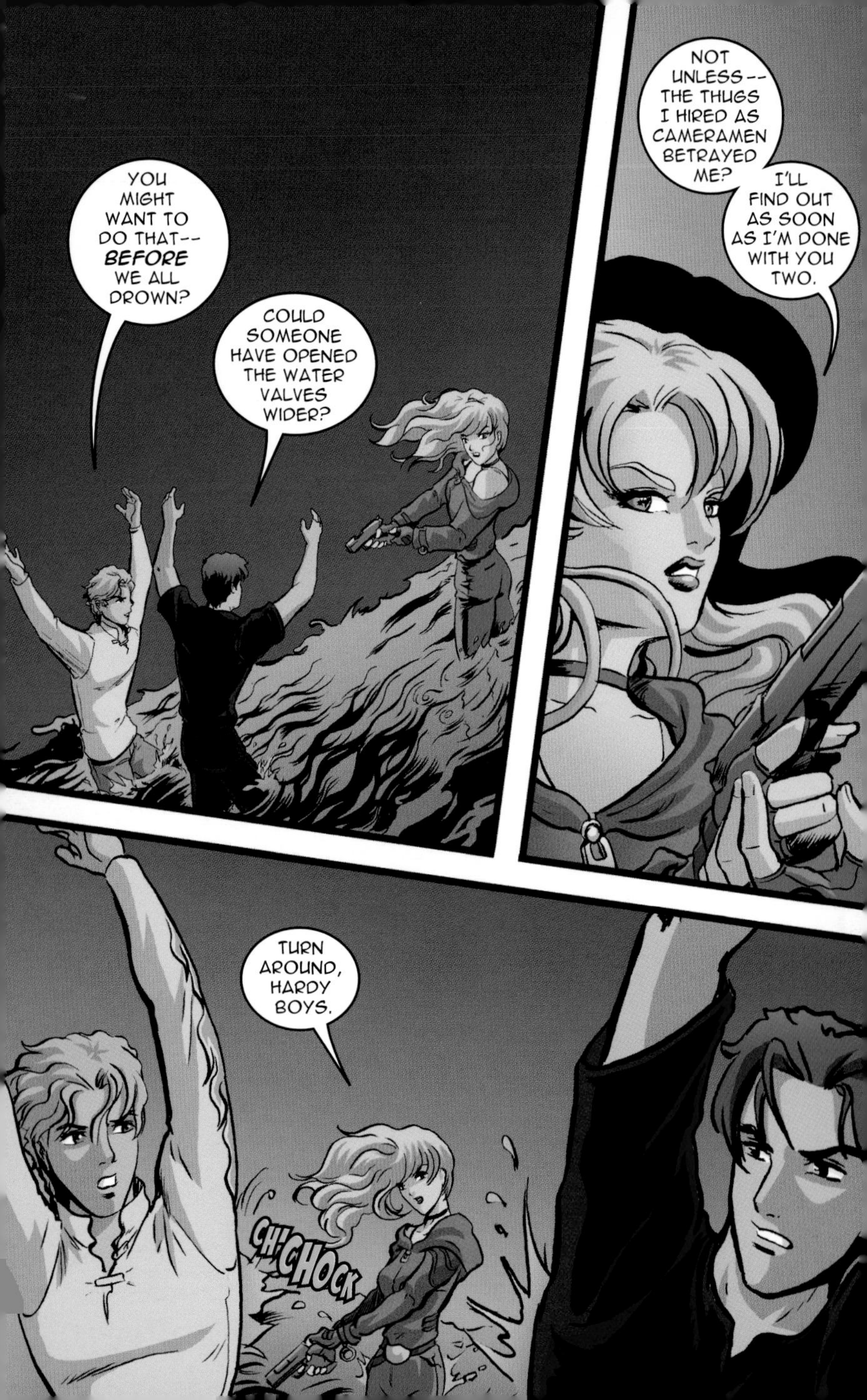
YOU MIGHT WANT TO DO THAT-- *BEFORE* WE ALL DROWN?
COULD SOMEONE HAVE OPENED THE WATER VALVES WIDER?
NOT UNLESS-- THE THUGS I HIRED AS CAMERAMEN BETRAYED ME?
I'LL FIND OUT AS SOON AS I'M DONE WITH YOU TWO.
TURN AROUND, HARDY BOYS.
CHI-CHOCK

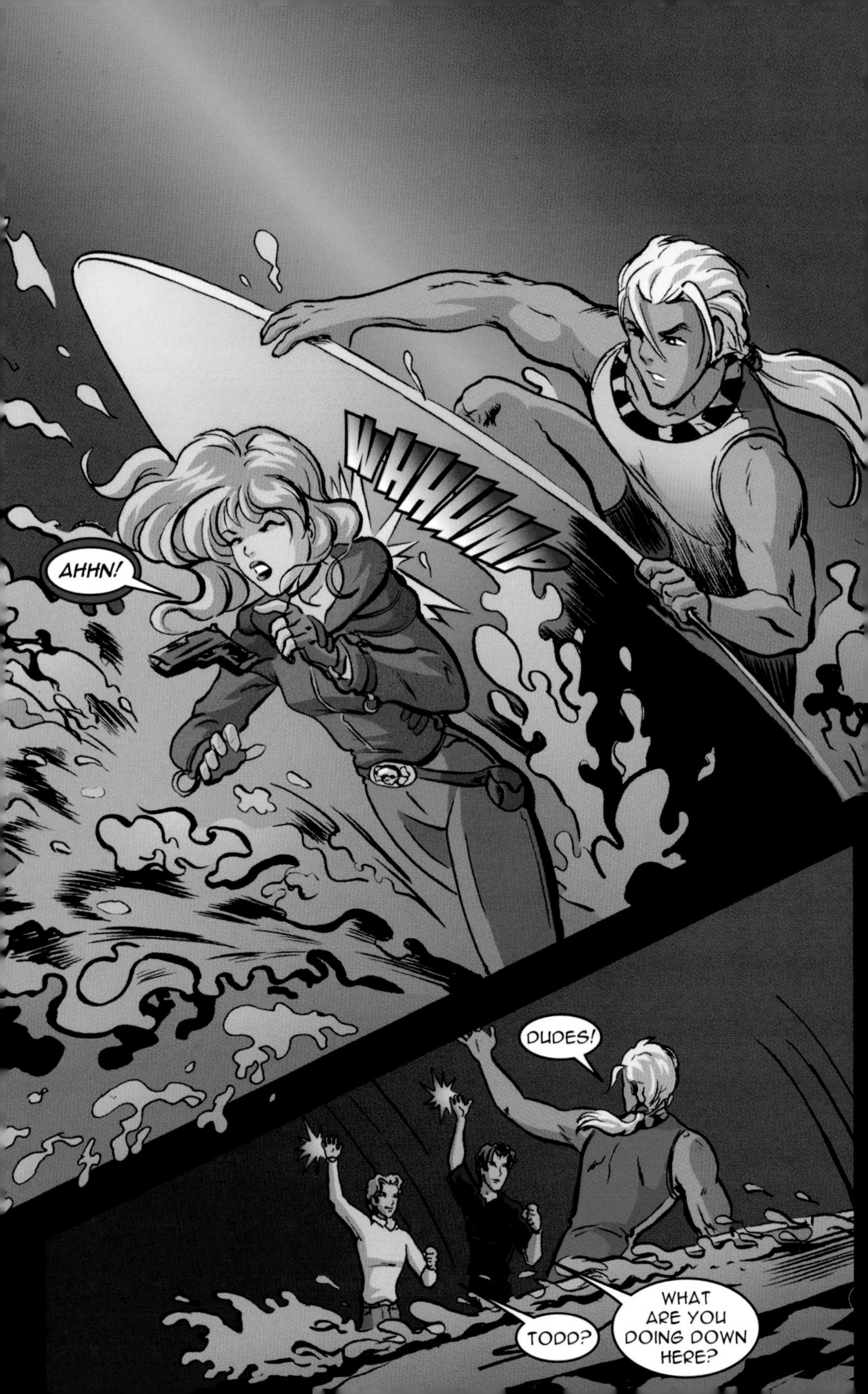
AHHN!
WHHUMP
DUDES!
TODD?
WHAT ARE YOU DOING DOWN HERE?

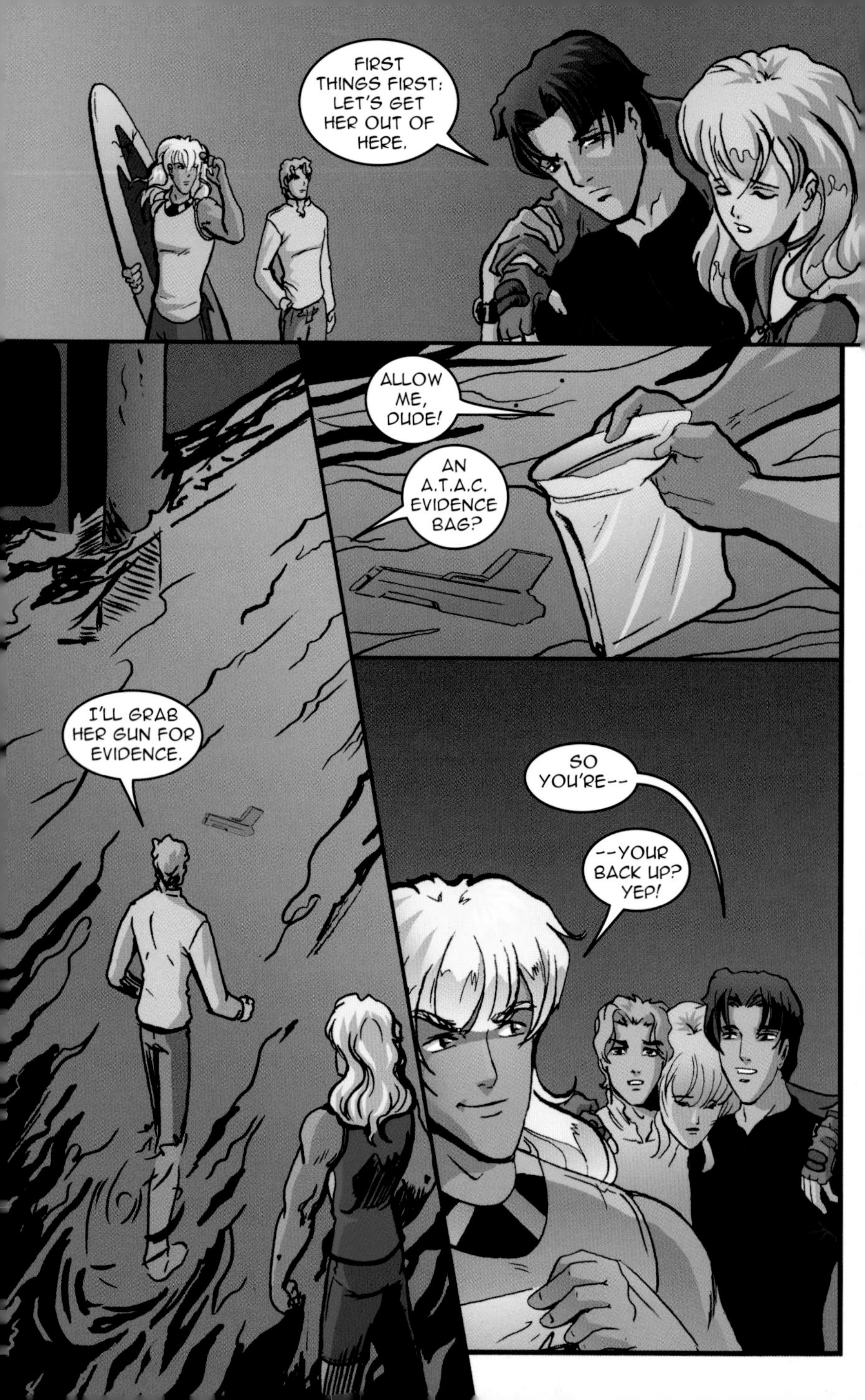
FIRST THINGS FIRST: LET'S GET HER OUT OF HERE.
I'LL GRAB HER GUN FOR EVIDENCE.
ALLOW ME, DUDE!
AN A.T.A.C. EVIDENCE BAG?
SO YOU'RE--
--YOUR BACK UP? YEP!

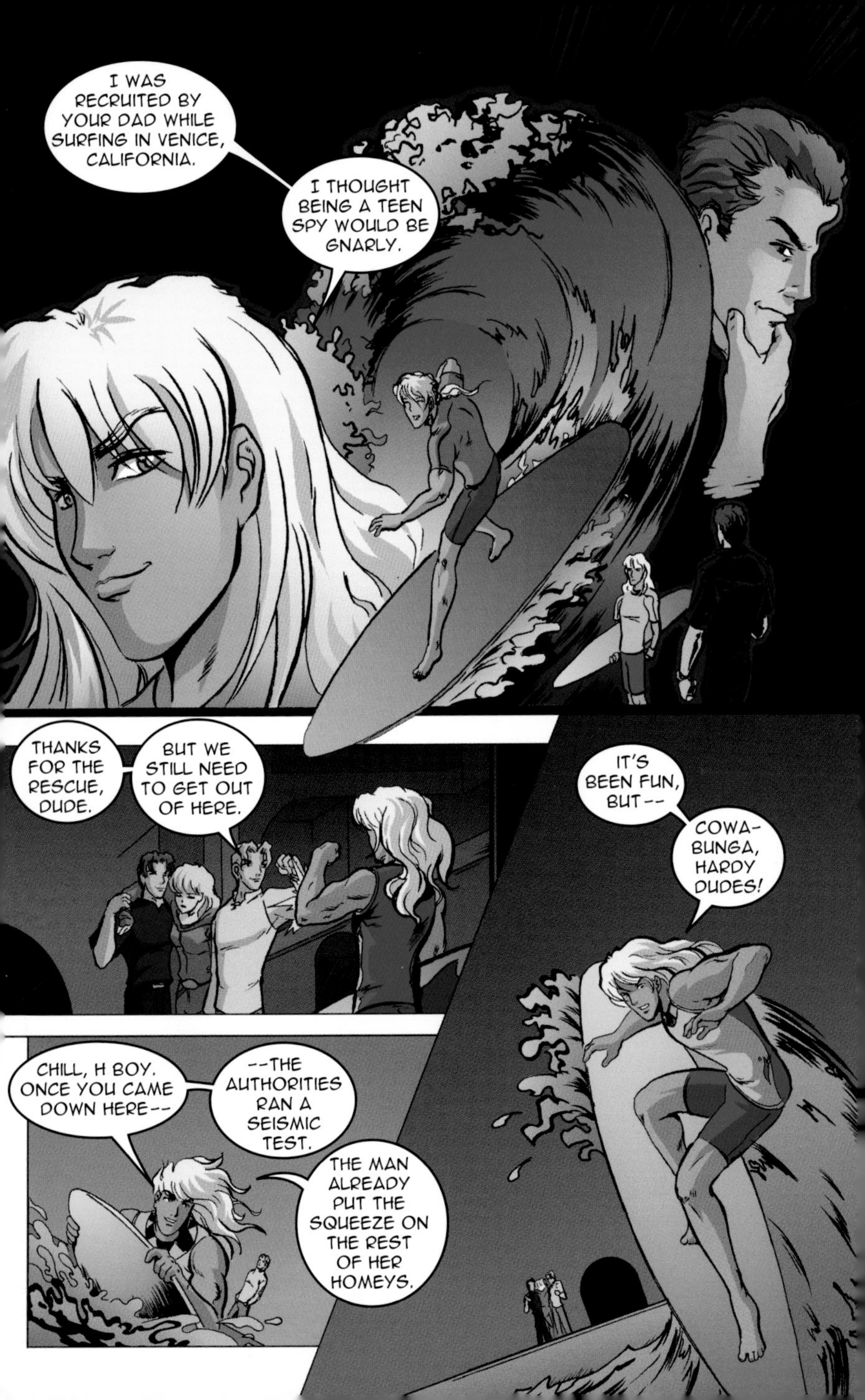
I WAS RECRUITED BY YOUR DAD WHILE SURFING IN VENICE, CALIFORNIA.
I THOUGHT BEING A TEEN SPY WOULD BE GNARLY.
THANKS FOR THE RESCUE, DUDE.
BUT WE STILL NEED TO GET OUT OF HERE.
CHILL, H BOY. ONCE YOU CAME DOWN HERE--
--THE AUTHORITIES RAN A SEISMIC TEST.
THE MAN ALREADY PUT THE SQUEEZE ON THE REST OF HER HOMEYS.
IT'S BEEN FUN, BUT--
COWA-BUNGA, HARDY DUDES!

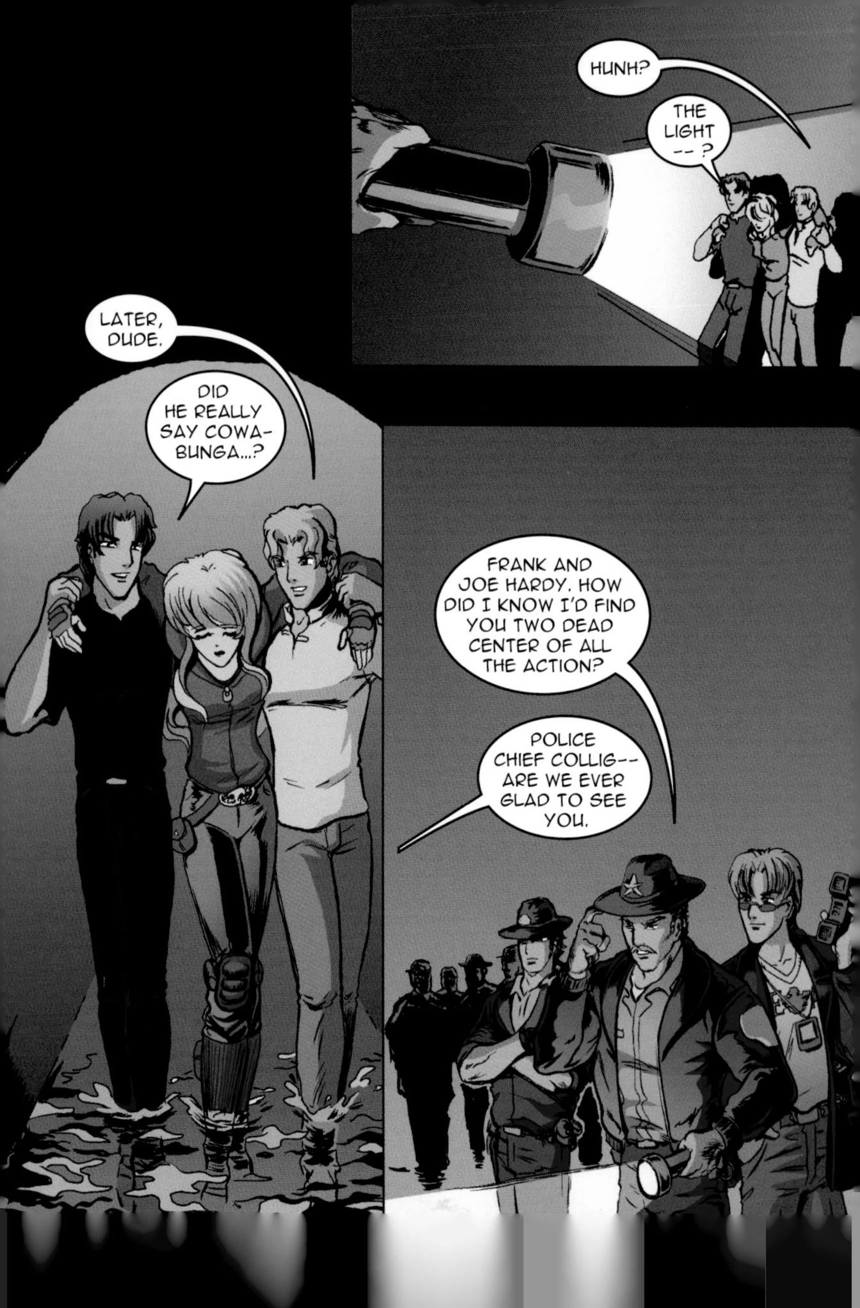
HUNH?
THE LIGHT -- ?
LATER, DUDE.
DID HE REALLY SAY COWA-BUNGA...?
FRANK AND JOE HARDY. HOW DID I KNOW I'D FIND YOU TWO DEAD CENTER OF ALL THE ACTION?
POLICE CHIEF COLLIG-- ARE WE EVER GLAD TO SEE YOU.

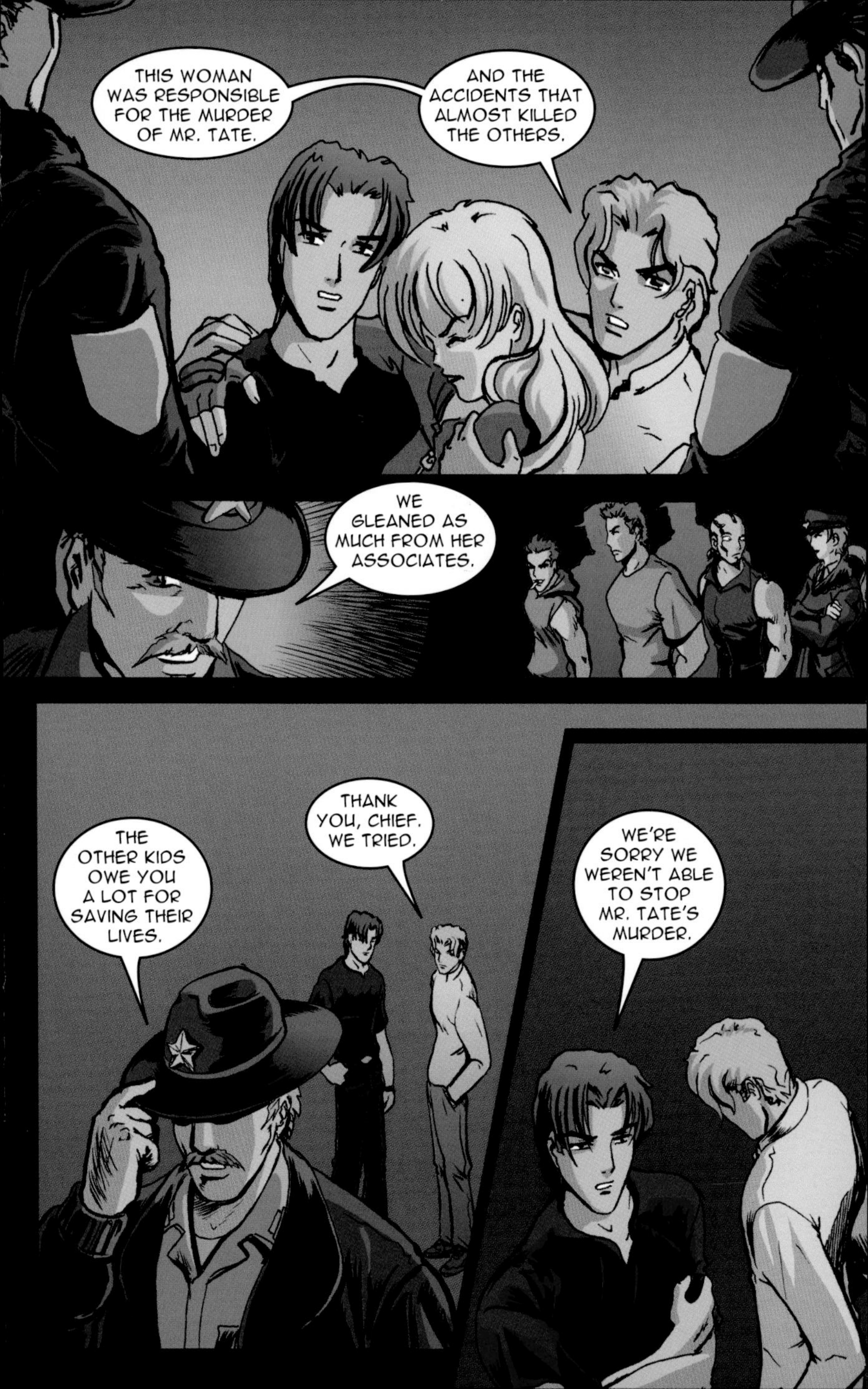
THIS WOMAN WAS RESPONSIBLE FOR THE MURDER OF MR. TATE.
AND THE ACCIDENTS THAT ALMOST KILLED THE OTHERS.
WE GLEANED AS MUCH FROM HER ASSOCIATES.
THE OTHER KIDS OWE YOU A LOT FOR SAVING THEIR LIVES.
THANK YOU, CHIEF. WE TRIED.
WE'RE SORRY WE WEREN'T ABLE TO STOP MR. TATE'S MURDER.

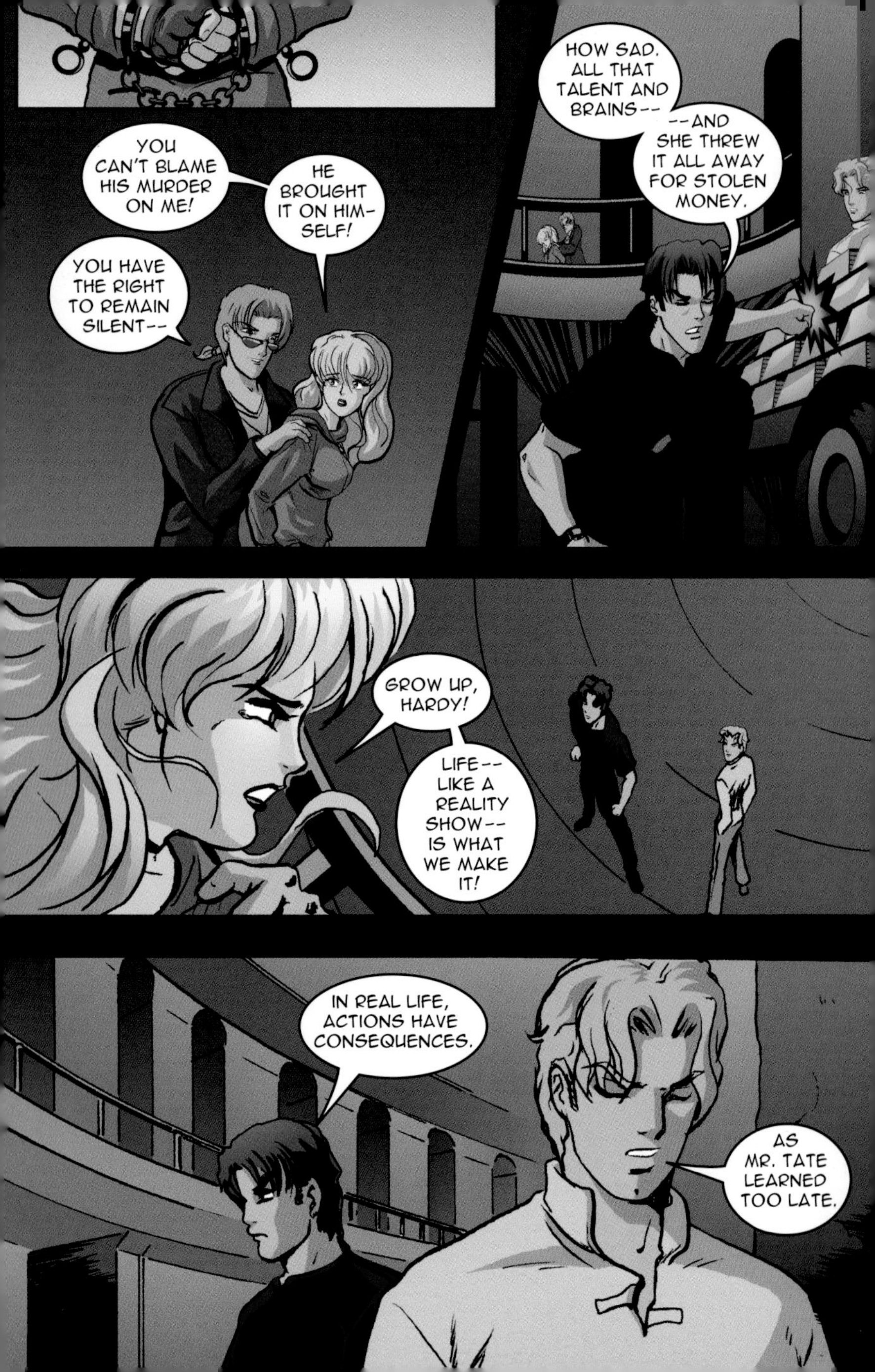
YOU CAN'T BLAME HIS MURDER ON ME!
HE BROUGHT IT ON HIM-SELF!
YOU HAVE THE RIGHT TO REMAIN SILENT--
HOW SAD. ALL THAT TALENT AND BRAINS--
--AND SHE THREW IT ALL AWAY FOR STOLEN MONEY.
GROW UP, HARDY!
LIFE--LIKE A REALITY SHOW--IS WHAT WE MAKE IT!
IN REAL LIFE, ACTIONS HAVE CONSEQUENCES.
AS MR. TATE LEARNED TOO LATE.

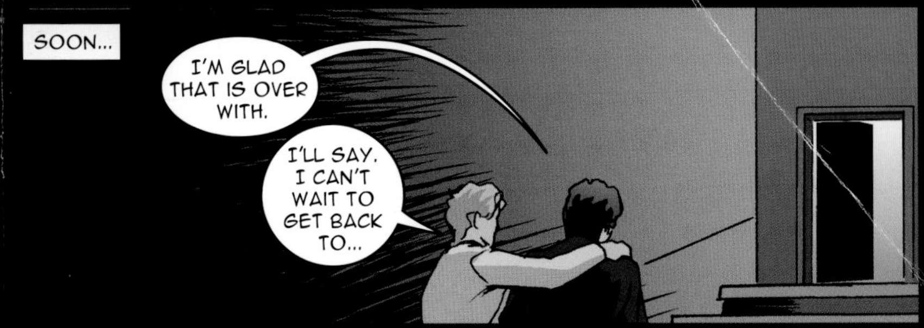
SOON...
I'M GLAD THAT IS OVER WITH.
I'LL SAY. I CAN'T WAIT TO GET BACK TO...

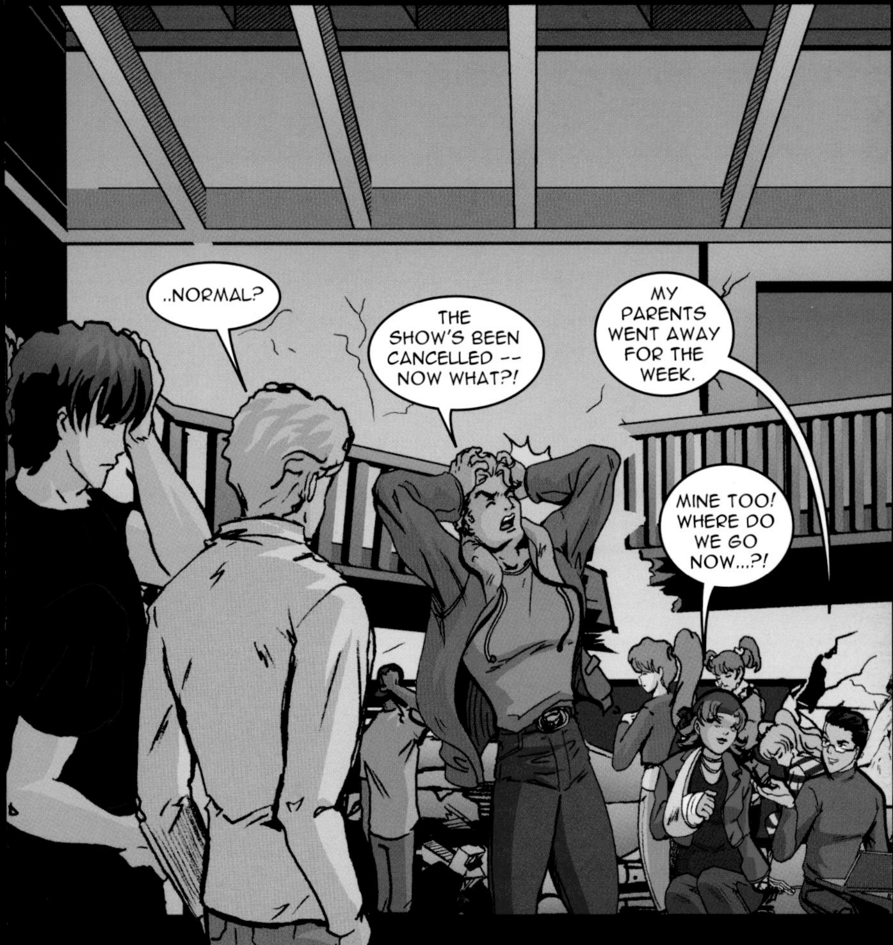
..NORMAL?
THE SHOW'S BEEN CANCELLED -- NOW WHAT?!
MY PARENTS WENT AWAY FOR THE WEEK.
MINE TOO! WHERE DO WE GO NOW...?!

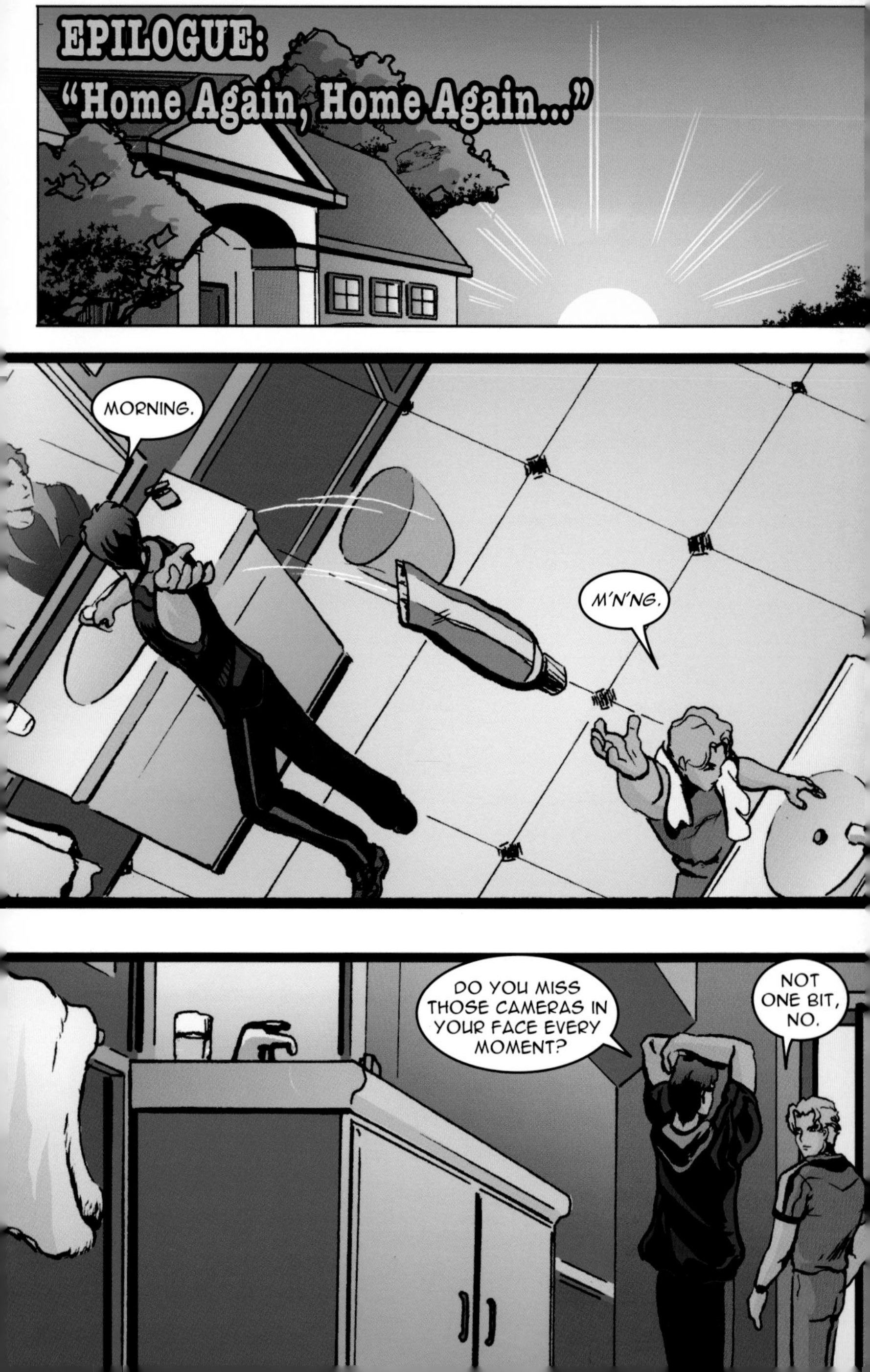
EPILOGUE:
"Home Again, Home Again..."
MORNING.
M'N'NG.
DO YOU MISS THOSE CAMERAS IN YOUR FACE EVERY MOMENT?
NOT ONE BIT, NO.

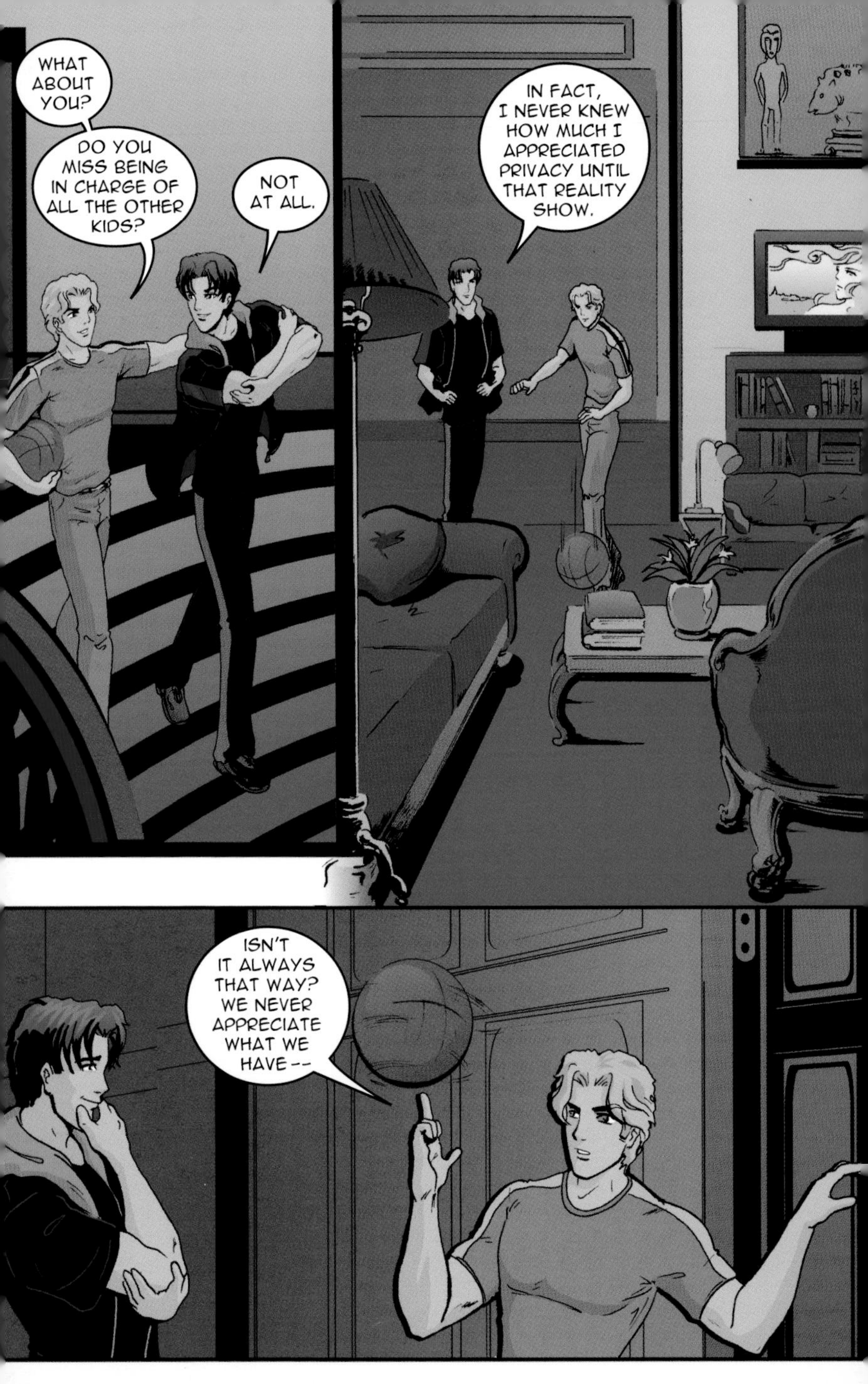
WHAT ABOUT YOU?
DO YOU MISS BEING IN CHARGE OF ALL THE OTHER KIDS?
NOT AT ALL.
IN FACT, I NEVER KNEW HOW MUCH I APPRECIATED PRIVACY UNTIL THAT REALITY SHOW.
ISN'T IT ALWAYS THAT WAY? WE NEVER APPRECIATE WHAT WE HAVE--

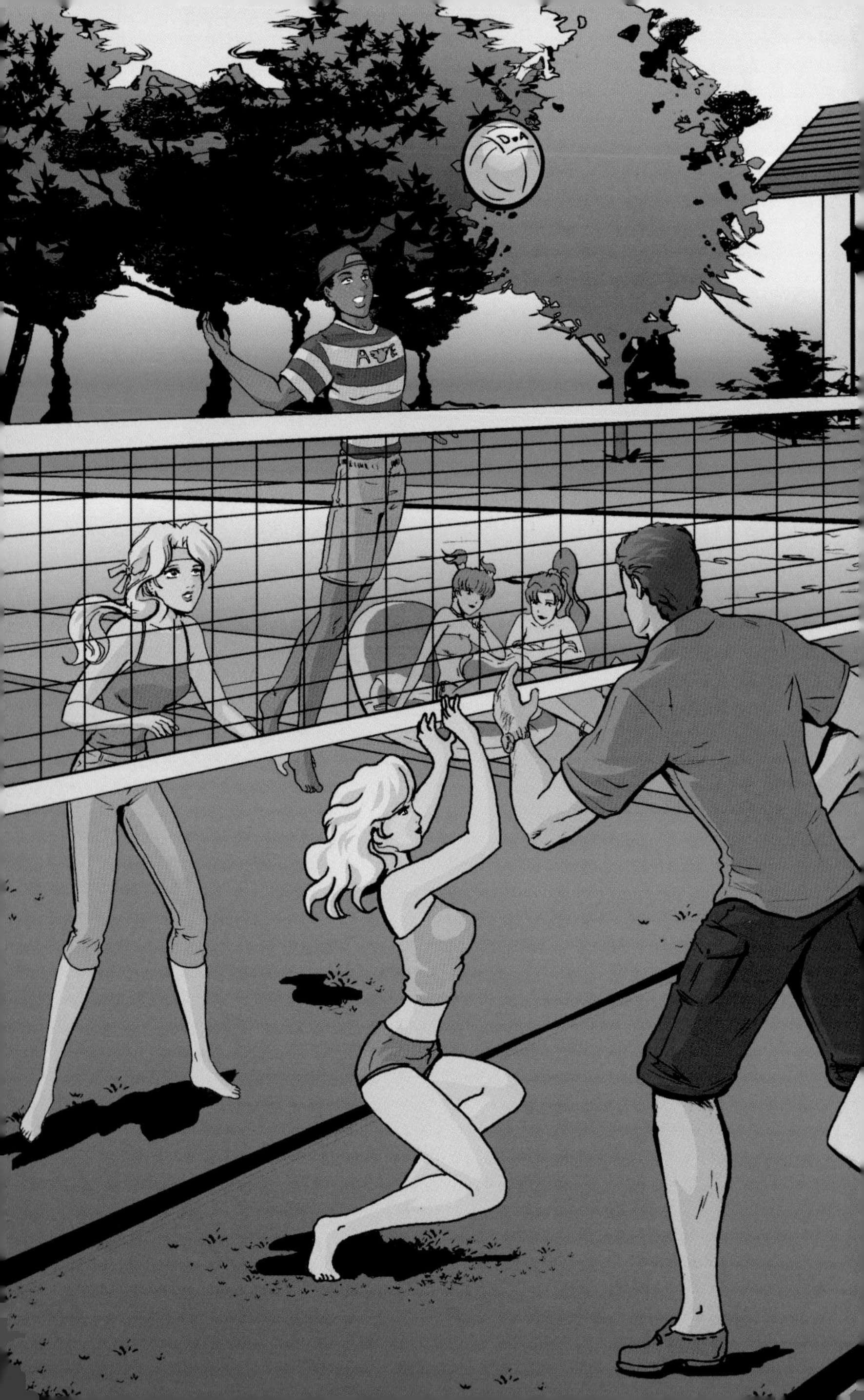

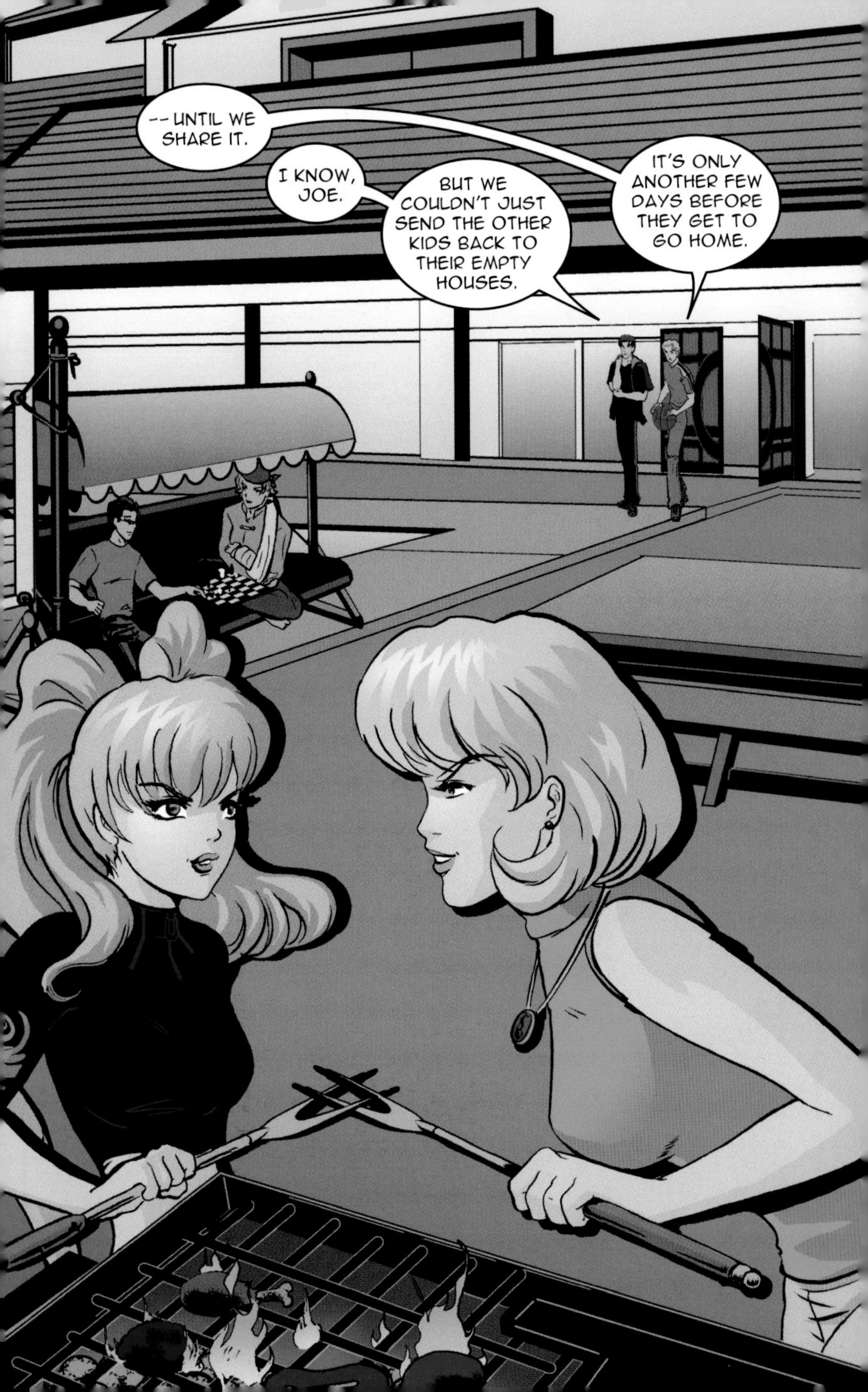
I KNOW, JOE.
BUT WE COULDN'T JUST SEND THE OTHER KIDS BACK TO THEIR EMPTY HOUSES.
IT'S ONLY ANOTHER FEW DAYS BEFORE THEY GET TO GO HOME.
--UNTIL WE SHARE IT.

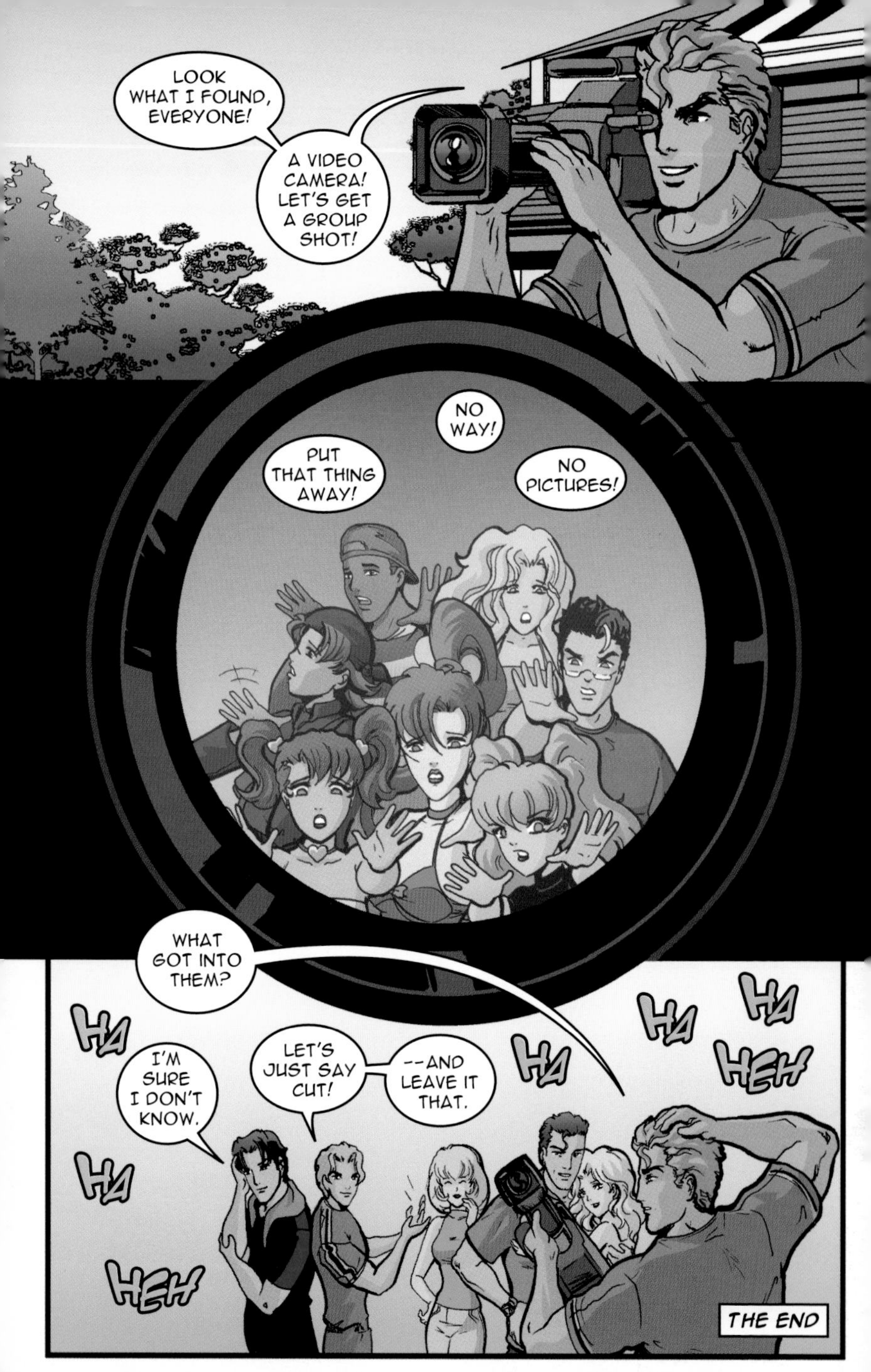

LOOK WHAT I FOUND, EVERYONE!
A VIDEO CAMERA! LET'S GET A GROUP SHOT!
NO WAY!
PUT THAT THING AWAY!
NO PICTURES!
WHAT GOT INTO THEM?
HA
I'M SURE I DON'T KNOW.
LET'S JUST SAY CUT!
--AND LEAVE IT THAT.
HA
HA
HA
HEH
HA
HEH
THE END

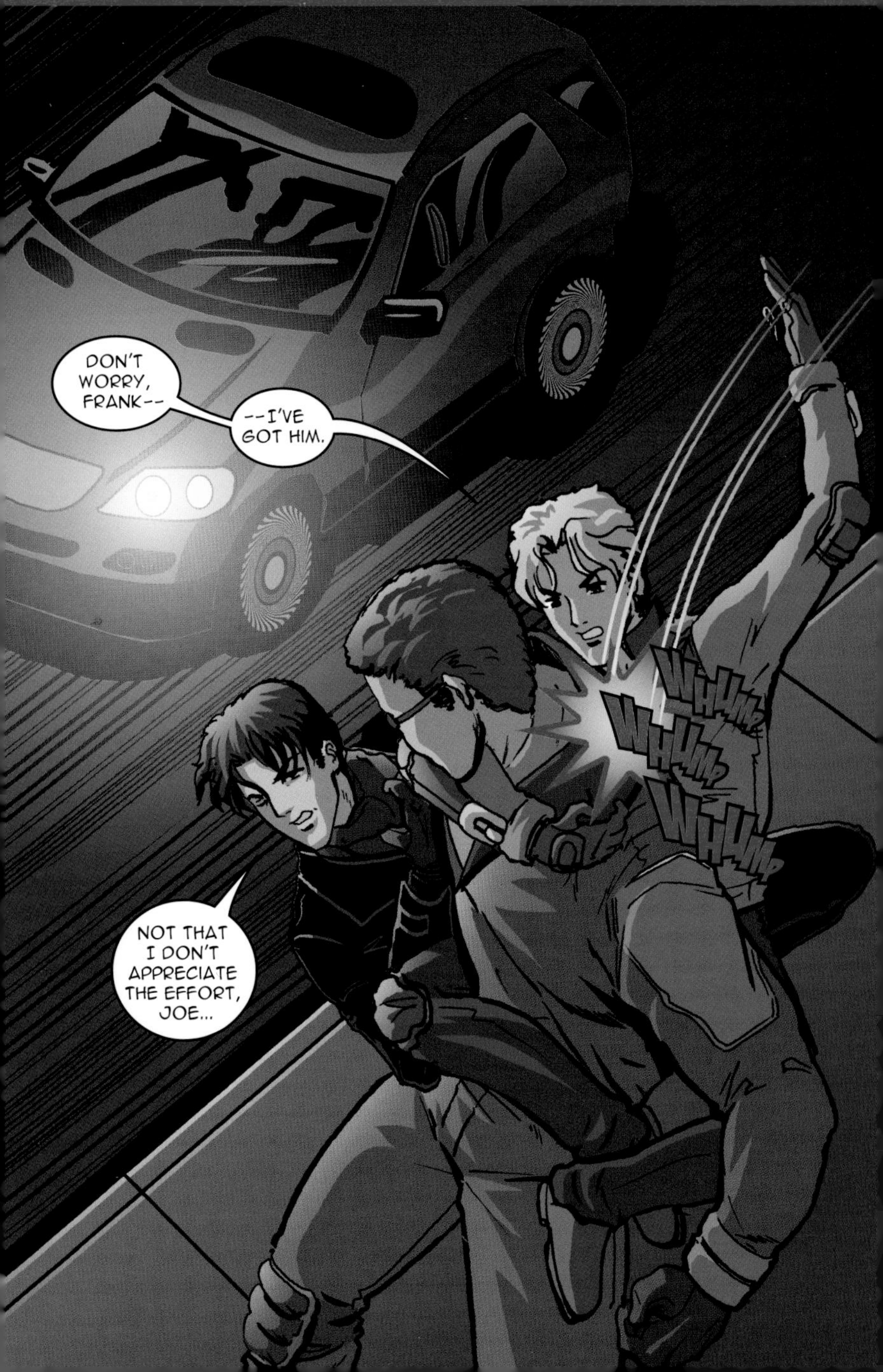
DON'T WORRY, FRANK--
--I'VE GOT HIM.
WHUMP
WHUMP
WHUMP
NOT THAT I DON'T APPRECIATE THE EFFORT, JOE...

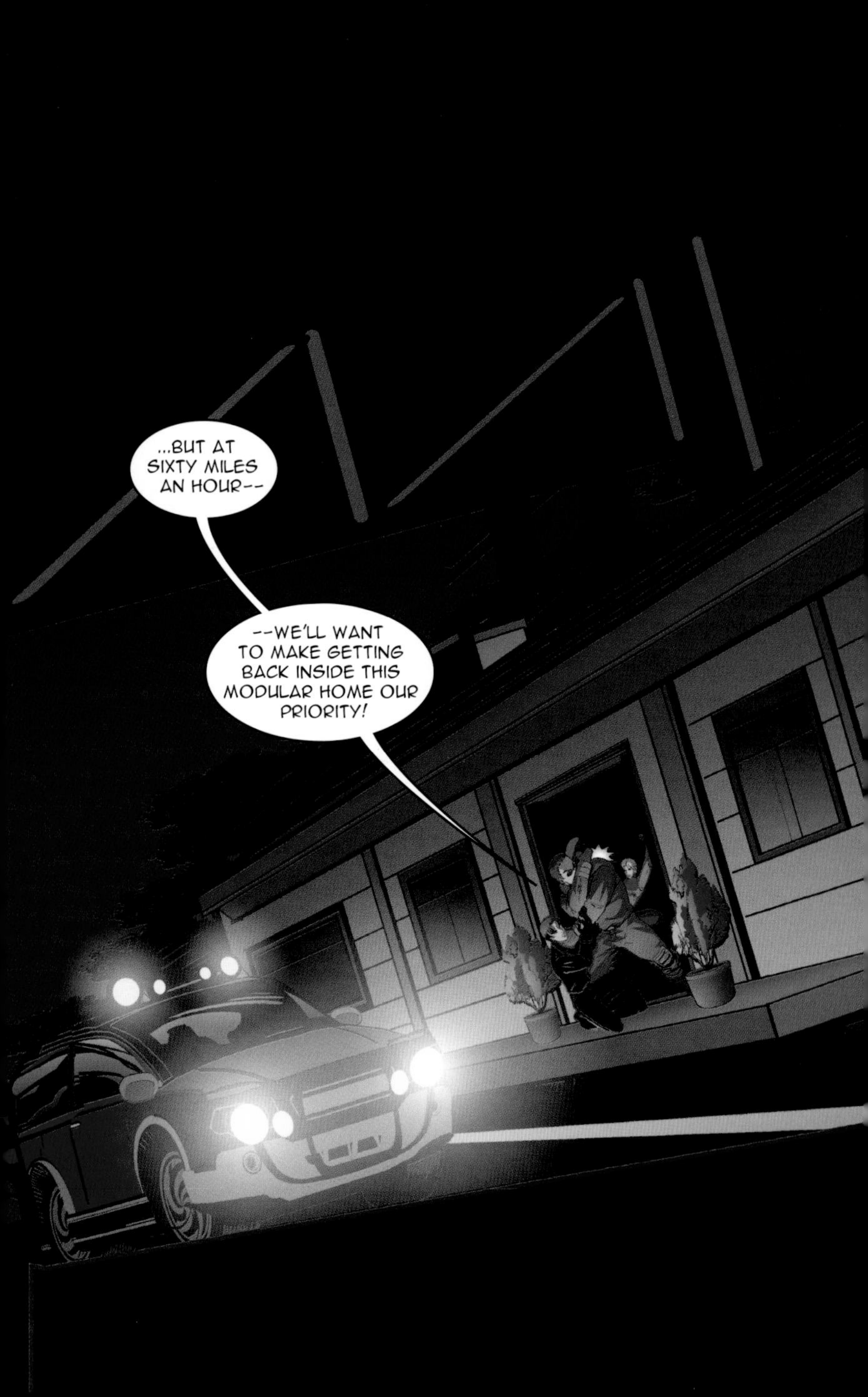
...BUT AT SIXTY MILES AN HOUR--
--WE'LL WANT TO MAKE GETTING BACK INSIDE THIS MODULAR HOME OUR PRIORITY!

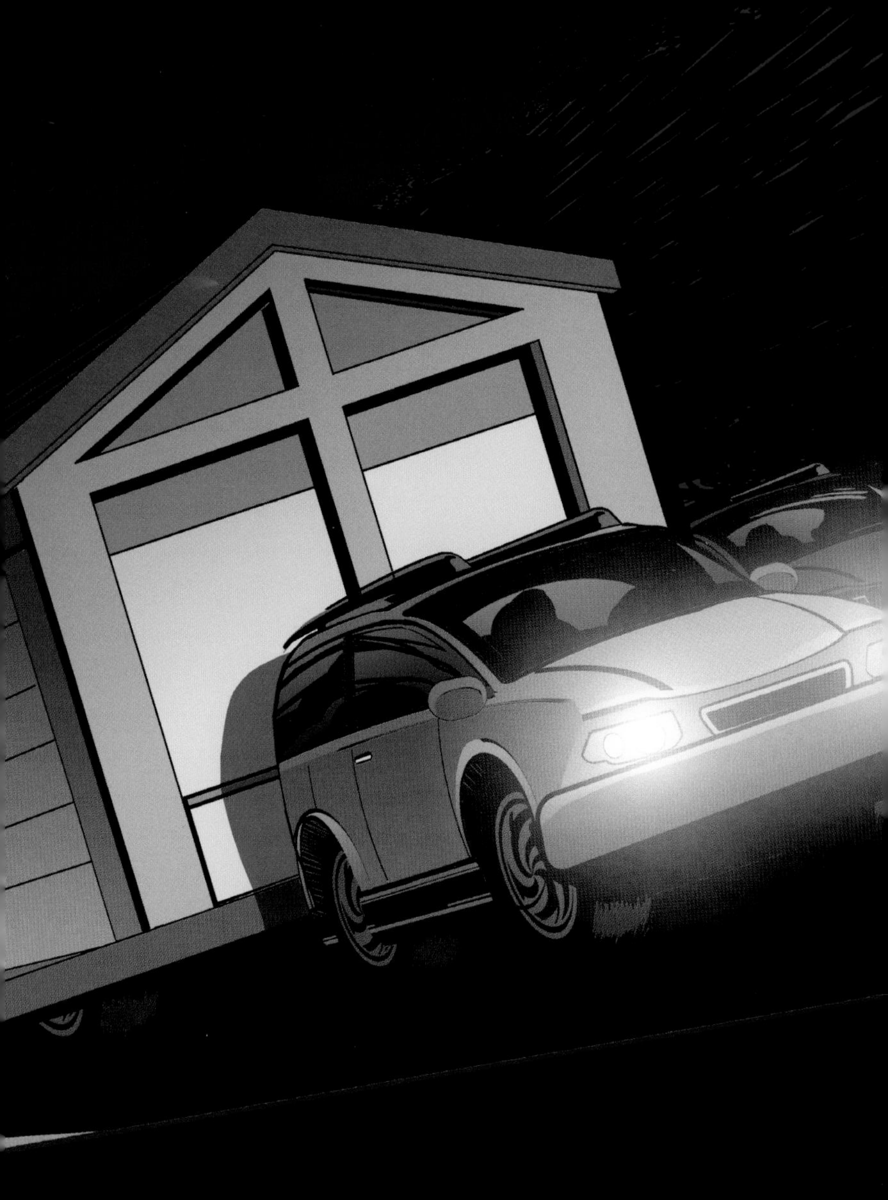

CHAPTER ONE:

“What A Long Strange Drive It’s Been”

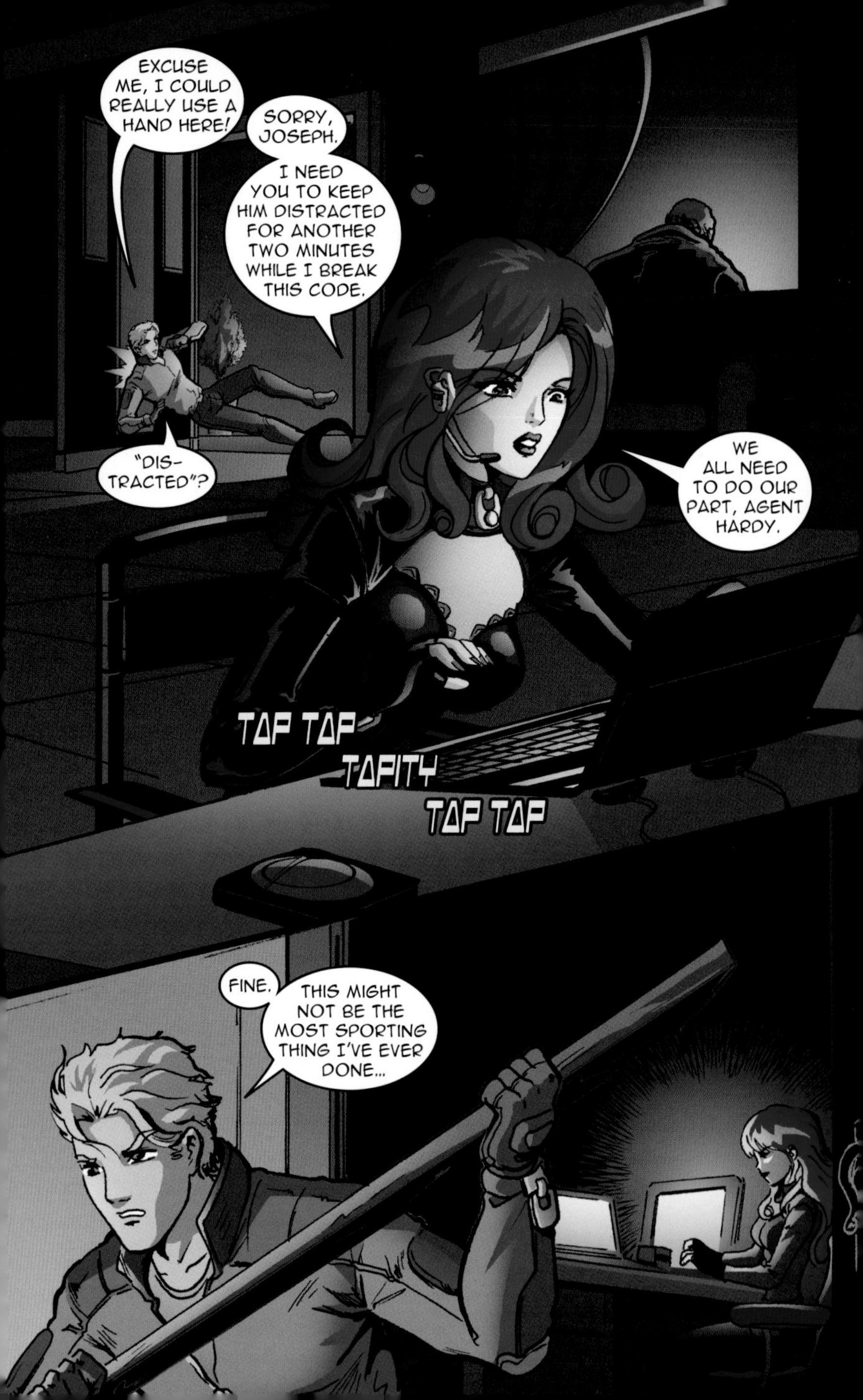
EXCUSE ME, I COULD REALLY USE A HAND HERE!
SORRY, JOSEPH.
I NEED YOU TO KEEP HIM DISTRACTED FOR ANOTHER TWO MINUTES WHILE I BREAK THIS CODE.
"DIS-TRACTED"?
WE ALL NEED TO DO OUR PART, AGENT HARDY.
TAP TAP
TAPITY
TAP TAP
FINE.
THIS MIGHT NOT BE THE MOST SPORTING THING I'VE EVER DONE...

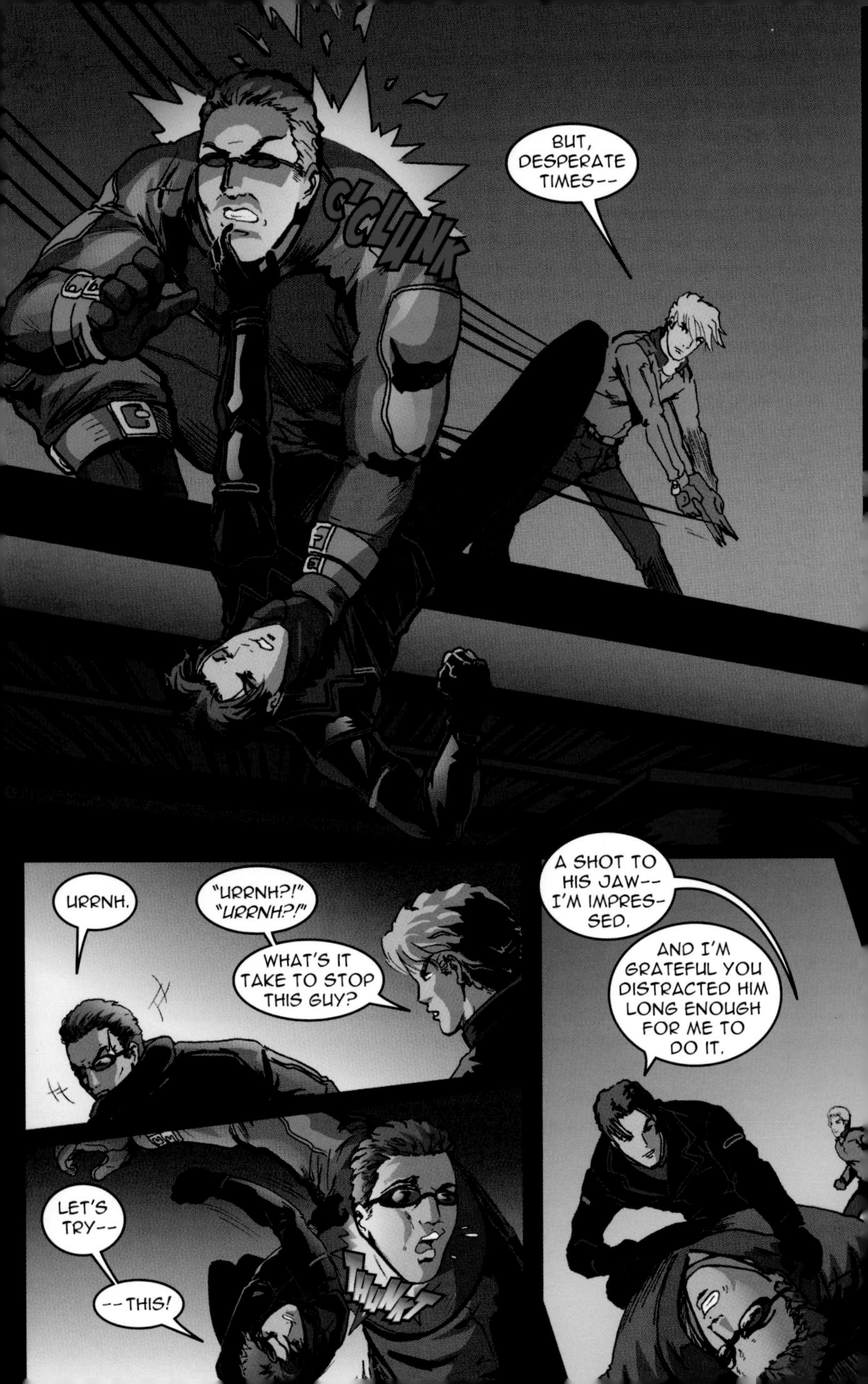
C'CLUNK
BUT, DESPERATE TIMES--
URRNH.
"URRNH?!" "URRNH?!"
WHAT'S IT TAKE TO STOP THIS GUY?
LET'S TRY--
--THIS!
THUNK
A SHOT TO HIS JAW-- I'M IMPRES-SED.
AND I'M GRATEFUL YOU DISTRACTED HIM LONG ENOUGH FOR ME TO DO IT.

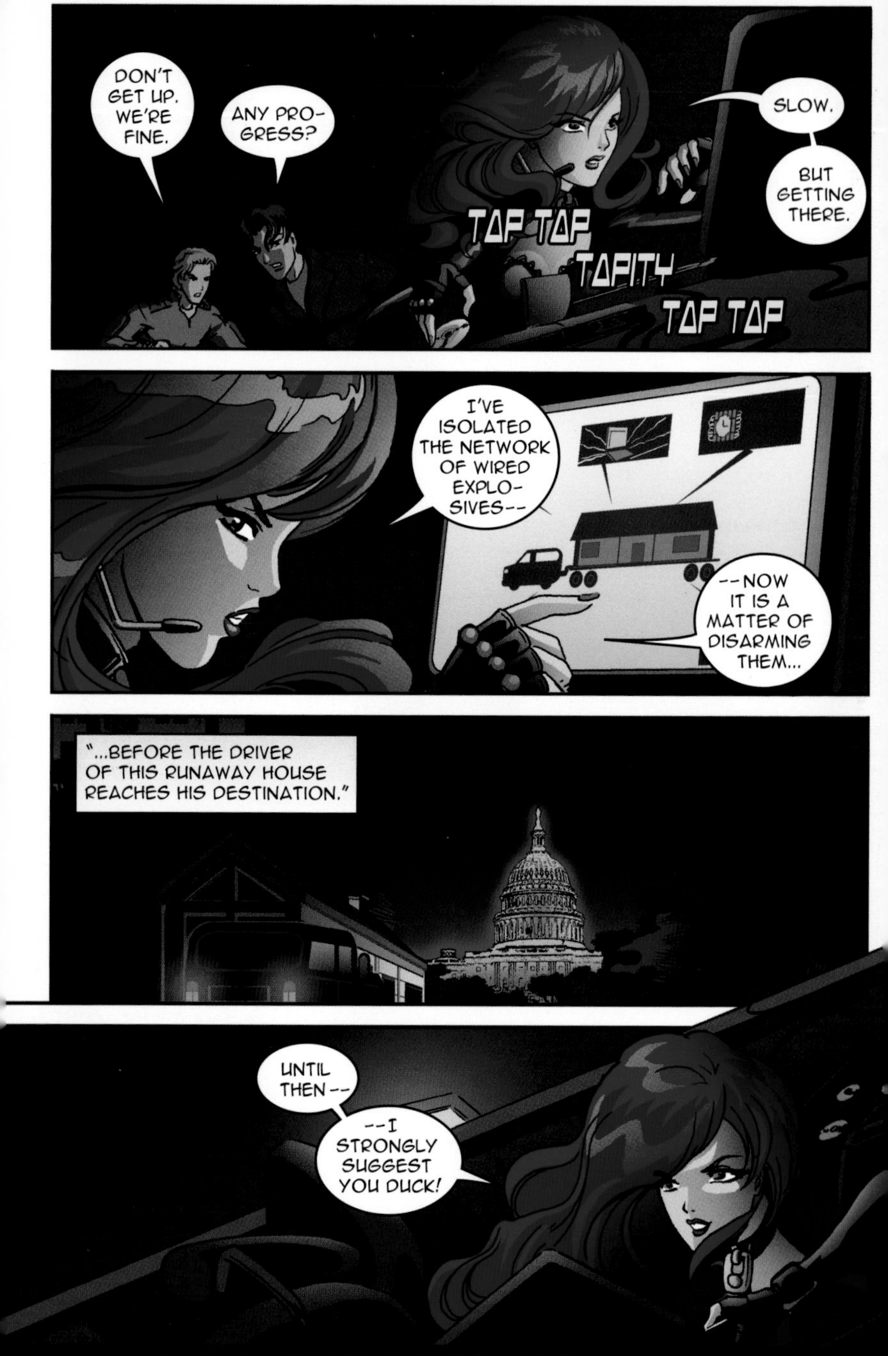
DON'T GET UP. WE'RE FINE.
ANY PRO-GRESS?
SLOW.
BUT GETTING THERE.
TAP TAP
TAPITY
TAP TAP
I'VE ISOLATED THE NETWORK OF WIRED EXPLO-SIVES--
--NOW IT IS A MATTER OF DISARMING THEM...
"...BEFORE THE DRIVER OF THIS RUNAWAY HOUSE REACHES HIS DESTINATION."
UNTIL THEN--
--I STRONGLY SUGGEST YOU DUCK!

NANCY DREW

A NEW ONE EVERY 3 MONTHS!

NEW STORY! FULL-COLOR GRAPHIC NOVEL
NANCY DREW
girl detective
#12
DRESS REHEARSAL
BASED ON THE SERIES BY CAROLYN KEENE
Stefan PETRUCHA
Sho MURASE
ON SALE NOW!
PAPERCUTZ

#1 “The Demon of River Heights”
ISBN 1-59707-000-9
#2 “Writ In Stone”
ISBN 1-59707-002-5
#3 “The Haunted Dollhouse”
ISBN 1-59707-008-4
#4 “The Girl Who Wasn’t There”
ISBN 1-59707-012-2
#5 “The Fake Heir”
ISBN 1-59707-024-6
#6 “Mr. Cheeters Is Missing”
ISBN 1-59707-030-0
#7 “The Charmed Bracelet”
ISBN 1-59707-036-X
#8 “Global Warning”
ISBN 1-59707-051-3
#9 “Ghost in the Machinery”
ISBN 1-59707-058-0
#10 “The Disoriented Express”
ISBN 1-59707-066-1
#11 “Monkey Wrench Blues”
ISBN 1-59707-076-9
NEW! #12 “Dress Reversal”
ISBN 1-59707-086-6
All: Pocket sized, 96-112pp., full color, $7.95
Also available in hardcover! $12.95 each.

NEW STORIES! FULL-COLOR GRAPHIC NOVELS
NANCY DREW
BASED ON THE SERIES BY CAROLYN KEENE
PAPERCUTZ

Nancy Drew
Boxed Set, #1-4
384 pages of color comics! $29.95,
ISBN 1-59707-038-6
Nancy Drew
Boxed Set, #5-8
432 pages of color comics! $29.95,
ISBN 1-59707-074-2

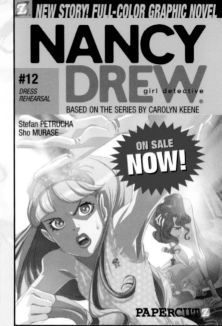

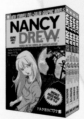

TOTALLY SPIES!

New Full-Color Graphic Novel!
#1
Totally Spies!
THE OP
PAPERCUTZ

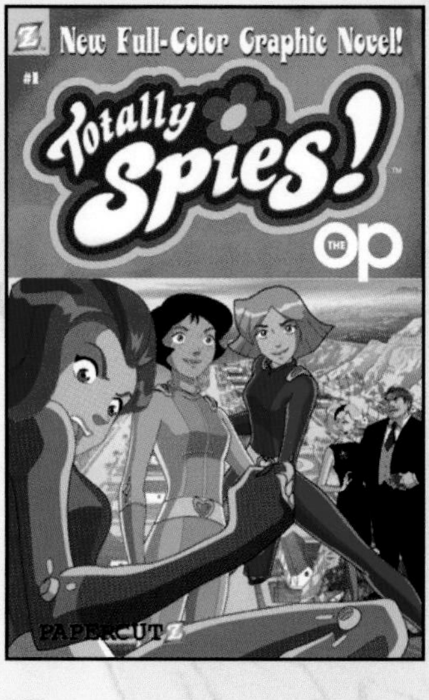

#1 “The O.P.” ISBN 1-59707-043-2
#2 “I Hate the 80’s” ISBN 1-59707-045-9
#3 “Evil Jerry” ISBN 1-59707-047-5
#4 “Spies in Space” ISBN 1-59707-055-6
Each: 5x7 1/2, 112pp., full color paperback: $7.95
Also available in hardcover! $12.95 each

www.papercutz.com

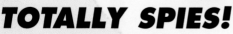

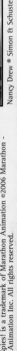